Death Ship *and* The Black Dragon

TWO CLASSIC ADVENTURES OF

TM

by Walter B. Gibson
writing as Maxwell Grant

plus **"The Man with The Shadow's Face"**
by Will Murray

SANCTUM BOOKS

This Sanctum Books edition is an unabridged republication of the text and illustrations of two stories from *The Shadow Magazine,* as originally published by Street & Smith Publications, Inc., N.Y.: *Death Ship* from the April 1, 1939 issue and *The Black Dragon* from the March 1, 1943 issue. These stories are works of their time. Consequently, the text is reprinted intact in its original historical form, including occasional out-of-date ethnic and cultural stereotyping. Typographical errors have been tacitly corrected in this edition.

International Standard Book Number:
978-1-60877-122-6

First printing: August 2013

Series editor/publisher: Anthony Tollin
anthonytollin@shadowsanctum.com

Consulting editor: Will Murray

Copy editor: Joseph Wrzos

Cover and photo restoration: Michael Piper

Published by Sanctum Books
P.O. Box 761474, San Antonio, TX 78245-1474

Visit The Shadow at www.shadowsanctum.com.

Volume 76

CONTENTS

Thrilling Tales and Features

Cover art by Graves Gladney
Back cover art by Graves Gladney and Modest Stein
Interior illustrations by Edd Cartier and Paul Orban

CHAPTER I
THE DOUBLE SNARE

THE last rays of sunset dyed the Golden Gate, adding a touch of crimson to the yellowed sky above the blue Pacific. Looking off from the high structure of the Golden Gate Bridge, a long, sleek steamship could be seen heading out to sea, her decks crowded with Alaska-bound passengers.

Soon, that sight was lost to the driver who had viewed it. He was across the bridge, north of San Francisco, dipping his coupé along a descending road that led away from the ocean. Headed somewhere beyond Sausalito, he was away from the sunset's glow, entering a gathering twilight that already gripped San Francisco Bay.

Headlights glimmered from the coupé; within the car there was the sound of a whispered laugh. The dusk that presaged darkness was to that driver's liking.

He was The Shadow, whose chosen paths were those that lay beneath the shroud of night.

Out of heavy traffic, the car was moving slowly, as if lingering until darkness deepened. Its lights were dim and therefore inconspicuous, but even that did not fully suit the mysterious driver. When he had reached a road at the bayside, he extinguished the lights altogether.

From then on, the car's course resembled a creep, while keen eyes guided it solely by the ribbon of grayish white that signified the narrow, winding roadway.

There came a place where a side road plowed off into the hillside, marked only by a thick blackness. Most drivers would have hesitated at turning into that byway, even though familiar with it, for darkness gave it the semblance of a bottomless hole. But The Shadow swung his car with cool precision, undeterred when it suddenly tilted sideways.

With tires crunching heavily, he leveled the car in the very spot he wanted, a deep ditch below the road level. When the wheels began to climb, he halted.

Parked in the bed of a dry stream, the coupé was placed where occasional travelers along the side road would not discover it, thanks to clumps of bushes that flanked the roadside above. Well tucked from sight, The Shadow listened for sounds close by. Hearing none, he turned on the car's dome light.

The glow showed a figure attired in tuxedo; but the face above was obscured by the brim of a slouch hat. Despite its broad brim, the hat seemed ordinary enough, until long-fingered hands drew the folds of a cloak up from the car seat.

Once that black garment had settled on its owner's shoulders, the dark hat blended with the attire. The long hands drew on gloves of the same jet-black hue, to produce the final touch that made The Shadow a grotesque being quite different from the human driver who had brought the coupé here.

Paper crinkled as The Shadow spread it. His eyes studied a neat chart that showed not only the obscure road, but a pathway that led to the bay. The latter was indicated by wavy lines, with a jutting block that obviously marked a pier.

Moving a forefinger along the line of the path, The Shadow finished by reaching for the light switch. A *click* brought darkness to the coupé.

In that gloom, no eyes could have discerned the shape of The Shadow. Nor could ears have detected the almost soundless exit that he made from the car. The only traces of his subsequent course were the occasional blinks of a tiny flashlight that moved along the path to the bay.

Those flashes, however, were muffled by the folds of The Shadow's cloak. After some fifty feet, they ceased entirely. Sure of his route, The Shadow was proceeding in complete darkness.

Night had come in sudden fashion, but The Shadow could distinguish between shades of blackness. There was a smoothness, like that of polished ebony, that marked the waters of the bay; a bulkiness about the darkness that formed the shoreline. The Shadow's goal formed a pencil streak that marred the bay's smooth sheen. That goal was an old pier that stretched into deep water.

WITH fifty yards to go, The Shadow halted; he had sensed motion in the darkness near him. His caution was rewarded when he heard stealthy footsteps prowling near. They passed; still listening, The Shadow caught other, fainter sounds. Picking the right spot, he saw the guarded blink of a flashlight.

His suspicions were proven. A small cordon of prowlers were on duty, watching the neighborhood of the pier. From further sounds and another flashlight's blink, The Shadow determined that the watchers were drawing closer. Evidently they intended finally to congregate at the pier itself, and that prospect forced The Shadow to a single decision.

This was his chance to pierce the cordon before it became too tight; to be at the one place where enemies would not expect to find him: namely, at the pier itself.

There was swiftness to The Shadow's approach as he covered those final fifty yards, but speed did not mar his ability at keeping silence. When he reached a squatty structure that formed the land end of the pier, he looked back to detect another telltale sparkle from a flashlight. His penetration had not been discovered.

The pier was a wide, high platform, and the building at the land end of it served as a boathouse. The building was set low, and it was necessary to pass through it to reach the space beneath the pier, where The Shadow knew that a small vessel was kept. For tonight's venture was no aimless quest on the part of the mysterious being in black. The Shadow was delving into an enterprise as mysterious as these of his own creation.

He had come here to investigate the newly invented Z-boat designed by Commander Rodney Prew, formerly an officer in the United States Navy.

Off to the northeast were distant lights that marked Mare Island, where naval officers expectantly awaited tomorrow's announcement regarding the purpose of Prew's new craft. To the south, The Shadow could see the glow of San Francisco, a city that had sheltered the secret meetings of plotters whose purposes were as hidden as their methods.

Through stray clues, The Shadow had divined that the future of the Z-boat was at stake, although there had been no surface indication of such circumstance. It was more than a hunch that had brought The Shadow here tonight; he had the definite fact that if any stroke should be intended, it would have to be made before tomorrow.

From the time when the Navy Department had learned of Commander Prew's private construction of a new type of warcraft, he had been given a limit in which to complete his preliminary work. Tomorrow, when that period expired, polite officers in navy uniforms would sail down from Mare Island and take over the ship beneath the pier.

Whether Prew, or others, wished to prolong the secrecy surrounding the Z-boat was still a mystery in itself. So, for that matter, was the presence of the men on shore. On previous excursions here, The Shadow had found no guarding cordon. The only watchers had been a few men stationed on the Z-boat itself.

Previously, The Shadow had gained access to the little boathouse only to find it deserted, with farther passage blocked. At the door where he stood now, black against the darkened weather-beaten wood, he soon made sure that the interior of the boathouse was as dark and silent as it had been before. That made it expressly suited to his requirements.

While outside lurkers were closing in upon the pier, becoming more confident as they progressed, The Shadow could be awaiting them in an even better lurking spot. Whatever their purpose, he would be well equipped to learn it when they arrived, as well as having the element of surprise in his own favor.

THE SHADOW took one last survey. Off on the bay, he saw dwindling lights, merely those of a plying ferry. Gazing toward San Francisco, he observed a more ominous sign; sudden swaths of brightness that came from big searchlights playing a huge circle upon the bay. Their sweep formed an absolute barrier between this spot and San Francisco, but they never altered in their circuit.

Those were the lights of Alcatraz, constantly on the watch for any creeping craft that might try to reach The Rock, where hundreds of criminals held almost impossible dreams of rescue. The Shadow remembered one time when Alcatraz had been invaded, but he himself had nullified that enterprise.*

Thanks to The Shadow, Alcatraz was again impregnable; and watchers on the fortress island were unwittingly returning the favor. Their searchlights, it seemed, were sufficient to prevent any troublemakers from using the water route to or from this pier where Prew's Z-boat was veiled from public view.

That speculation ended, The Shadow began operations upon the boathouse door. It was locked, but none too strongly, for it was intended to be inconspicuous, since the inner barrier between house and pier was the one that actually counted. The Shadow had worked on this lock before, and he picked it this time with very little trouble.

Easing inside, he closed the door behind him, letting the spring lock latch by degrees. Then, with his flashlight close to the floor, he crossed the single room until he reached the inner door. It offered a different problem; it was not only locked, but bolted from the other side.

Skillfully, The Shadow tapped the woodwork with silent, gloved finger. He was checking on a previous finding: the exact location of the bolt. From beneath his cloak he produced a tiny drill, set it at the exact spot required.

Pressure on that drill's spring handle would drive a hole through the woodwork, enabling him to get at the bolt. The Shadow's thumb was poised, when something stopped him.

It was a creak, that sounded first as if it came from the outer door that he had locked behind him. A whisper of breeze stirred through the darkness, then faded. Next a footfall, as evasive as the trifling breeze.

It couldn't have come from the outer door; The Shadow was sure that he would have heard a key at work. But, so far as he remembered, there was no other entrance to this boathouse other than the two doors, and he could account for both of them!

Then he recalled the gasoline cans. They had stood in an inner corner, grimy and covered with cobwebs, big containers that The Shadow had not moved from their place. Nor had he looked for them tonight. Assuming that they had been removed, the sound could have come from that corner.

THE drill slid beneath The Shadow's cloak. His deft fingers were on the butt of an automatic. He was faced toward the corner that he suspected; at the same time, he was drawing away from the inner door, knowing that it might prove to be a danger spot.

Calculating upon stealthy moves in darkness, The Shadow was showing no haste. He was waiting for another footfall to reveal the location of an adversary. But the sound he wanted did not come. Instead, there was a *click* from the wall, away from the corner where the cans had been.

With that sound came light, the brilliance of a hundred-watt bulb, hanging from the ceiling to a

*See *Shadow Over Alcatraz* in *The Shadow* Vol. 16.

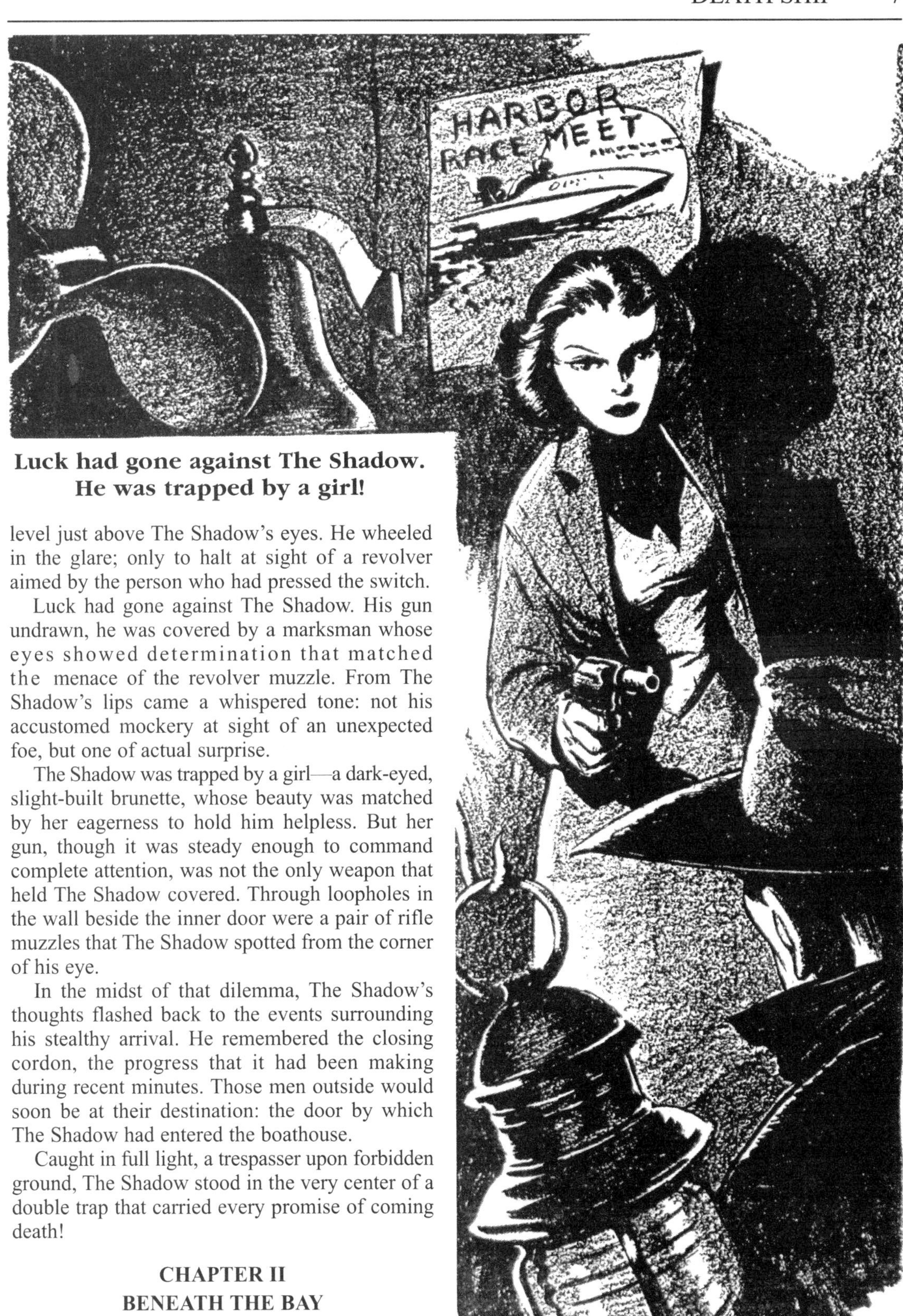

Luck had gone against The Shadow. He was trapped by a girl!

level just above The Shadow's eyes. He wheeled in the glare; only to halt at sight of a revolver aimed by the person who had pressed the switch.

Luck had gone against The Shadow. His gun undrawn, he was covered by a marksman whose eyes showed determination that matched the menace of the revolver muzzle. From The Shadow's lips came a whispered tone: not his accustomed mockery at sight of an unexpected foe, but one of actual surprise.

The Shadow was trapped by a girl—a dark-eyed, slight-built brunette, whose beauty was matched by her eagerness to hold him helpless. But her gun, though it was steady enough to command complete attention, was not the only weapon that held The Shadow covered. Through loopholes in the wall beside the inner door were a pair of rifle muzzles that The Shadow spotted from the corner of his eye.

In the midst of that dilemma, The Shadow's thoughts flashed back to the events surrounding his stealthy arrival. He remembered the closing cordon, the progress that it had been making during recent minutes. Those men outside would soon be at their destination: the door by which The Shadow had entered the boathouse.

Caught in full light, a trespasser upon forbidden ground, The Shadow stood in the very center of a double trap that carried every promise of coming death!

CHAPTER II
BENEATH THE BAY

NORMALLY, danger was The Shadow's call to action. Experience had shown him that the greater the odds against him, the more he could win through speedy tactics. He possessed that rare instinct which enabled him to take chances, confident that his own boldness would produce the needed breaks in his favor.

Yet that faculty was not The Shadow's greatest boon. More valuable than his daring was his ability to recognize situations wherein the opposite tack was necessary.

This was one such case. Caught as he was, The Shadow saw instantly that this trap, as it stood at present, was unescapable. However swift his action, he could bring nothing but his own doom as a consequence, unless he managed first to shape a coming course.

The girl was determined in her manner. Her grip on the revolver showed that she knew how to use it, and there was a steadiness of her slender forefinger that indicated a hair trigger in back of it. Those guns that jutted from the inner wall were waiting only for the girl's decision, ready to take over any effort in which she might fail.

It was policy, therefore, to let the brunette believe that she had gained full control. When her tension lessened, a similar slackness would result among the invisible gunners who covered The Shadow through the loopholes.

The very tone of The Shadow's whispered laugh was a proof of his instinctive decision. The girl did not realize the thought behind it; she took the tone for what The Shadow intended it to convey: an expression of bitter resignation. His hands, as they came upward, shoulder high, were reluctant enough to complete the pretense.

The girl's finger eased. Though he ignored the wall guns, The Shadow was sure that they had also lessened in their menace. His calculations concerned those outside watchers, moving in to block the land exit from the boathouse. There would be a few minutes before they could be grouped outside the door. The Shadow intended to make the most of that interim.

His head tilted slightly upward. His eyes caught the glow of the hundred-watt lamp, six feet away at an angle to his left. The girl was farther away, at the side wall, facing across the boathouse, but she saw the glitter of The Shadow's eyes. Her gaze became intense; she was trying to make out other features beneath the hatbrim. Failing in that, she moved a step forward, then halted.

"Stand where you are!" announced the girl, in a low, steady contralto. "And let me remind you that it is customary for strangers here to declare themselves!"

There was a pause; then The Shadow's whisper, sibilant, with a trace of mockery.

"Perhaps both of us are strangers to these premises," he countered. "Since you have thrust yourself into this situation, your own introduction should come first."

The girl's lips became scornful.

"My name is Claudette Marchand," she told The Shadow. "That is something you already know. Anyone who has meddled in Commander Prew's business knows that I am his confidential secretary. You are not the first person who has sought to bribe me into betraying the secret of his invention."

WHILE she talked, Claudette was crouching slightly forward, endeavoring to gain a real glimpse of The Shadow's face. Whether she believed that she would recognize him, or was merely putting on a bluff, The Shadow could not discover.

One reason for his laxity in the matters was The Shadow's interest elsewhere. His gaze had lowered, as if to escape the girl's stare. His real purpose was to pick the place from which Claudette had bobbed into the boathouse.

The answer lay in the corner. There, near the inner wall, The Shadow saw a trapdoor with an iron ring. Unquestionably it led to steps below. That trapdoor had been covered by the big gasoline cans on The Shadow's previous visits.

"Perhaps"—Claudette had moved another step forward—"you have heard of Felix Sergon?"

She paused, having pronounced the name emphatically, with a hardness to the "g," and her eyes were looking sharply for some response from The Shadow. Observing none, she repeated the name disdainfully:

"Felix Sergon, who calls himself an adventurer and soldier of fortune, but who is actually an international spy. I have his picture here"—her free hand brought a small photograph from the sash of her dark dress—"and if you would care to see it more closely—"

She ended with a gesture, as though she sought to compare the photo with The Shadow's face, once she could manage to see beneath the hatbrim. The Shadow's eyes went toward the picture; he saw the portrait of a flattish square-jawed face topped by short-clipped hair.

Felix Sergon—both the name and the picture were recognized by The Shadow. But whether Claudette Marchand actually believed that The Shadow might be Sergon was another question. She was clever, this girl, crafty enough to be trying to outsmart the black-cloaked intruder whom she had so cunningly trapped.

What she did not count upon was The Shadow's own skill at bluff. He hadn't forgotten those bristling guns at the inner wall, nor the creeping men who by this time had neared the outside door. He seemed, however, to be interested only in the preservation of his own identity.

Hands still high, The Shadow drew away, turning so that his back was toward the wall. The shift was natural, as was his sudden crouch.

Though Claudette saw no danger from the move, she was canny enough to recognize that the changed position might produce unforeseen complications. She dropped back a few steps, steadying her gun. Again, her contralto tone was firm:

"Stand where you are!"

The shift had brought The Shadow closer to the hanging bulb. It was just above the level of his hatbrim. For the first time in gazing toward The Shadow, Claudette could look past him to the inner wall.

Not only could the girl see the ready guns; she should have heard the creeping past the outer door that betokened the arrival of the outside prowlers, for The Shadow caught that sound. But there was a change in Claudette's expression, a curious bewilderment that made her waver. Something made her momentarily forget The Shadow, and that was the only urge he needed.

Claudette Marchand, alone, could have frustrated The Shadow's next move; for the gunners at the loopholes were looking at his back and did not realize what was happening until the stroke was underway.

ALL the while that he had kept his hands half raised, The Shadow had been pressing his right elbow against his ribs. His purpose had been to keep a half-drawn automatic from tumbling to the floor. It was the gun for which he had started a reach when Claudette sprang the surprise with the big light.

The Shadow wanted that automatic in a hurry, to serve him in the present situation, and he acquired it in a unique style.

With a sudden upward fling of his right arm, he hooked the gun muzzle in the crook of his elbow, jerking it out from beneath his cloak. It popped into sight like a jack-in-the-box, flipping over to the left. The fingers of his left hand were ready for it; they took the gun butt in midair.

The Shadow did not wait to find the trigger. As he dived rightward, toward the floor, his left hand made a backhand slash, using the .45 as a bludgeon. Cold metal smashed the hot glass of the dangling electric-lightbulb.

The light was gone with a sharp explosion that sounded like a gunshot. Hitting the floor in a long roll, The Shadow lashed one foot toward Claudette. He tripped the girl just as she tugged away at the revolver trigger. Her gun was popping uselessly as she rolled beside The Shadow.

A moment later, other guns were splitting the blackness with their flaying tongues. The men at the loopholes were shooting for The Shadow; but to no avail. He was below the line of their fire; he had found Claudette in the darkness and was sprawling her, gunless, against that inner wall.

Guns stopped their chatter. There were gruff shouts from behind the partition, the yank of bolts. Simultaneously came the ripping of the outer door that The Shadow had latched when he entered. Flashlights flickered there.

Into that glow came an avalanche of blackness. The Shadow was on his feet, flinging forward, sledging with his automatic to hew a path through the opposition. He ran into a cluster of men, who met him with bare hands.

By all the laws of previous experience, The Shadow should have left that crew sprawled about the doorway. Instead, he met a startling setback. The effect was exactly as if The Shadow had been a rubber ball thrown against a wall. His lunge ended the moment that hands encountered him. He was bounced back, half across the boathouse, in a reverse somersault that carried him a dozen feet.

There were more lights, coming from the inner doorway, now wide open. The Shadow saw ugly faces in the glow, gun muzzles turned in his direction. The whole scene was kaleidoscopic, whirling, blinking, before his dazed eyes. All that The Shadow could actually sense was a round ring of metal that his fingers had encountered on the floor, near the corner.

He realized what it was and gave a hard tug, felt the trapdoor yield. With a twist of his flattened body, The Shadow went through the space that fortune had provided him just as the roar of guns blasted above his head.

There was a ladder that Claudette had used when she had hidden beneath the trapdoor, but The Shadow did not find it. Instead, he took a dozen-foot plunge that ended in a splash. The feel of that cold water was grateful, for it offered a refuge and ended The Shadow's daze. Ten feet below the surface, he groped for a space beneath the pilings that might offer him another exit.

He found a way through; holding his breath, he squirmed under water; then, with lungs that seemed about to burst, he made for the surface. Coming up into light, The Shadow grabbed for the slimy rung of a ladder, shook the water from his face and stared at the sight before him.

HE had gone beneath the inner wall of the boathouse. Under the old pier, he had found the long space where the Z-boat was moored. Lights from the side walls showed a craft that was some sixty feet in length, shaped like a speedboat but with a streamlined oval deck.

On the blunt, narrow stern of the odd craft The Shadow saw the name, *Barracuda.* Hauling himself half up the ladder, he spied an odd-shaped cockpit in the middle of the vessel. The space looked deep, and it was fronted by what appeared to be a half-domed windshield. But The Shadow was interested in persons, rather than the boat.

He caught a glimpse of Claudette Marchand, as her head disappeared inside the boat. Men were with her—the same murderous gunners who had fired at The Shadow only a few minutes before. Then all were gone except one, whose back was turned. Shoulders looming from the cockpit, that fellow rasped an order.

There was a swift churn of propellers. Hooked tight to the pier ladder, The Shadow avoided their slash. The *Barracuda* started forward with a roar, just as the last man turned about. He saw The Shadow, yanked a revolver and aimed for the black-clad shape against the ladder. As the gun barked, The Shadow recognized the man's face.

That vicious marksman was Felix Sergon, the very man whose name Claudette had so shrewdly mentioned to The Shadow!

Sergon's hasty shots went wide. He hadn't a chance to guide them as the *Barracuda* lurched out into the bay. The speedy boat left a wake of foamy white beneath the pier, and The Shadow saw Sergon thrust away his gun, to manipulate the half-domed top of the cockpit. Then the strange craft was in the open, thrumming away at a racing pace.

Holding to the ladder, The Shadow watched. The pier pointed almost southward, in the exact direction that the *Barracuda* had taken. The boat was out of sight against the darkened waters, but it was leaving a line of whiteness that The Shadow could follow.

Though he had not prevented Sergon's getaway, The Shadow saw only a short-lived flight for the new master of the *Barracuda.* A ship like that could not travel San Francisco Bay without challenge, once it had been spotted. If seen immediately, the *Barracuda* would be blocked off before she could reach the Golden Gate, the only outlet to the open ocean.

It seemed a certainty that the *Barracuda* would be spied. For the speedy Z-boat was driving straight for the most guarded zone in all the bay—the stretch of open water that was swept by the great searchlights from Alcatraz!

There was no way for the ship to go around that barrier. As the white wake faded, The Shadow watched, confident that he would see the *Barracuda* bathed in floodlights that awaited it. He could trace the line that it had cut, almost to the near edge of a sweeping searchlight. The glow was coming to receive the *Barracuda*!

Then The Shadow was staring at something that amazed him. The searchlight had swung about; it was flinging its beam back along the Z-boat's route, showing even the widening wake the craft had produced.

But that was *all* that The Shadow saw!

Open water, nothing more. The thrum of the Z-boat's motors had ended utterly. For once, The Shadow gazed in awe—he, the amazing being whose own career had been studded with exploits that to others seemed incredible!

The *Barracuda*, the mystery ship invented by Commander Rodney Prew, had vanished completely, almost instantly, beneath the waters of San Francisco Bay!

CHAPTER III
CROSSED BATTLE

SCARCELY recuperated from the struggle in the boathouse, The Shadow found it difficult to analyze the chain of recent experience. From the start, events had built up in rapid succession to that amazing climax, the total disappearance of the *Barracuda.*

Tonight, The Shadow had expected to find Commander Rodney Prew in personal command of the Z-boat, for tomorrow the ship was scheduled to be delivered to the government. Instead, The Shadow had encountered Claudette Marchand; her sudden entrance, her naming of Felix Sergon, the very man who had already taken charge of the *Barracuda*, were in themselves suspicious incidents.

Yet, from those events and certain recollections of minor happenings, The Shadow was piecing an explanation. More facts were needed to fit the whole into place, but those could be gathered later. Tracing backward, The Shadow was considering the importance of learning why the *Barracuda* had vanished, rather than where the ship had gone.

That brought his thoughts to the real beginning of his adventure—when he had managed a stealthy passage through the lurkers on the land side of the pier. He remembered the surprise that those watchers had given him when he tried to cleave his way through them, and the recollection brought him a mental jolt that equaled his physical experience.

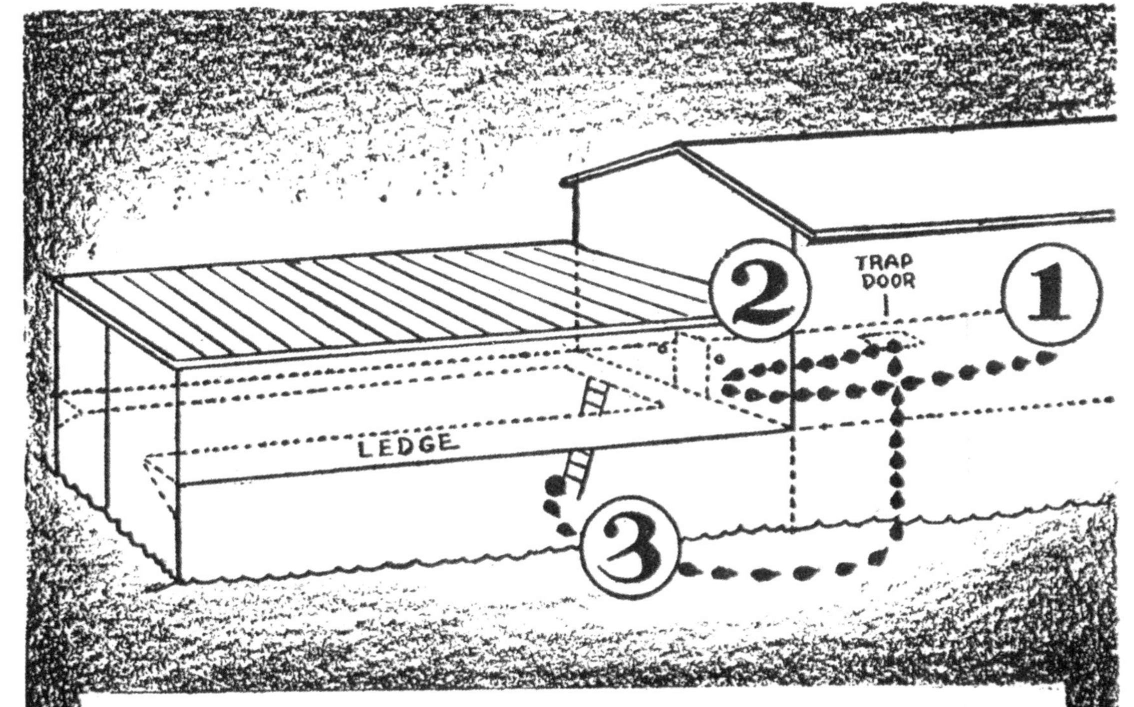

1. Jutting out into the water, north of San Francisco, lies an old boathouse connected to a pier. It is here that an ex-naval officer has been experimenting with a Z-boat. Through darkness . . .

2. . . . approaches The Shadow, anxious to gain information about this new type of water craft. Piercing a cordon of watchers, he makes entrance to the boathouse and is about to enter the pier when he is surprised and held at gun point by a girl. Knowing . . .

3. . . . the outside cordon is about to close in, and not wanting to be caught between two fires, The Shadow acts quickly and manages to escape down a hidden trapdoor.

Whoever those fighters were, they had not gone aboard the *Barracuda* with Felix Sergon and Claudette Marchand. There was a chance that they were still about these premises, perhaps unsatisfied that they had completely disposed of The Shadow!

There was grim satisfaction in the thought. If those chaps constituted Sergon's land crew, they might supply a lot of information if properly questioned. Moreover, The Shadow had a personal score to settle with those battlers who had treated him like a rubber ball.

Coming up the last rungs of the slippery ladder, The Shadow stepped onto the ledge that adjoined the boathouse. He took a curious look at the hidden space where in the *Barracuda* had been moored.

It was like a dock, beneath the old pier, with runways on both sides and this end platform where The Shadow stood. Farther out, at the bay end of the pier, he could see a pair of metal doors, swung inward. They had evidently been opened at Sergon's order, shortly before the departure of the *Barracuda.*

More important was the door that led into the boathouse. It was bolted, as it had been when The Shadow first arrived. Perhaps Sergon had recognized The Shadow before the cloaked fighter had taken his dive through the trapdoor. Maybe he had expected that The Shadow would emerge from the trapdoor chamber and engage the land crew, possibly with better results on the second attempt.

There could be other reasons, but they did not matter at this moment. The crux of it was that The Shadow had reversed the situation. He was beneath the pier, the land crew still in the boathouse, and it was unlikely that they had guessed where he had gone.

Best of all, The Shadow had a way of finding out what the others were about. All he had to do was peer through one of the loopholes that Sergon and his men had used for their guns.

Each of the loopholes was equipped with a little metal shutter that could be opened only from The Shadow's side. The things worked on swivels, and in turning one The Shadow was careful to cover it with a gloved hand, to hide any light from the illuminated space beneath the pier.

Eye to the loophole, he saw the glow of a flashlight. It was in a corner of the boathouse, the very corner where The Shadow had wriggled through the trapdoor. As he watched, The Shadow saw the light turn downward.

They were looking for him!

Or was it only one person who handled the search? The light was steady, its bearer beyond it, for nothing came between The Shadow and the light. Somehow, it didn't seem to indicate that a group was present. A lone man would make the situation all the better. One could talk as well as half a dozen.

SINCE surprises were in order, this looked like The Shadow's turn to spring one. He relished the idea of suddenly snagging that lone prowler without the man's pals learning it. If they came around to investigate, they would probably search beneath the trapdoor.

But that was not where The Shadow would be, once he had made the capture. His plan was to take a prisoner and bring him back to this ledge beneath the pier.

Closing the swivel shutter in noiseless fashion, The Shadow moved to the connecting door. He drew back the bolts without the slightest scrape. The next move was one that required consummate skill.

Pressing against the edge of the door, The Shadow was prepared to block completely the space when he eased it open. Moving from light into darkness was a difficult performance, but one that The Shadow had often managed.

Hand on the doorknob, The Shadow paused. There were sounds that caught his attention, not from the boathouse but from the open pier above.

Those sounds accounted for the absent members of the land crew. Apparently they had suspected that The Shadow might have found his way from the watery pit. They were prowling the pier, probably looking from its edges. They were making creaking sounds just above The Shadow's head.

Calculating that it would be some time before the others returned to the boathouse, The Shadow resumed his task of moving through the doorway. Since haste was unnecessary, he eased inward by very slow degrees, concentrating entirely upon the gleam of the flashlight that still pointed down into the pit.

There were louder creaks above, but The Shadow gave them no concern, until suddenly a sharp, splintering sound ripped the weather-beaten timbers.

That noise echoed through the boathouse. It alarmed the man at the trapdoor. He sprang about, swinging the flashlight. Instantly, The Shadow whipped back and slammed the door. His hand went for a bolt, but there was no time to throw it.

Looking upward, The Shadow saw a gaping hole above. The men on the pier had used a crowbar to pry away a whole section of the planking, and they had managed it with a single leverage!

It was more important to draw a gun than to shove the bolt, but The Shadow lacked opportunity to reach for his remaining automatic. A face was coming downward through the space above, with it shoulders and extended arms. The Shadow sped his own hands upward to meet the downward lunge.

The figure that struck him was slight but wiry. Hands snaked past his arms, pinned them and took a grip about his neck. The Shadow reeled backward as the attacker struck.

One glimpse of his opponent's face told him who these men were, and explained why they had handled him so effectively in the boathouse. They were Japanese, skilled in jiujitsu tactics.

The previous encounter had given this Jap confidence that he could handle The Shadow alone. He was grinning as the cloaked fighter bent in his grasp, struggling to counteract the hold. The smile left him, though, when a gloved hand poked forward and shoved his chin straight back.

All the while during that quick struggle, The Shadow had been watching a second face at the hole above. His sudden rally was intended to bring the next Japanese down from the pier. The fellow took the bait.

He dropped through to aid his pal, never believing that he would find The Shadow alone when he arrived.

Just as the second attacker hit the ledge, The Shadow settled matters with the first. Applying a grip that not only broke the fellow's hold, The Shadow showed the jiujitsu expert a new trick in his own art.

Coming up from a stoop, The Shadow supplied a twisting snap that flung the man clear over his shoulder into the water between the runways.

COINCIDENT with the Jap's splash came a clatter from the boathouse door. The man from the other side sprang into sight, to see The Shadow snatch the one who had just dropped through from the pier. Another instant, The Shadow was using one Japanese as a missile to stop the other's drive. The pair went sprawling into the boathouse.

Rolling to their feet, they were back to the attack, only to be tumbled anew into the darkness. Their only advantage was their ability to fall. This time they were the rubber balls, taking bounce after bounce, trying to keep up the struggle until the man from the water rejoined them.

The Shadow was ready when that moment came. Wheeling in through the doorway, he spilled his two adversaries, then made a sudden drive out to the ledge.

The drenched Jap from the ladder was diving across to grab him, when The Shadow took a long leap forward. His lunge had all the appearance of a spring out into the water, when his hands, stretching high, caught the edge of the very opening that Japanese had ripped in the pier above.

Long legs swung away in pendulum fashion as the driving Japanese missed them. Then, with a hoist, The Shadow went up through the gap and rolled to the surface of the pier above.

The dripping Japanese matched his speed. By the time The Shadow had twisted to thrust an automatic down through the hole, two of them had taken the third on their shoulders and were shoving him up through. Viciously, the Jap made a grab for The Shadow's gun hand and managed to hang tight while another Oriental was coming up. The second Jap paused long enough to haul up the last man; and it was that error that turned the whole struggle to The Shadow's favor.

With less than a second to spare, The Shadow shook away the Jap who gripped him and made a wheel to the pier edge. Coming about, he opened fire with his automatic.

His purpose was not to drop the Japanese, it was to scatter them; and he succeeded. Scrambling toward the low roof of the boathouse, they yanked out revolvers and returned the fire. They couldn't see The Shadow, for he withheld his fire after the opening shots. They were making themselves targets by the flame from their own guns.

Creeping along the fringe of the pier, The Shadow was coming in upon the nearest Japanese, who was still shooting blindly in the darkness. The sound of barking guns drowned the hum of an approaching boat. The first evidence of its arrival came when a searchlight blazed squarely across the pier.

The Japanese were caught in the glare. Their guns quit talking; like The Shadow, they heard a brisk command from the boat. They knew what the ship was—a navy cutter from Mare Island. Someone had reported that the end of the pier was open, and the navy boat had come to investigate.

Not waiting to argue, the Japs used their acrobatic skill to scramble across the boathouse roof and dive from sight, just as a rifle volley opened from the cutter. There were commands to cut off their flight along the shore. The cutter swashed away from the pier, turned its searchlight in a new direction.

NONE of the sailors had spied The Shadow. He had been in the glare only for a moment, then had dropped completely from sight through the hole to the hidden dock below. This was his chance to turn matters to his own advantage. The Japanese were slippery, but by cutting through the boathouse, The Shadow hoped to overtake at least one of the trio.

Their route was shorter. They were across the boathouse, onto solid land before he even arrived inside the squatty building; but that mattered little. The Shadow depended upon the cutter's roving searchlight to give a fleeting glimpse of at least one fugitive. The Shadow still held to his conviction that one prisoner would be enough.

He was almost across the boathouse; two more strides would have brought him to the outer door, when a cataclysm struck.

To The Shadow, the shock was only momentary. His stride was halted by a blast of flame, a mighty

Long legs swung away in pendulum fashion as the driving Japanese missed them.

heaving of the floor, a crackle of timbers all about him. A chunk of a wooden beam thudded his head with a jolt that he did not feel, amid that thunderous burst. He was tossed in air, ricocheted like a human projectile, to land amid a torrent of shattered timbers at a spot where there no longer was a floor.

A charge of dynamite had exploded beneath the old pier, skyrocketing its center high into the night with a force that crumpled the boathouse into a mass of unrecognizable debris.

Flying wreckage showered the cutter; the shock of the blast flattened sailors to the deck. The only casualty was the searchlight, which was shattered by a flying timber that struck it end-on. By the time the crew had nosed the boat ashore, pursuit of the Japanese was useless.

For half an hour, sailors searched the remnants of the ruined pier and pried into the splintered fragments of the boathouse in hope of finding at least one of the Orientals that they had spied.

Finally satisfied that there had been no victims, they gave up the hunt.

The cutter headed back to Mare Island, to report. Thick night gripped the wreckage beside the shore, with silence that was stirred only by the monotonous lick of tiny waves.

Sweeping searchlights from Alcatraz came short of that ruined mass of blackness, as if loath to reveal the spot where The Shadow lay entombed.

CHAPTER IV
HIGH TIDE

THE explosion north of Sausalito was stop-press news for the San Francisco papers. By midnight, special editions were on the street, selling as fast as newsboys could peddle them. The story, though meager in its details, had every element that made it sensational.

Though navy authorities insisted that the mysterious Z-boat was yet untested; that its purpose, as well as its design, were purely matters for speculation, the newspapers refused to believe it. Big headlines proclaimed that the missing ship was a type of vessel that might revolutionize all warfare.

They based that cry on the fact that navy boats were looking for the *Barracuda* all over San Francisco Bay and in waters off the Golden Gate. The department had stated the ship's name, claiming that Commander Prew had previously announced it, and that indicated that other details were being withheld.

But the newspapers were wrong.

Only one observer had seen what had happened to the *Barracuda*; he, alone, could have solved the mystery of why the ship had disappeared. His name did not appear in the newspaper accounts; if it had, he would have been listed as dead.

That person was The Shadow.

By the time the final editions were on press, rival newspapers had scooped one another with more news. One item concerned Commander Rodney Prew. The former naval officer was not aboard the *Barracuda*, as first supposed. He had been seen in San Francisco nearly an hour after the cutter had visited the rifled pier.

That was just about the time when news flashes had come over the radio. Learning that the *Barracuda* was gone, Prew had staged a disappearance of his own. Naval authorities were looking for him, without success.

Such news was sensational, but it was matched by the story that a rival newspaper carried. That sheet stated on positive authority that Japanese had been seen by the crew of the navy cutter. Reports concerning Japanese were not unusual in California; they might be blamed for anything short of an earthquake. But when such news was solidly backed, it carried weight.

The fate of the *Barracuda* had suddenly swelled to a matter of international importance, promising all sorts of startling developments. But no one, not even the most fanciful of news writers, predicted the next development that came.

It happened just before dawn, miles off the California coast, where a coast-wise steamer was plowing northward through the long swells of the Pacific. She was the *Yukon*, the same ship that The Shadow had seen sailing from the Golden Gate.

ALL was quiet aboard the *Yukon* when a lookout sighted a low gray hulk ahead. His quick call brought the *clang* of bells, the reverse of motors that halted the steamer promptly. The thing that the lookout saw resembled a half-sunken derelict just off the starboard bow; but, curiously, the *Yukon* had ridden over it.

The mystery was shattered by a sudden scuffle that began at the steamer's stern. Shots were fired; crew members, dashing there, were confronted by a squad of masked men who had come over the ship's rail.

Managed by a broad-shouldered leader whose jaw showed wide beneath his mask, the boarders had shot down three of the steamship's crew. Though few in number, they held the upper hand, and they had assured their success by first placing accomplices aboard the *Yukon*.

Treacherous crew members accounted for the ease with which the masked raiders had come aboard. Fuming officers of the *Yukon* found themselves covered by revolvers that mutineers had drawn. They could not resist, for fear that others might turn out to be parties to the plan.

With the crew subdued, Felix Sergon and his followers proceeded with outright piracy.

Men from the *Barracuda* visited the cabins of the *Yukon*, pounded upon doors and made passengers turn over their valuables. They cowed the purser in his office, threatened him with torture, until he opened the strongbox and turned over its contents.

Gorged with funds from wealthy tourists, satiated by the capture of a large payroll that was being carried to Alaska, the pirates retired to the stern and dropped down by a rope ladder. With them went the deserters from the *Yukon*, half a dozen in number. The last to remain on deck was Felix Sergon, still unrecognized because of his mask.

Sergon's bluff was a perfect one.

He was holding off the entire crew with a single gun, watching for the first hand that might start a move. In his hard rasp, he told them that there were still traitors among them, and he called upon such men to follow after he had reached the *Barracuda*.

Thrusting away his revolver, Sergon coolly went over the side. From the deck of the *Yukon*, shaky officers and seamen watched him board the strange-decked craft, with its half-domed cockpit.

It wasn't until the *Barracuda* started slowly away that Sergon suddenly pulled off his mask. Too distant for his face to be recognized, he gave a contemptuous wave back toward the *Yukon*. That was when the men aboard the steamer realized that his talk of other traitors had been a fake.

The *Barracuda* was off again, heading indolently southward as though its master feared no pursuit. Within its hull, the stolen Z-boat was carrying loot that totaled close to one hundred thousand dollars.

By the time the pirate craft was a speck on the horizon, radio flashes were issuing from the *Yukon*. Sergon had not bothered to cripple the steamship's wireless, though he could easily have done so. He did not seem to care how widely, or how soon, his act of piracy was reported.

The news brought prompt action. Numbers of destroyers steamed out from San Francisco Bay, accompanied by other searching craft! They had orders to find the *Barracuda*, and if occasion demanded, to sink her on sight.

Airplanes zoomed seaward from all along the coast, hoping to aid the sea search. But finding the *Barracuda* by day proved as difficult as at night. Again the strange ship had vanished, this time with more than a bay to hide her. Seemingly, the whole expanse of the Pacific Ocean had become the Z-boat's own preserve.

One phase, at least, of the mystery was solved. Though Commander Prew had not been located, naval authorities announced—without his corroboration—that the *Barracuda* must unquestionably be a submarine, probably one that was capable of submerging to great depths. Nothing else could account for the way in which the ship had vanished, even from the sight of ocean-patrolling seaplanes.

AMID wild speculation and resultant rumors, the public was interested only in the sea search for the *Barracuda*. Little attention was drawn to certain work that took place on the bay shore, not many miles from Sausalito. There, searchers were probing the ruins of Prew's boathouse, hoping to find some chance clue to the missing *Barracuda*.

The work proved as slow as it was fruitless. When shattered timbers were pulled away, they revealed nothing except other chunks of wood below. At times, the task became precarious. Broken beams slipped, almost plunging the workers into the debris.

Near sunset, there was a warning clatter while men were prying at a fragment of a wall. Everyone made a scramble as the ruins gave way and tumbled deep among the pilings.

One man couldn't quite grab the hands that snatched for him. He was caught in a vortex of caving ruins and barely managed to wriggle free. He splashed into the water beneath, and was almost senseless when rescuers dragged him out.

A piece of falling wood had struck the worker's head, which caused others to form the almost obvious conclusion that anyone trapped in the charred ruins could never come out alive.

It was lucky, they decided, that no one had been entombed there the night before. Such a person might have lived until morning, but he wouldn't have had a chance, after these workers began to tear the ruins apart.

Such was the verdict when the men quit work. With nightfall, guards went on duty, to see that no prowlers approached the wreckage of the boathouse. Nor did the guards venture too close, for they remembered the close call that a man had experienced only a few hours before.

That was why none of the guards heard the first sounds that came from the shattered ruin, a stir that belied the opinion of those who were sure that no one could be alive there.

The noise was scarcely louder than the lap of the waves that broke the hush of night. In fact, those licking waters of the bay were responsible for the stir beneath the ruined boathouse. The debris had settled, the tide had risen—dried timbers were receiving their first taste of water. So was the human form within the ruins.

The lap of water against his face revived The Shadow from a state of semiconsciousness. For the first time in many hours, he sensed more than a vague medley of sounds that had seemed to come from undefinable distances.

He was wedged in a water-filled space of blackness, so tightly that he could scarcely move. When he pushed one hand painfully upward, it slithered against a roundish slimy object, a piling that had remained unshattered by last night's blast.

Dimly, the past recalled itself to The Shadow. He remembered the cataclysmic destruction of the boathouse. Gradually, he realized how he had fared.

Struck by a flying timber, The Shadow had rebounded toward the corner by the open trapdoor. He had missed the buckling floor, to land between the upright pilings beneath. The flood of wreckage had piled about him; one chunk had actually wedged in between the pilings, just above his head. That had been fortunate. The piece of wood had acted as a buffer.

Today, The Shadow had gone lower, with the settling timbers. Men had worked around the pilings, pressing them apart. That accounted for his being above the level of the rising tide, and it made his present plight more precarious than ever. Soon,

The lap of water against his face revived The Shadow from a state of semiconsciousness.

the tide would be high, above the level of his head.

WITH all his strength, The Shadow tried to withdraw his legs from the pressure of the pilings. He failed. Stretching his arms, he gripped the wedged beam above his head, ready to risk loosening an avalanche of broken wood, if it came free. Again, he worked to free his legs, without result.

Desperate minutes, those, climaxed when the water came above The Shadow's face. The tide was high and he was completely beneath it. Too late to give a shout to those on shore, even had he guessed that men were there.

With every ounce of gathered strength, The Shadow pulled upon the wedged beam. It seemed useless, for the strain upon his legs was proof complete that he could not release them. Yet the effort brought results. Though The Shadow's body did not budge an inch upward, the beam came down.

Those pilings formed a long, narrow angle, spreading toward the top. To work up from their scissors grip was impossible, but to spread them by pressure from the top, was a feasible procedure. The beam that The Shadow gripped was the very wedge he needed.

Hauled down by The Shadow's desperate effort, it pressed the pilings inches wide. Slimy wood offered no friction, and those inches were enough.

Just when The Shadow's breath gave out, his legs wrenched free. The beam stopped its descent despite his haul. Instead, The Shadow was coming up. His legs were no longer anchored; it was the beam's turn to stick fast. Chinning up to the cross-piece, The Shadow took long, grateful puffs of air.

A few minutes later, he was astride the beam, reaching gingerly among the cluttered wreckage that was jammed above. Vaguely, he recalled past clatterings and knew that men must have been at work. Chances were that the rubbish had settled tightly. Any space would be worth an attempt at exit. Working his hands above his head, The Shadow found a gap.

Then he was burrowing upward, dragging his numbed body between massive slivers that seemed to bite like claws. At times, his jostling shoulders brought tremors from the mass about him, and when he reached the looser space above, his journey had reached its most precarious stage. His body was half clear; he was resting his weight on one arm, when he felt the whole mass shift.

Mere seconds might have carried The Shadow into a new, and less lucky, burial, if he had not remembered those pilings in the darkness beside him. He shot both arms in the right direction, embraced a bulky object with all the grip that he could give.

Then The Shadow was swinging clear, clutching the piling above the level where the slime began, while broken boards and shingles rumbled away beneath him, to bring splashes from the water below.

Shouts came from the shore. Watchers had heard the new crash and suspected that someone was prying into the ruins. The pilings here were wide enough for The Shadow to twist between them and brace himself during the brief search that followed.

The guards were cautious in their approach; their flashlights did not reveal the blackened shape that might have been one of the pilings among which it rested.

Deciding that the rubbish had settled of its own accord, the watchers groped back to the shore. The Shadow, as soon as the lights drew away, let himself downward, out beyond the pilings. Too weary even for a short swim, he worked his way from post to post, until he crawled on land.

THE guards tonight were not as crafty as the Japanese who had been on shore the night before. This group were still flashing their lights, and it was easy to avoid them. But The Shadow did not entirely trust his numbed legs. Instead of rising, he crawled on hands and knees, skirting bushes, keeping low each time he rested, until he found the pathway up to the road.

He hoped that any search had been confined to the shore itself, and that proved to be the case. The Shadow's coupé was exactly where he had left it, buried deep in the ditch of the side road. He started the motor; when it had warmed up, he carefully reversed the car, lest its noise reach the shore.

The guards, it seemed, were out of earshot; for when The Shadow paused to listen from the main road, he heard no sounds from below. Using the road as a gray-streaked guide, he started the car forward in the darkness and came to the nearest bend.

There, The Shadow risked his lights. He shoved the gear into high and pressed the accelerator. With a purr, the coupé was returning over its course of the night before, taking its owner back to San Francisco.

Once in that city, The Shadow would begin his own campaign to solve the riddle of the missing *Barracuda.*

CHAPTER V
THE NEXT QUEST

AMONG the exclusive apartment hotels of San Francisco, the Leland Arms boasted not only the best location, but the most imposing array of guests. Many of the persons who strolled its club-like lobby were individuals of worldwide note.

Along with other services, the management kept

close tabs upon its guests. That was done politely, unobtrusively, all for the benefit of the persons concerned. Persons of fame or wealth might encounter annoying situations when they stopped at some hotels, but never at the Leland Arms.

Tonight, the guest record showed one important checkmark. One guest, Mr. Lamont Cranston, from New York, was missing without due reason. Usually, when guests left the hotel, polite clerks learned where they intended to go. Last night, a slip had been made in Cranston's case.

The record showed, though, that he had departed without luggage and that he had not checked out. That made it very plausible that something might have happened to Mr. Lamont Cranston. Everyone, from clerk to doorman, was anxiously hoping for his return.

Shortly after nine o'clock, a feeling of relief swept over the personnel. It was occasioned when a taxicab stopped at the Leland Arms, and discharged a tall passenger in evening clothes, who gave a short nod to the doorman. By the time Lamont Cranston entered the lobby, every attendant there had received the doorman's flash that he was back.

The clerk inquired politely where Mr. Cranston had been and learned that he had visited friends in Oakland. A bellboy was bringing in a large suitcase, so the clerk supposed that Cranston must have taken some luggage after all. Probably he had dressed in evening clothes before leaving Oakland for the trip across the bay.

There was certainly nothing in Cranston's appearance to betray where he had actually spent the preceding night. His calm, almost masklike face showed no traces of an ordeal; his immaculate attire indicated that he had remained fastidious ever since he had left the hotel the night before.

In fact, no greater contrast could have been imagined than Cranston, as he stood at present, compared to a bedraggled, water-soaked figure that had quite recently dragged itself from the ruins of a bay-shore pier.

Such contrasts, it happened, were The Shadow's specialty.

Persons who encountered The Shadow invariably marveled at his speed of action. Conversely, those who met Lamont Cranston were impressed by his leisurely manner. He displayed it in the lobby of the Leland Arms—first, when he motioned the bellboy toward the elevator; again, when he loafed over toward the newsstand.

There, Cranston bought a newspaper that fairly screamed with news, but he glanced at the headlines in blasé fashion.

Such things as a missing Z-boat, a vanished commander, Japanese plots, piracy on the high seas, were scarcely of moment to Lamont Cranston. When he wanted excitement, he hunted big game in Africa or Asia. When he read newspapers, he concentrated upon the stock market reports.

That, at least, was what he seemed to do, when he seated himself in a corner of the lobby; but during his turning of the pages, Cranston brought the front page in between the spread. Behind that newspaper, his eyes took on a sharpness as he eagerly read details that he was scanning for the first time.

Odd that he, The Shadow, the only person to see the *Barracuda* vanish, should be the very one who needed information!

THE newspaper told much, yet very little. From the deluge of events, it was difficult to separate the kernels from the chaff. There were theories, however, that interested The Shadow, since they smacked of facts given out from official quarters.

First was the matter of Commander Rodney Prew. By rights, the inventor of the Z-boat should have been at the pier, instead of at his club, where he had last been seen. If Prew had not expected the things that had happened, why had he run out so suddenly when the news came?

Confronted with that question, the newspaper had sought an answer and had found a good one. Prew's past had been investigated, bringing much to light. His resignation from the navy, a few years ago, had actually been his method of escaping a court-martial.

Prew, it seemed, had been in command of a destroyer flotilla, and had put his ships to an unauthorized speed test. While higher officers were weighing the matter, he had left the service. It was after his return to private life that he had begun his development of the mysterious Z-boat.

Even there, Prew was due for criticism. He had not offered the ship to the government until authorities had learned of its construction. Prew's sudden willingness to turn the ship over to the navy, his insistence that such had been his original intention, was something that seemed very much a subterfuge, in light of recent events.

Intimation No. 1 was that Commander Rodney Prew had deliberately intended to sell his Z-boat to any foreign power that might make the highest bid. The fact that he was in San Francisco when the ship vanished, had all the earmarks of an alibi.

Next was the question of the Japanese.

Why had they been at the pier, trying to keep undercover, at the very time when the *Barracuda* had left?

There was a good answer to that one. The Japanese were anxious to buy the Z-boat; they had, perhaps, completed a deal with Prew. Naturally enough, they would be on hand to cover up when the *Barracuda* departed.

Prew, of course, was not on hand to deny any charges made against him. But the Japanese, as usual, had representatives in Washington who were polite, as well as emphatic, in their denials that they knew anything about the *Barracuda*.

That, from the newspaper's standpoint, was merely the same old effort to bluff the American public. One whole page cited instances of Japanese diplomacy dating from the year 1853, when Commodore Perry had sailed into the Bay of Yeddo to show the shoguns what a modern fleet looked like.

Since that year, the newspaper insisted, the Japanese had always been overinterested in acquiring exclusive rights to new types of war vessels, and that applied to the Z-boat *Barracuda*.

Those points settled, what about the ship itself? Why had the *Barracuda* gone in for piracy? Who was its commander, identified only as a man with a harsh voice and a jaw that looked like iron?

The newspaper did not mention the name of Felix Sergon, which indicated that it had not been learned. But Sergon's part in the scheme was quite neatly covered. The theory was that Commander Prew had paid him to run off with the *Barracuda* and turn it over to the Japanese. The subsequent deed of piracy was simply a Nipponese ruse to obscure the real facts.

The unknown commander of the Z-boat had probably received word by radio that Japanese agents had been spotted near the pier. Following prearranged orders, he had pretended to go in for piracy, to make it look as though he had started the venture on his own.

Into this medley, the newspaper had injected the feminine question, bringing up the name of Claudette Marchand. She, like Commander Prew, had disappeared, but she had not been seen after the *Barracuda* had been reported strayed or stolen. So it seemed that the fate of Claudette Marchand was the real mystery in the case.

She might have disappeared either with the *Barracuda*, or with Commander Prew. It was possible that she had met with foul play. One thing alone was certain: that the missing girl knew much that had happened and could tell a great deal, if found and questioned.

With that, The Shadow agreed.

FOLDING the newspaper, The Shadow laid it aside, with the stock market reports on display. In Cranston's style, he strolled to the elevator and rode up to his room on the fifth floor. The bellboy was still waiting there with the suitcase, for he had expected Cranston to bring the key.

Unlocking the door, The Shadow turned on the lights. He pointed to a trunk rack; the bellboy placed the suitcase there and received a generous tip. Closing the door, The Shadow strolled about the room in a fashion that still suited Cranston.

First, he ran his forefinger along the crack of a bureau drawer. Next, he stopped at a closet, to give the knob of the door a slight tug. He inserted a key in the lock of a trunk that stood in a corner and gave it a double twist.

The laugh that whispered from Cranston's fixed lips was the echoed mockery of The Shadow.

Supposedly, no one knew that The Shadow was in San Francisco. There were certain persons, however, who could have learned of his presence last night. Those parties, by all ordinary calculations, should never have identified The Shadow as Lamont Cranston. Nevertheless, that very identification had been accomplished.

Before leaving the hotel room, The Shadow had waxed an almost invisible hair across the crack of the bureau drawer. That telltale object was gone, sure proof that the drawer had been opened during his absence.

He had left the closet door closed only to a point where it would normally remain shut, but he had not let the latch spring into place. His careful pull on the doorknob should have brought the door open. It had failed to do so. Someone else had opened that door, and closed it afterward but had let it latch.

As for the trunk, it had a double lock. Some person had finally opened it with a special key, but in relocking it, had been satisfied with a single turn. The Shadow's own experiment with the lock proved that it was not set as he had left it.

Persons unknown had entered this room and searched it thoroughly. In light of recent incidents, they could have had but one purpose: to find out facts pertaining to The Shadow. Not only were they crafty, they had penetrated the Cranston disguise—which proved them extraordinarily clever.

But whatever they had found could not have mattered. The Shadow had left nothing in this room that could have proven their suspicion.

That, however, did not settle the matter for The Shadow. Instead, it gave him an immediate question—one quite as close to the mystery of the *Barracuda* as it was to his own personal security, since the two had become identified.

Whatever else The Shadow had in mind could wait until he had interviewed the man who had instigated the search of the hotel room. That man, The Shadow felt sure, would not be difficult to find.

Stepping to the suitcase that he had brought with him from another hotel, The Shadow opened it and brought out a fresh cloak, along with a flattened slouch hat.

Placing those garments so they would appear as a topcoat resting across his arm, The Shadow paused beside the window and gazed across the lighted slopes of San Francisco, to an area where lights of many colors threw a weird glow against the foggy sky.

Again a laugh stirred from motionless lips. That mirth was The Shadow's prophecy of an adventure soon to come.

CHAPTER VI
A JAPANESE WELCOME

IT is supposed that the recent Japanese invasion of Chinese soil began with the conquest of Manchuria. To a degree, that idea might be amended. Long before they set up the puppet state of Manchukuo, the Japanese were biting into Chinese territory, not in Asia but in North America.

Their sphere of action was San Francisco's Chinatown, where, by wise and timely purchases, the Japanese used business methods to acquire Chinese properties. Hence, strictly speaking, San Francisco no longer possesses a Chinatown. Instead, it has an Oriental quarter where natives of warring nations dwell together in comparative peace.

The lights that The Shadow viewed from his hotel window were those of Chinatown, but his thoughts concerned a Japanese establishment. Riding by cab to the Oriental district, he traveled along a street where Japanese signs stood out conspicuously among those of Chinese merchants.

From the window, The Shadow saw the very sign that he wanted. It bore the title:

ISHI SOYOTO
Oriental Merchandise

Soyoto's shop was closed. It was a small place tucked between two Chinese stores, but above were darkened windows that might be Soyoto's residence. The Shadow told the cab driver to turn the corner.

By the time the taxi had wheeled into a dark street, its passenger was no longer Lamont Cranston. His shoulders enveloped in his black cloak, his head topped by the slouch hat, The Shadow let a bill flutter into the driver's lap and made a silent and rapid exit from the cab.

The taximan didn't speculate on where his passenger had gone. He decided that the less he bothered about it, the better. It wasn't often that money dropped into his lap, and he wasn't anxious to park too long on a backstreet in Chinatown. The cab scooted away as if something was after it.

From the gloom of the street below, The Shadow looked for a way to reach Soyoto's upstairs premises. The more he studied them, the greater the problem became. There was no rear door to the place, and the windows, from their look, were barred.

All that was in keeping with what The Shadow knew about Ishi Soyoto.

He had never met the Japanese in question, but he knew that Soyoto was something more than an ordinary merchant. There had been times when The Shadow had looked into Japanese affairs, and he was familiar with important messages that bore the signature of Ishi Soyoto.

As Cranston, he had visited the shop in daytime, to find it a sleepy place, quite out of keeping with Japanese enterprise. Nor was Soyoto ever in the place.

That fitted with The Shadow's opinion that Ishi Soyoto was an unofficial representative of certain important factions in Japan, the very man who might employ a group like the acrobatic Japs who had given The Shadow a battle on the bay shore.

Keeping close to the dingy wall, The Shadow avoided occasional pedestrians in the darkness. His course took him back toward the corner that the taxicab had turned. Just short of the lights, The Shadow stopped to observe a little shop with dimly lighted windows.

It bore a Chinese sign, and it looked like a tea shop, but through the window The Shadow could see stacks of dust-laden chests along the shelves. A sleepy-eyed Chinaman was squatting in a corner chair, apparently expecting no customers.

This place, like Soyoto's store, looked dead, so far as business was concerned. True, a Chinese merchant might be content to let business drift along with time; but he could scarcely be expected to stay open evenings, if he adhered to such philosophy.

The Chinese tea shop, as The Shadow studied it, looked like a tribute to Soyoto's craftiness. Anyone looking for a secret entrance to a Japanese headquarters would not expect to find a route leading through a Chinaman's store.

SCARCELY had The Shadow formed that opinion before he drew back instinctively to a space away from the window. Someone had come in from the corner—a little man, who was sneaking along the narrow street. The Shadow could hear the fellow's breathing, as he stopped in front of the tea house for a cautious look about.

The man slid into the shop. Swinging back toward the window, The Shadow caught a glimpse of the visitor. The fellow was a Japanese, and he passed unchallenged by the Chinese proprietor. Opening a door beyond a stack of tea chests, the Jap stepped from sight.

Five seconds later, a patch of blackness fell upon

the threshold of the tea shop. It sidled through the open door, grew to a strange, grotesque shape once it was inside. A low whisper was audible among those cobwebbed walls.

The sleepy Chinaman looked up; his lips opened to drop a long pipe that was pressed between them. When he found his voice, the Celestial gulped a name:

"Ying Ko!"

He had recognized The Shadow. Long had that master of mysterious methods been known among Chinese as Ying Ko. He was recognized as a foe to all who dealt in evil. Arrived with unexpected suddenness, he had every appearance of a being bent on vengeance.

The effect on the lone Chinaman was exactly what The Shadow had anticipated.

That Celestial was troubled with a guilty conscience, not because he had ever dealt in crime but because he was in the pay of Ishi Soyoto. He knew of fellow countrymen who would not be pleased to know that his store served as the back door to a Japanese headquarters.

He recognized that such word would reach them, should Ying Ko choose. The expression of his face showed plainly that he was ready to follow any orders that The Shadow might give.

Stepping close to the Chinaman, The Shadow toned low words in singsong language. The Chinaman nodded. He was to remember nothing of Ying Ko, should he be questioned later. That was a plausible suggestion; after all, who could ever see Ying Ko, should Ying Ko choose otherwise?

Reasoning thus, the Chinaman wondered why The Shadow had paused at all while en route to the hidden door. The mystery was explained when The Shadow put questions in Chinese. Those queries had the tone of commands, and the worried Chinaman oozed answers. By the time he was through, he had blabbed every detail that he knew regarding the secret route to Soyoto's upstairs rooms.

With a whispered laugh that made the Chinaman cringe uneasily, The Shadow wheeled past the tea chests and opened the door. He glided into darkness, to pick a course along a passage. He went by a stairway, came to a door, but instead of opening it he pressed a panel shoulder high in the wall.

A door slid open; it closed as soon as The Shadow had crossed the threshold. Counting six paces forward, The Shadow turned to his right and probed another panel. A second sliding door revealed steep stairs, dimly illuminated from above. The Shadow followed that flight to the top, then stepped across the final step.

He had avoided a move that would have sounded an alarm. Everything was as the Chinaman had told him, and the best was still to come. Moving along another passage, The Shadow stopped at a door on the right. It seemed locked, and he could have worked for hours at the keyhole without result. The trick lay in the doorknob. It worked like the dial of a safe.

Three to the left, two to the right, four to the left—the door was open. Twisting into a darkened room, The Shadow closed the door behind him and moved along beside the wall. At the corner, he stretched his arms as a brace, moved his foot forward and tested the floor. It gave with a slight creak.

Again, the Chinaman had revealed the truth. This room was floored by an oversized trapdoor, set to drop an unwary intruder into depths below.

Edging along the next wall, The Shadow reached another door. There was no trick to this one, but he employed the utmost care when he turned the knob. As he eased the door inward, The Shadow saw a mild glow that permeated a lavishly furnished room.

On one side were windows; on the other, the usual door by which persons entered. That door, the Chinaman had told The Shadow, was always guarded by men stationed in an anteroom.

NEAR the center of the room was a large desk. Behind it, his back toward the windows, set a bespectacled Japanese. He was attired in a native costume, and wore a bluish jacket with a golden sash that showed above the level of the flat-topped desk. Beside him lay some open books, all printed in Japanese characters on thin double pages of rice paper.

In contrast, however, were other objects close by. A cradle telephone rested on the desk; just beyond was a news ticker, that began to *click* as The Shadow watched. The Japanese turned to watch the tape that came from the ticker, and his move and its noise gave The Shadow perfect opportunity to step into the room and shut the door behind him.

There was no doubt as to the identity of the man at the desk. His wizened face, his thin hair, the large-rimmed spectacles, fitted the descriptions of Ishi Soyoto. Busy with the ticker, Soyoto could not hear The Shadow's approach. He was still turned away when his black-clad visitor had reached the desk.

The Shadow drew an automatic, leveled it across the desk so that its muzzle would loom before Soyoto's eyes the moment that the bespectacled man turned about. Indeed, The Shadow found himself gripped by a rare emotion: that of impatience. He was anxious to see Soyoto's reaction when he faced the gun.

It would be the first object that Soyoto would see, for the room was lighted solely by a desk lamp that threw its glare directly upon the big .45 projecting from The Shadow's gloved hand.

The ticker ceased its clickings. Soyoto tore away the tape, dropped it upon the desk along with other paper strips. He swung his swivel chair around, coming face to face with the gun muzzle. He eyed it with interest, so fascinated that he did not look upward to meet the gaze of The Shadow.

In a troubled manner, Soyoto made clacking noises with his tongue. They indicated distress at the realization of an invader, but that note was well-feigned.

Before The Shadow could catch the real significance, men were upon him. They rose from hidden spots behind the desk and big chairs that sided it. There were four of them; they came with a simultaneous leap, wiry fellows who caught The Shadow before he could wrench away. He was dragged back from the desk; his gun tilted upward, away from Soyoto.

Too late to offset the tactics of those jiujitsu specialists, The Shadow could have resisted only with gunfire. His finger was on the trigger, his deft wrist whisked from gripping hands soon enough for him to aim as he pleased. In that one maneuver, The Shadow had counteracted the Japanese attack, and it was sufficient for him to gain a real advantage of his own.

But The Shadow did not fire. He let the gun pivot in his hand as proof that he could use it; he lowered the weapon toward the floor. Ishi Soyoto saw the gesture and gave a pleased grin. Again, he made the *clack-clack* that he used as signal to his followers.

Hands released The Shadow. The jiujitsu crew stepped back. Soyoto arose from his swivel chair, made a polite gesture toward another chair near the desk.

"Your visit is a welcome one," said Soyoto in short-clipped English. "Pray be seated, so we can discuss matters—Mr. *Cranston*!"

The Shadow let his gun slide beneath his cloak. Peeling away his gloves, he held them in one hand, while he removed his hat with the other. He was indicating that need for subterfuge had passed, and again Soyoto looked pleased.

Dropping the gloves in the hat, The Shadow placed the latter on the desk. His face came into the light; scrutinizing the firm features of Cranston, Soyoto delivered a nod of recognition. He watched The Shadow take the opposite chair. Speaking in Japanese, Soyoto ordered his servitors to retire.

They filed away in solemn procession through the door that led to the anteroom. Alone with The Shadow, Ishi Soyoto politely proffered a pack of cigarettes. The Shadow took one, Soyoto another. Both lighted them from the match that the thin-haired Japanese supplied.

Leaning back in his swivel chair, Ishi Soyoto indulged in another of his wide-mouthed grins. Then, his face becoming more solemn, Soyoto began to speak. His tone was serious, his expression sincere.

For with all his cunningness, Ishi Soyoto had recognized that his neat trap might have failed him had The Shadow chosen battle instead of conference.

CHAPTER VII
SOYOTO'S MESSAGE

"I HAVE awaited you, Mr. Cranston," declared Soyoto, in his choppy English, "because I know much about you. One who is so clever as to be The Shadow should surely learn of those who have learned of him."

While propounding that logic, Soyoto kept his eyes fixed upon the calm face of Cranston. Through his thick spectacles, the Japanese was trying to scrutinize beyond the impenetrable mask that formed The Shadow's features. Gaining nothing, Soyoto puffed his cigarette, blew a slow coil of smoke from between his lips.

"Of course," he said, politely, "we know that you are not Lament Cranston. The face that you wear is a disguise—like your cloak, like this hat"—he gestured toward the desk—"that you have obliged me by laying aside.

"But since you choose to appear as Cranston, we respect your wishes. To me, for the present at least, you are Lamont Cranston. Is that to our mutual like?"

"Quite," replied The Shadow. "It intrigues me, Mr. Soyoto, to meet someone who has guessed the identity that I occasionally use."

Soyoto listened intently to The Shadow's tone.

It was not a sinister whisper; it was a calm, even form of speech, almost a leisurely drawl. It was a voice that suited Cranston, and Soyoto admired the thoroughness with which The Shadow clung to his present role.

"This meeting is most fortunate," resumed Soyoto. "It is an honor to speak with one so wise. I am glad to greet The Shadow as a friend. It may be that we can exchange much knowledge."

It was evident that Soyoto was fishing for facts, and his statement indicated that he might supply some of his own. There was a flicker of interest on the maskish face of Cranston. Whether genuine or merely an expression to encourage further statements from Soyoto was something that baffled the Japanese.

"Perhaps you would like me to speak first," suggested Soyoto. "Very good, Mr. Cranston. It all has been a very bad mistake. We—myself and others—have no interest in the ship called the *Barracuda*, except to prove that we did not steal it."

He picked up strips of tape from the desk, smoothed them and passed them across to The Shadow. They were typed in Japanese characters, and Soyoto nodded knowingly when he saw The Shadow read them. Most of them were confidential reports from Washington, further denials on the part of Japanese regarding the *Barracuda* matter.

Soyoto reserved one strip for himself, stroking it between his fingers while he kept the printed side away from The Shadow's view.

"The facts are these," declared Soyoto. "Commander Prew invented a new ship. What he intended to do with it, we do not know. It is said he did not wish to give it to his government, though he had promised to do so. Whether that is true or false, I cannot say. But it is certain that Commander Prew did not offer his ship to my government in Tokyo."

There was a slight smile forming on Cranston's lips. Soyoto seemed to understand it, for he leaned forward and added wisely:

"Commander Prew did not steal his own ship. That was done by another. One who has not yet been named. Perhaps you can tell me, Mr. Cranston, just who that person might be."

Soyoto was fingering the tape, referring to it with a glance down his spectacles. That was why The Shadow quietly replied:

"The man's name is Felix Sergon."

There was a bow from Soyoto. He placed the tape in The Shadow's hands. It was a report, in Japanese, naming Sergon as the man who had taken the *Barracuda*.

"YOU understand in full," declared Soyoto. "I am free to tell you why my men were present last night. They were seeking Sergon—not to aid him, but to learn his schemes. Felix Sergon is a very dangerous man. We do not trust him in Japan."

Soyoto's choppy statement had the ring of sincerity, but he was not sure that he had convinced The Shadow.

"You think, perhaps," continued Soyoto, "that we might trust Sergon if he brought the *Barracuda* to us. Not so, Mr. Cranston. But we are very anxious to have Sergon believe that we would buy the ship. That would give us opportunity to trap him."

"Consider these things, Mr. Cranston." Soyoto was leaning back in his chair, smiling wisely. "My government seeks friendship with America. That is why I am in San Francisco. My purpose is not to spy, but to create good will. Unfortunately, that policy has been misunderstood.

"Our only course is to aid your government to regain the missing Z-boat. To do so, we must entice Felix Sergon. We must make him believe that he will be welcome in Japan. That is why we have not stated his name to your government."

Soyoto waited for The Shadow's reaction. He thought he caught a slight nod from Cranston. Soyoto's logic was twofold: first, there was sense to the situation as he had stated it; again, there was the chance that if the Japanese openly declared the name of the man who had taken the Z-boat, they might be subject to further misunderstanding.

Ever clever, Soyoto was letting The Shadow form that second conclusion of his own accord. Once sure that The Shadow had considered it, Soyoto leaned forward with a new suggestion.

"You wonder, perhaps," he began, "why I have mentioned Felix Sergon to you. It is only because you first admitted that you knew who he was. From that, Mr. Cranston, I understand that you have kept all information to yourself. Since that is your policy, we are both in accord.

"Therefore, we can work together. There are facts that each of us should know. Facts, perhaps"—Soyoto was stroking his smooth chin—"that we do know, separately. It would be wise for us to exchange them."

"For what purpose?"

Soyoto evidently expected The Shadow's cool-toned question. He had an answer for it.

"That we may find Commander Rodney Prew," declared the Japanese, "and begin our search for Felix Sergon."

Soyoto's intimation was that Prew had secretly engineered the theft of the *Barracuda*, using Sergon as his tool. He seemed honest in the inference, but there was something deep behind it. The Shadow called the turn.

"To find Prew," he remarked, "we must locate others who knew something about the *Barracuda*. By others I refer to persons associated directly with Prew."

Each time he spoke it, The Shadow stressed the

word "others," and that shot hit home. He knew that Soyoto wanted to learn something regarding Claudette Marchand. In turn, he guessed that there might be another party in the game, someone known to Soyoto. The conjecture proved correct.

"There are two others," agreed Soyoto. "A woman, Prew's secretary, who was at the pier. Also a man, who provided funds to help Prew build his ship."

Cunningly, Soyoto avoided mention of names, pretending that he knew neither one. The Shadow seemed to take the bait.

"If I tell you one name," he suggested, "will you aid me in learning the other?"

"With much pleasure," agreed Soyoto, "as soon as my agents discover it."

The Shadow seemed to weigh the agreement; then, in Cranston's quiet tone, he declared:

"The girl's name is Claudette Marchand."

Soyoto promptly made a note of it, his face very serious. That, to The Shadow, meant that Soyoto was smiling inwardly. It hadn't taken many minutes to analyze Soyoto's way. Whatever his thoughts, the man's facial expression showed the opposite.

"Claudette Marchand," repeated Soyoto. "I should like to know what became of her."

This time, he was smiling, as though merely curious. He was actually telling The Shadow that he was very anxious to acquire that information. Calmly, The Shadow gave it.

"She went aboard the *Barracuda*," he told Soyoto, "along with Sergon and the rest."

For once, Soyoto showed unfeigned elation.

"Ah, that explains it!" he exclaimed. "It was she who dealt with Sergon. It is most likely"—he was cocking his head as he spoke—"that she did so at Prew's order.

"My men"—he spread his hands depreciatingly—"are sometimes very inefficient. They saw the Marchand woman, but believed that she escaped ashore in the confusion."

THE ticker beside the desk was clattering; Soyoto turned, pulled out a length of tape. He read it, shrugged as he folded it. The Shadow saw him tuck the strip beneath his sash.

"More conflicting reports from Washington," declared the Japanese. "All this is very bad. We must wait, very patient, until we can learn more. I thank you, Mr. Cranston, for your visit. This"—he wrote something on a little card—"is my telephone number. Call me whenever you wish."

The Shadow received the card. Soyoto came from behind the desk, stepped toward the outer door. Donning hat and gloves, The Shadow followed. Hand on the doorknob, Soyoto bowed.

"My servants," he said, "will conduct you downstairs. Good evening, Mr. Cranston."

Concealed by the lowered hatbrim, The Shadow had noticed something by the door. It was a light switch with two buttons—one pearl, the other black. The pearl button was pressed inward, indicating that the light was on.

But Soyoto's desk lamp connected with a floor plug. There was no light that the wall switch controlled. Instantly, The Shadow sensed the real purpose of that switch.

It controlled an electric hookup that enabled the servants in the anteroom to hear all that happened to Soyoto's office. That was why Soyoto had been willing to interview The Shadow in private. All along, The Shadow had suspected a catch; he had at last found out what it was.

He was willing to deal with Soyoto on the man's own terms. But any departure from the actual agreement would have to end that policy. From something that he had noticed about Soyoto, The Shadow was convinced that the deal was already void. Soyoto, having learned what facts he wanted, had neglected to state others of his own.

"Good evening, Mr. Soyoto," returned The Shadow, still using his quiet tone. "But permit me to wait a few minutes, while I write out my own address, the one where you can always reach me."

The Shadow raised his left arm, as his hand pretended to reach for something beneath his cloak. With his elbow, he nudged the black button of the wall switch, cutting off the current that controlled the hidden microphone. Soyoto saw the action, started a sudden cry.

The shout did not leave Soyoto's lips. The Shadow's hands were at his throat, clutching it tight. The pair reeled across the room, missing heavy chairs by inches, until they reached a darkened corner past the desk. There, the brief struggle ended. Soon afterward, a black-shrouded figure glided through the fringe of light and opened the door to the anteroom.

Soyoto's jiujitsu crew awaited. One Jap looked into the office, saw his master in the swivel chair, which was turned toward the electric ticker. He closed the door, nodding for another to conduct The Shadow to the street. The route that they took was a direct one, through the closed shop below.

Returning, the guide found the others babbling in conference. They were wondering why Soyoto hadn't called them. They decided that the man from below should report that The Shadow had left the outer door.

At last, the man agreed to do so. He opened the door to Soyoto's office and peered in the direction of the desk.

The Jap spoke, but Soyoto did not answer. Calling excitedly to the others, the fellow rushed in and reached the desk. He and the others found out why Soyoto had not answered.

Their bespectacled master was bound in his chair, his ankles strapped by a leather belt, his wrists girded with his golden sash and twisted through the slats of the chair back.

Soyoto was gagged with a black handkerchief that The Shadow had evidently provided. He had tucked it low behind Soyoto's collar, so that the knot had failed to show when the guards looked in from the anteroom. Turned with his face from view, the gagged Japanese had appeared to be watching the ticker in a natural pose.

The moment he was released, Ishi Soyoto began to give excited orders in his native tongue. His servitors nodded their response and surged from the room. Soon they were rushing through the Chinese tea shop, to reach a car that was housed in an old garage across the rear street.

Unbluffed by Soyoto, The Shadow had outwitted the crafty master of the Japanese. To amend that defeat, Ishi Soyoto had dispatched his own crew of fighters along The Shadow's trail.

CHAPTER VIII
DEATH'S TRAIL

A TAXICAB was wheeling madly through the hilly streets of San Francisco, away from heavy traffic. In it rode The Shadow; between his gloved fingers stretched a strip of ticker tape. It was the last message that had come to Ishi Soyoto. The Shadow had plucked it from the pocket beneath Soyoto's sash.

The light from a corner showed the typing on the strip. It was in Japanese characters; The Shadow had already translated it. The message referred to a man named Carl Methron. It stated that his servant had learned where Methron had gone. He was living at the Hillview Apartments; his apartment number there was 6B.

To The Shadow, Carl Methron could be no person other than the silent partner who had backed Commander Prew's construction of the *Barracuda*. In his analysis of Ishi Soyoto, The Shadow had classed the Japanese as being truthful, but with a canny ability to reserve certain facts.

Soyoto's talk of a backer was genuine. Perhaps he had intended later to reveal the man's name, but it had been evident that he knew it all the while. One reason for Soyoto's reservation was his lack of knowledge concerning Methron's whereabouts.

Ishi Soyoto had wanted to be the first to question Carl Methron. Afterward, he might have passed facts along to The Shadow. In that policy, however, Soyoto had violated his own agreement. Perhaps he felt himself justified; if so, he could not object to The Shadow's own code of ethics.

By tying up Soyoto, The Shadow had simply turned the situation about. He—not Soyoto—would be the first to drop in on Methron. What Prew's backer would have to say, Soyoto could learn later—when The Shadow chose to inform him.

Though the Hillview was some distance from the center of the city, The Shadow knew of the place and had given the taxi driver the shortest route to reach it. At this speed, The Shadow was not worrying about Soyoto's henchmen, even should they follow. He was sure that he had gained a dozen minutes at the start, and that he was increasing that margin.

If Methron happened to be in his apartment, which was likely at this late hour, The Shadow could whisk him away before the Japs arrived. If Methron wasn't there, The Shadow could watch the place. Soyoto's men had ways of bobbing up from nowhere, but they usually had to pick their setting. This time, if the need came, the advantage would be The Shadow's.

Twisting a final corner, the taxi screeched to a stop coming down a steep street. It halted near the side door of the Hillview, and The Shadow did a quick glide to a small parking lot. From that darkness, he watched the taxi pull away.

As it went past the corner, a man stepped into sight and took a look toward the side door. The man was wearing a doorman's uniform; seeing no passenger from the cab, he went back to his post at the front of the apartment house.

That left the path clear for The Shadow, but he maintained caution when he entered the side door. Within the lobby was a newsstand, a glum-faced man behind it. He was looking toward the side door, but he did not see The Shadow pass. No eyes could have spotted the cloaked shape that kept to the deep gloom of the lobby wall.

Straight ahead was a stairway; as usual with many apartments, its lower steps were barely visible from the main lobby. They were white, however, being made of imitation marble, so The Shadow paused before he reached them. He timed his next maneuver to a moment when the man at the newsstand turned away.

Long, silent strides took The Shadow six steps upward. Pausing, he peered back toward the newsstand. The man had looked in his direction, was screwing his eyes as if he had seen something. Then the fellow gave a shrug. He had noted nothing more than a disappearing streak of blackness.

ONE thought pleased The Shadow while he was moving up to the sixth floor. If the Japs arrived, they couldn't risk using that inside stairway. They would have to take a slower route, up an old fire escape that The Shadow had noted at the back of the building.

Hence, it would not be difficult either to intercept them or avoid them. The Shadow could choose whichever policy he wanted, when the time came.

The door of 6B was locked. It had a large, old-fashioned keyhole of the simple type that serves as encouragement to burglars. This floor was the top one, well away from observation. Unlocking that door would have required only a few seconds if The Shadow had not calculated that someone might be inside the apartment.

Therefore, he used his skeleton key as carefully as if he had been working on a difficult lock. When a slight scrape came from the keyhole, he paused to scratch a bit of wax from the key handle.

The key was hollow, filled with oil. Released, the fluid oozed into the lock. When The Shadow turned the key again, not a sound resulted.

Bracing the door as he opened it, The Shadow prevented any creaks. He stood inside the living room of a simply furnished apartment, that was almost totally dark. After listening for sounds, The Shadow began operations with a tiny flashlight.

He came across a telephone unconnected with the downstairs lobby, for it bore an individual number. He saw a desk with a few papers lying on it, but none proved important. However, an open suitcase in the corner contained some empty envelopes tucked near the bottom.

One of these was addressed to J. H. Wiggin, Hillview Apartments, San Francisco. In a corner it bore the return address of Commander Rodney Prew, with a post office box in Sausalito.

The envelope indicated that Carl Methron used the name of Wiggin whenever he occupied this apartment. That, in turn, could explain why Ishi Soyoto had encountered some trouble locating him.

Deciding to investigate the bedroom, The Shadow went in that direction. He no longer required the flashlight, for the bedroom had windows on the front street and lights from below supplied a slight illumination.

In one corner, between the windows, was a bureau, its top drawer half open. Gliding there, The Shadow introduced one hand, his flashlight with it, to produce a gleam within the drawer. The muffled light showed that the drawer was empty.

Snapping off the flashlight, The Shadow removed his hand and reached for the next drawer below. At that moment, his eyes saw a mirror that backed the bureau. The corner was too dark to reveal his face in the glass; but glimmering, distant in the mirror, was a sight that made The Shadow halt short.

That reflection came from a revolver muzzle

From beneath his cloak, The Shadow drew an automatic ... aiming the .45 as he came.

aimed directly toward The Shadow's back from somewhere across the room!

THERE wasn't a sound as The Shadow eased low. Once beneath the level of an intervening bed, he turned his head to locate the gun's exact position. It projected from a closet door in another corner of the room. Chance light, striking the mirror, had reflected it.

Once spotted, the gun could be observed again, although The Shadow had failed to notice it when he first entered. The crack of the door was on the side away from the living room, which had been to The Shadow's advantage at the time when he arrived. But, despite his caution, there were ways in which he might have betrayed his presence.

If so, the man behind that gun was merely waiting for the intruder to come into the window light. Once there, The Shadow would be an absolute target for a capable marksman, with a range so short that one shot should be enough.

Flattened to the floor, The Shadow began a circuitous creep toward the closet. He was below the window level, but he could still see the gun, and the hole in its rounded end looked ominous. Any venturer less confident than The Shadow would have decided upon retreat; for, as the cloaked creeper advanced, the gun muzzle seemed to lower straight for his eyes.

The Shadow recognized that as an optical illusion, one upon which he himself had often depended when dealing with a group of foemen. From the right perspective, a gun would always yawn at a man who faced it, even thought he managed to gain a slight angle of safety.

Nevertheless, it was increasingly difficult to believe that the gun was not on the move. The closer The Shadow came, the more certain it seemed that he was covered, until he was almost at the closet door. There, he waited, holding back even the slightest sound of his own breathing.

He was below the path of the gun. His nerve had served him. Counting that he would not be seen along the blackened floor; calculating that the silence of the gun meant that its owner had not guessed his position, The Shadow had reached a vantage spot.

From beneath his cloak, he drew an automatic. Inching upward, aiming the .45 as he came, he reached for the doorknob with his free hand.

Whether the man in the closet was Methron, alias Wiggin, or some invader here ahead of The Shadow, the only policy was to meet him with a silent attack. Gunshots would not help The Shadow's present investigation, and he had no desire to injure an opponent who might turn out to be a friend. But it would not do to parley with a man who was thrusting a gun muzzle from the edge of an open closet door.

Surprise was the only method. The Shadow provided it when he gave the door a sudden yank. Literally, he flung the door away from him as he came upward with a twist. He caught a flash of the revolver striking downward; as he grabbed for it, he took the full weight of a bulky adversary who came from the closet with a heavy lunge.

CATCHING that gun fist, The Shadow tried to shove it aside. He met with stiff-armed opposition, and with it, the revolver roared. A solid slug sizzled so close to The Shadow's ear that it left a tingle. Slinging his gun hand around the bulky man's neck, The Shadow rolled with him to the floor.

He had pinned the revolver beneath him, where it could do no harm. His own gun was turned full about, poking its cold-muzzle against the sprawled man's neck. The Shadow's whisper added further threat, unless the fellow released his grip on the revolver. But he still clung to it.

One knee on the man's arm, The Shadow gave a tug. Never had he met a grip like that. He couldn't budge the revolver from the fingers that clutched it. It was recollection of that sharp shot, only a few seconds before, that kept The Shadow at work. In a flash, the explanation reached him.

Withdrawing his own gun, The Shadow relaxed his grip on the revolver barrel. Springing to his feet, he found a floor lamp close beside the closet door. Pulling the cord, he turned to view the thing that lay on the floor.

The light disclosed a stiffened figure in pajamas; above the jacket, a contorted face with goggly eyes. That countenance was bloodless, except for a clotted brick-red patch above a baldish temple.

Whoever the man might prove to be, he was stone dead; had been so for many hours. Murdered by a blow upon the head, he had been planted in the closet, a revolver in his fist. *Rigor mortis* had set in upon the corpse, accounting for its stiffness and the grip with which the dead hand clutched the gun.

The Shadow's own grab had pressed the man's trigger finger. The shot that had so nearly meant The Shadow's doom had come during a duel with a dead antagonist!

CHAPTER IX
THE OUTSIDE CALL

FINISHED with his brief survey of the murder victim, The Shadow considered a subject that concerned himself. His plans for the immediate future depended upon whether or not the gunshot had been heard.

Turning off the light, he peered from the window.

Below, he saw the doorman stalking back and forth in front of the apartment house. That was a good sign, for any sound of gunfire would probably have brought the man inside.

Perhaps the shot had been heard in some other sixth-floor apartment, but had not yet been reported. To learn if that had happened, The Shadow made a trip to the outside hall, only to find complete silence. So far, so good.

In the hallway, The Shadow found an exit to the fire escape. He listened there, but heard no sounds from below. The fire escape was not far from Methron's living room. When he returned there, The Shadow opened a window from which he could listen occasionally for any sounds of approaching Japanese.

Back in the bedroom, The Shadow restored the light and took a look into the closet. Hanging there were the dead man's clothes. Search of the pockets produced evidence of the victim's identity. The man was Carl Methron.

There was nothing to tell why Prew's backer had met his grisly finish, nor did superficial clues offer any trace to the murderer. There was a small address book in one pocket and it contained Prew's post-office address, but that simply substantiated something that The Shadow already knew; namely, that Carl Methron had conducted business with Commander Rodney Prew.

The address book, like the envelope in the suitcase, was an item that the authorities should find; so The Shadow replaced it in the pocket where he had found it.

He was moving out into the living room to listen at the window, when a buzzing sound began close by the wall. Almost instantly, The Shadow identified it. The sound was from the telephone bell, muffled by Methron or his murderer, to prevent it from being heard outside the apartment.

That buzz produced a moot question.

Was this a genuine call, or had someone observed the light that The Shadow had temporarily turned on in Methron's bedroom? Instinctively, The Shadow rejected the first answer and settled on the second; then reason compelled him to believe that the call was pure luck.

Methron's front window was too high above the street for the light to have been seen. Moreover, fog was settling so thickly that the glow could not have been noticed from any nearby building.

That call could prove vital. The proper move was to answer it, but to do so in efficient fashion. If the caller actually wanted to talk to Methron, The Shadow would need some pretext to keep him on the wire.

It wouldn't do to take Methron's voice, for The Shadow had never heard it. During those seconds while he sought some other answer to the problem, The Shadow heard the buzz repeated. He knew that he couldn't wait much longer, for the person at the other end might become impatient or suspicious.

The Shadow needed a quick inspiration. It came to him as he clenched one gloved hand.

From inside the glove came a crinkle. It was the ticker tape that The Shadow had tucked there. He remembered one detail of that message—a reference to Methron's servant, who had supplied information to Ishi Soyoto.

That servant must have been a Japanese.

The Shadow's decision was made. He could fake a Jap's voice well enough to get by, because they had a mode of speech that was almost uniform, particularly among those who acted as house servants.

Despite his decision, The Shadow paused before moving over to the telephone. He had caught another sound—one that made him listen for a moment, then urged him to hurry his new-made plan. The new sound was a *clang* from the fire escape, somewhere near the ground level.

Soyoto's crew was here. The sooner The Shadow answered that call and finished with it, the better.

HE bounded to the telephone. Scooping up the mouthpiece, he spoke in a clippy tone:

"Who speaking, please?"

For a few seconds there was no answer, although The Shadow could tell that the wire was open. Then came a voice that seemed to have a forced growl:

"I want to talk to Mr. Wiggin."

"Not here at present," replied The Shadow. "He give order to take message."

The man at the other end thought that over much too long to suit The Shadow, tensed, not on the man's own account but because sounds were audible from higher on the fire escape. At last:

"No message," came the growl. "I'll call him later."

In Japanese style, The Shadow introduced a quick suggestion:

"Give number, please."

"Give what?"

"Give number, so master can call. You wait. He come back soon."

It was the term "master" that clinched the matter. The Shadow cleverly avoided reference to Methron by name, and also dodged the name of Wiggin. Evidently the caller decided that the supposed servant must be completely in Methron's confidence, for he didn't hang up. His voice lost something of its growl, as he parried:

"How soon?"

"Very soon."

Something *was* due to happen very soon, as

louder scrapes from the fire escape foretold. Lifting his shoulder, The Shadow pressed it against the end of the receiver, to wedge the latter in place against his ear. His left hand free, he drew an automatic, to greet the invading Japanese.

While still in that pose, he heard the voice repeat a number; and the name of the telephone exchange located it as near the waterfront. Lips close to the mouthpiece, The Shadow asked:

"How long you stay there?"

"Fifteen minutes," decided the speaker. "I can't wait any longer. Tell Mr. Wiggin to call as soon as he comes in."

A receiver clicked at the other end. The Shadow let his own receiver nestle on the hook. Sounds had ceased from the fire escape; the Japanese were coming in by the hallway. It wouldn't take them long to unlock the easy door of the apartment, for their previous search of The Shadow's hotel room told that they were expert at such work.

There was still time, however, for The Shadow to prepare a surprise. The best location would be the bedroom. He was in there by the time a key was rattling in the outside lock, and his first move was to open the front window.

There was a narrow ledge outside it, and The Shadow peered along that shelf, to see where it would lead if needed as an emergency exit.

The moment that he raised the window, he heard a scurry from below. Someone had dashed out to talk to the doorman; the arrival was the glum-faced clerk who had been behind the lobby newsstand.

He started to gesticulate upward. Immediately, the doorman whipped off his big blue coat and flung it across a brass rail beside the outside steps. He and the clerk started a dash into the apartment house.

The doorman's haste to get rid of his coat, and the fact that he wore an ordinary suit beneath, gave the whole thing away. They weren't employees here, they were San Francisco detectives; stationed on some special duty. Their purpose was less important than the reason for their alarm.

Someone a few floors below must have heard the Japanese intruders ascending the fire escape and sent word to the lobby. The dicks were coming up to find out who the invaders were.

The Japanese were already in Methron's living room, creeping through with very little stealth, for they were unfamiliar with this apartment. The Shadow had an excellent chance to leave them with an empty nest. He was at the window; the ledge offered safe passage to any apartment on the entire sixth floor.

But if he slipped away, there might be consequences of a most unfortunate sort. The Japs didn't know that they had been discovered. If they stopped to puzzle over Methron's death, to look for vain clues, they would be trapped here. Driven desperate, they would try to fight their way out.

There would be casualties; whether Japanese or detectives, the result would prove bad. It would mean another clouded issue, with ensuing complications. The affair at the Sausalito pier had been unfortunate, because The Shadow believed Soyoto's statement that the Japanese had been there to hinder Felix Sergon, rather than to help him.

If Japanese were reported on the scene where Methron's body lay, suspicions would be increased. They might be blamed for a murder which was certainly not their work; the presence of a batch of them would indicate that they had come to carry away the body.

There was only one way to defeat the present dilemma. It required one of the greatest nerve tests that The Shadow had ever undergone. He deliberately threw away sure safety in order to accomplish it.

INSTEAD of swinging through the window, The Shadow waited until the creeping Japanese were actually in the room. Then, as his left hand thrust away his automatic, he reached for the lamp cord with his right.

He overcame the momentary hesitation that gripped him. Yanking the cord, he wheeled full about, raising both hands as high as he could reach.

Death was closer than when the bullet from Methron's revolver had whizzed past The Shadow's ear. As his cloaked figure turned, to become a helpless target, all four of Soyoto's men bounded to their feet, pointing their guns as they came.

The Shadow saw fingers that were actually quivering on triggers, as the Japs recognized the fighter who had so recently tricked their master.

They managed, however, to withhold their fire, but kept their guns leveled. Slanty-eyed, they squinted suspiciously. Though they had expected to find The Shadow here ahead of them, they had not counted upon his prompt surrender. Their faces betrayed the conflict in their minds.

Soyoto must have instructed them to use their guns as threats; to depend upon their superior number if The Shadow fired first. For Ishi Soyoto, of all persons, was anxious to regain an understanding with The Shadow. Whatever Soyoto's real purpose, whether he dealt in truth or lies, he knew that a deed once perpetrated could not be revoked.

The Shadow took advantage of the timely indecision among the Japanese. His tone came sinister, strange in its utterance, for he spoke in the language of their native Nippon. He seemed to be speaking for Ishi Soyoto, reminding them of their most important duty here. They had been sent, so said

The Shadow, not to wage battle but to find Carl Methron and bring him alive to Ishi Soyoto.

That was impossible. With a sideward sweep of one gloved hand, The Shadow pointed to the figure on the floor. The Japanese saw Methron's body for the first time; they heard The Shadow's statement that the man had long been dead. Methron could have told The Shadow nothing; but there was something that The Shadow could tell these Japanese.

Hearing a chance sound, he lifted his hand again, one finger pointed as a signal for them to listen. What they heard was the rumble of an elevator coming upward. Turning his finger toward the door, The Shadow added a command.

"Go at once!" he ordered. "Go back to your master, before you are found here. Tell him all that you have seen here. Bear him the message that I have acted as his friend. He will believe you."

The Shadow's hand swung to the light cord. He tugged it before a solitary Japanese could make a move. His silhouette vanished from the window frame so suddenly that no eye observed the direction it had taken. That climax decided the Japanese. The Shadow's advice was wise. To ignore it might mean rebuke from Soyoto.

As final urge, they recognized that The Shadow, again in darkness, could be a formidable foe. They realized, too, that any minute might place them between two fires, for the elevator was certainly bringing newcomers to the sixth floor.

THERE was a scramble as the Japs made for the hallway. Stumbling over one another, they reached the fire escape and began a mad tumble downward. From the door of Methron's apartment they heard a strange laugh—one that seemed to brook trouble for others, rather than themselves, should they be wise enough to continue their flight.

The elevator had reached the top of the shaft. As its door slid open, The Shadow swung toward the large globe that contained the single hall light. His hand performed a juggle with a drawn automatic. Catching the gun barrel, The Shadow slashed the butt against the ceiling light.

Men from the elevator heard the crash, saw the light disappear. They sprang for The Shadow in the darkness, were met by something that they could not see—a shape that seemed all shroud and muscle, as it spilled them right and left. A streak of blackness swept into the elevator; the door went shut.

Racing down the stairway, the detectives hoped to cut off the unknown fighter's escape. By the time they reached the second floor, they had overshot their mark. The Shadow had stopped the elevator at the third. He was out through a window to the fire escape, taking the route by which the Japanese had already completed their flight.

A few blocks from the Hillview Apartments, a strange shape emerged like a creation from the fog, to enter a taxi that was parked near a corner. A hand shook the sleepy driver, a calm tone gave him a destination near the waterfront. The cabby came to life as if impelled by a ghost.

Unfortunately, the fog delayed the trip. Half an hour later, The Shadow left the cab waiting, while he prowled a neighborhood so thick with mist that even building walls were invisible. By this time, the man who had called by telephone would be gone, making the search fruitless, even if The Shadow found the place from which the call had been made.

Returning to the cab, The Shadow gave the driver an address near the center of the city. Chilled both by the fog and wonderment regarding his mysterious passenger, the driver had turned on the radio to while away his shivery moments.

A news flash arrived during that return ride. A local station was broadcasting an important announcement. All persons were urged to report any sign of a man answering to the description of Commander Rodney Prew. The creator of the Z-boat *Barracuda* was wanted for a known crime—the murder of a man named Carl Methron, otherwise known as J. H. Wiggin.

The repeated words of that announcement covered the low, whispered laugh that toned in strange significance from the lips of The Shadow.

CHAPTER X
ALONG THE WATERFRONT

IT was the next night, and fog again lay over Frisco. But the misty atmosphere was not the only message that had crept in from the Pacific. At dawn that day the *Barracuda* had appeared again, just off the coast some fifty nautical miles south of the Golden Gate.

She had popped up in the fog, to lie awash while her masked crew boarded a passing steamer, intent upon new deeds of piracy. This time, they had not been aided by traitors on board the steamer. They had cast a hooked rope up to the rail and managed a surprise arrival, headed by their broad-shouldered leader, whose wide jaw again displayed its iron thrust.

The attack had been an easy victory for Felix Sergon, but the fruits of conquest had proven small.

The very fog that had enshrouded the *Barracuda*, enabling her to roam at large, had caused Sergon to mistake a tramp freighter for a coastwise liner. Instead of wealthy passengers and a cash-filled strongroom, the pirates had found only a penniless crew and a mixed cargo that contained nothing more consequential than a shipment of canned goods.

Sergon had rifled those supplies. Estimates indicated that he and his fellow pirates had carried away enough Alaska salmon and California tuna to last them for a year. Unless their act had been merely the result of crooked instinct, it meant that they expected to defy all searchers for many months to come.

It was lucky for Sergon, perhaps, that he had not found the passenger liner he wanted. During the fog, naval vessels were staying close to such ships, acting as their convoy. The freighter had been proceeding alone, and by the time she had radioed the news, the *Barracuda* was well away.

Meanwhile, there had been other news in San

They sprang for The Shadow in the darkness, were met by ... a shape that seemed all shroud and muscle.

Francisco, sensational enough to sweep the entire country.

Dead Carl Methron had been identified as the silent partner of Commander Rodney Prew. The murdered backer was definitely recognized as the only man, outside of the Z-boat's inventor, who could have revealed important data concerning the *Barracuda*.

The details of the Methron case were as follows:

San Francisco police had been told that a man answering the description of Commander Rodney Prew had been seen, some days before, leaving the Hillview Apartments. Whom he had visited there was not known; nor had there been much likelihood of his return. Nevertheless, two detectives had been assigned to the apartment house, one to pose as doorman, the other as newsstand clerk.

Last night, prowlers had been reported on the fire escape. The detectives had hurried to the sixth floor, intending to begin investigation from the top downward. They had encountered darkness; with it, a mad fugitive who had gone through them like a whirlwind.

Chase had proven useless; but in apartment 6B the detectives had found a dead man—first identified as J. H. Wiggin; later, from papers on the body, as Carl Methron. A forgotten envelope in a suitcase, a small address book in Methron's pocket, had connected the dead man with Commander Prew.

Investigation proved that Methron had backed various commercial projects, with varying success. He made a specialty of aiding obscure inventors in the development of new devices, with a share of the profits as his return. There was every reason to suppose that Methron had put money into Prew's building of the Z-boat.

Examination of the body proved that Methron had been dead approximately twenty-four hours. That tied in with the sudden disappearance of Commander Prew, and produced a theory so iron-clad that it was accepted as fact.

THE first assumption was that Commander Prew had personally ordered the theft of his own ship. Previously, the only motive attributed to Prew was a desire to sell the *Barracuda* to some higher bidder than the United States government.

Now, there was a second motive, upon which the first depended. Whatever Prew's underhand scheme, he would have had to keep it from his silent partner, Methron.

Obviously, he had decided to wait until the *Barracuda* was safely away before discussing the matter with Methron. He could have hoped to broach the subject cleverly, winning Methron over to the circumstance, provided all had gone well. But there had been trouble at the Sausalito pier. Not only had the Z-boat's departure been rapidly discovered; Japanese troublemakers had been seen on the grounds.

Prew's first knowledge of those circumstances had come when he had heard the radio news flash at his club. Prew had left there promptly, and at last the law knew the reason why. He could only have gone to see Methron, hoping to reach the promoter before the latter knew the facts.

Possibly Methron had already caught the news, for there was a radio set in his apartment. It was easy, in any event, to picture him listening to Prew's arguments and remaining unswayed. The one detail that Prew could not possibly have explained away was the presence of Japanese at the pier.

Finding Methron's patriotism too staunch, Prew had only one way to hush the man. That was by cold murder.

The fact that drove home the clincher to this theory was Prew's knowledge of Methron's whereabouts. For reasons of his own, perhaps fear of conniving enemies, Methron had adopted the name of J. H. Wiggin and had rented his apartment under that alias. It was the one place where he could slip to safety in time of stress, and the only person definitely known to be acquainted with the matter was Commander Rodney Prew.

The little address book with Prew's name in it did not prove the fact. That was probably why Prew had left it in Methron's pocket, for he could later deny any knowledge of Methron's alias or residence.

But the envelope, overlooked in Methron's suitcase, was addressed to J. H. Wiggin, with Prew's return address, and it was written in the missing commander's own hand!

From The Shadow's viewpoint, these facts had value. He was particularly pleased, however, because he had not been identified as the intruder who had crashed his way out through the sixth-floor hall.

Popular opinion held that the man who engineered that flight must have been Rodney Prew, secretly returned to the scene of his crime by way of the fire escape.

More than one man had been reported on the fire escape; hence it was supposed that Prew had followers. There, again, was a case of suppressed identity, much to The Shadow's liking. Not a single person had guessed that the men on the fire escape had been Japanese.

The Shadow was weighing that lucky factor as he stalked the fog-laden darkness of the San Francisco waterfront. He had just made a call to his hotel, using the tone of Cranston, to learn that another person was also pleased because of the persuasive arguments that The Shadow had used with those Japanese who met him in Methron's apartment.

A valuable collection of ancient Japanese paintings had arrived at the hotel, addressed to Mr. Lamont Cranston. They had come from I. Soyoto & Co., with a bill for thirty-five hundred dollars stamped "paid."

Just a token of Soyoto's appreciation, because The Shadow had helped his men out of a bad mess in which they did not belong. Nevertheless, the gift applied to that incident alone. It did not change The Shadow's analysis of Ishi Soyoto and his methods, where other matters were concerned.

Nor did it help The Shadow's present quest.

All day, he had been along the waterfront, loitering in the rough attire of a stevedore. He had located the telephone from which last night's call had been made. It was in the back room of a waterfront dive, and could be reached by an alley exit without passing through the main section of the grogshop.

Who was the man who had telephoned Methron, and why had he made the call?

There were several possible answers. One was strongest in The Shadow's mind, but it needed more facts to bolster it. All day, The Shadow had sought further evidence; when night came, he had donned cloak and hat to speed his work.

The Shadow's process was a constant patrol of the waterfront, on the chance that the man who had telephoned was located somewhere near.

IT was a simple matter of trial and error, playing for some lucky discovery, and praying that it would come. A complete reversal of The Shadow's usual deductive methods, but in this instance something of a hunch. There was no reason why the call should have been made from the waterfront, except as a matter of convenience.

Doubtlessly, the unknown man would not use that same telephone again, after learning that Methron had been murdered. But there was reason to believe that he would come from hiding, once sure that everything was safe.

Since The Shadow was the only investigator watching this part of San Francisco, the entire neighborhood appeared serene. It was the perfect setting, particularly with the fog, to coax a man out from cover.

The great clock of the ferry house tower was donging eleven when The Shadow stopped beside a dock so ancient and neglected that it had sunk almost to the water level. He had made a careful study of piers along the harbor and had disregarded this one because of its unimportance.

That very unimportance, however, gave it value as a base for The Shadow's excursions. The space above the old dock was thick with fog, and that white gap made an excellent landmark. Moreover, it was the one place where The Shadow ran no risk of blundering into passers whom he did not care to meet.

Echoing clock strokes lingered in the fog, but amid those fading *clangs*, The Shadow was conscious of a creaking sound not far away. After the next booming tone, he located the noise; it came from the place least expected—the very center of the old, forgotten dock.

The Shadow's own strides were noiseless as he headed out along the dock. He heard the buzz of low voices; from a dozen feet away, he sighted the glow of a feeble lantern. Because of the fog, the men had risked the light, never guessing that it could become a beacon for an invisible prowler.

So close that he could have stretched a hand to reach them, The Shadow saw rough, unshaven faces beside the lantern. Grimy hands came into sight; one man counted off a batch of banknotes from a large wad and passed them to another.

"That ought to be enough, Rusty," he gruffed. "But remember what the skipper said. Don't buy all the stuff in one place. It might look suspicious."

"Leave it to me, Salvo," returned Rusty. "Only, don't get the heebies if I'm gone over an hour. It ain't any cinch to find the right places, this late."

The men parted. As Rusty came shoreward, The Shadow flattened, to lie unnoticed. From the dock level, he watched Salvo's lantern settle downward until it was out of sight. There was a repetition of the former creak. When it ended, The Shadow crept up to investigate.

He found a trapdoor in the dock, one so cleverly fashioned that the most intense search might have failed to discover it. Long ago, the old dock had been patched with short lengths of board, now rotten with age. Those were braced with beams beneath, and someone had sawed an irregular hole from below, cutting along the edges and ends of the boards.

Remembering a flattish mass that had followed Salvo downward, The Shadow calculated which side of the trap was hinged. He found a crack on the other edge, that would enable him to lift the level door when the time came. But that would be later, just before the ferry clock tolled twelve.

THE time came. Calculating that his own entry, if noticed, would be attributed to Rusty, the man who had gone ashore, The Shadow dug his fingers deep between the planking. The creaky trapdoor came up, to show the light of the lantern.

For some reason, Salvo had left it hanging on a nail driven in a beam a few feet below.

The Shadow expected to see the blackness of water in the low space beneath the dock. There was

So close that he could have stretched a hand to reach them, The Shadow saw rough, unshaven faces beside the lantern.

water, but it lacked a deep color. Instead, a few feet below the surface lay a long mass of gray that looked like the body of some mammoth fish, stretching in both directions beyond the small circle of the lamplight.

Squarely in the center of that gray metal shape was a rounded opening that projected above the surface. It was half domed; the side that looked like a windshield was toward the outer end of the pier, leaving the open space so it could conveniently be entered.

In size, appearance, the half-sunken vessel resembled but one craft that The Shadow had ever seen: the missing Z-boat called the *Barracuda*!

CHAPTER XI
THE CAPTURE BELOW

CLUTCHING a curved iron bar that he found beneath the dock trapdoor, The Shadow let the trap come shut. Dangling from the bar, he lowered his feet into the cockpit of the Z-boat. Feeling the rung of a ladder, he lowered himself beside the half dome.

The lantern was only a few feet above him. Raising the glass, The Shadow blew out the flame. That, he imagined, was a duty expected of Rusty, when The Shadow began a downward grope into the Z-boat.

Instead of a cockpit, he found the space more like the conning tower of a submarine. That fitted with his own observation, the night when the *Barracuda* had vanished in the bay. By the time The Shadow had reached the bottom of the ladder, he heard a slithery noise above.

An inner part of the dome clamped downward, completely sealing the space at the top. Immediately afterward, slow gurgles were audible from the darkness within the Z-boat. Someone had heard The Shadow's arrival and had mistaken him for Rusty. The ship had started to submerge.

The walls at the bottom of the ladder were rounded, like the sides of a giant cheese box. Probing them, The Shadow could feel no opening. The darkness was clammy in its thickness; that steady gurgle, combined with the slow sinking of the floor, would have caused the average adventurer to wish he had remained on shore.

There was something insidious about the entire situation.

To begin with, the *Barracuda* was supposed to be miles out to sea, trusting to fog or ocean depths to hide her. Yet here was The Shadow aboard Prew's Z-boat, sinking in the fringe of San Francisco harbor!

The dock above was the cleverest of camouflage. The pier in Sausalito had been high enough to hide a boat that floated on the surface; this dock was not. But the Z-boat, when submerged, could be tucked almost anywhere. That was an angle the searchers had evidently overlooked.

It all indicated devilish ingenuity on the part of Felix Sergon, the master of modern piracy. It made the sudden submerging of the submarine seem like a snare, a planned event in case some challenger like The Shadow came on board.

Like anyone else in his present position, The Shadow had reason to be qualmish, but he wasn't. He still retained a well-formed theory, which, if correct, would work to his advantage. First sight of the hidden Z-boat had shaken his theory; but added thought had told him that it could even yet be correct.

If it proved to be right, it would work out even better than he had originally hoped.

The ship had settled to the bottom by the time The Shadow at last solved the secret of the circular wall. Reaching high, he found a crevice that formed a level line all about. It meant that the entire wall was a solid cylinder that could be lowered, to give access to the interior of the Z-boat.

There was nothing in the way of a hidden switch to start the cylinder downward, but The Shadow fancied that he would not have long to wait.

The gurgles had ended. Someone had closed the submerging tanks. That done, he might already be on his way to lower the cylinder wall of the conning tower. Keeping fingers on the dividing crack, The Shadow waited.

Soon, the wall began to sink. A chink of light appeared above The Shadow's head; it widened into a field of glow from a passage leading forward. Then the light reached the ladder by which The Shadow had descended, throwing full illumination into the rounded center.

Yet there wasn't a sign of The Shadow as the wall descended. He was crouching with it, keeping out of sight beneath its shelter. When the wall reached the floor, he would be seen, but he was depending upon the chance that the barrier would stop before it went that far.

THE stop came. A man was peering from the passage, staring across the edge of the big cylinder when it reached the level of his waist. The fellow was Salvo, his unshaven face looking perplexed. He was sure that Rusty had come aboard; that was why he had first closed the conning tower and submerged the ship.

Salvo's grimy hand was on a large switch by the wall. A tiny light was burning there, a signal from a wired rung of the ladder in the conning tower. Salvo started to press the switch upward, to raise the wall again; then desisted.

He figured that the signal wire had short-circuited and decided to investigate. He laid both hands upon the wall rim and stared across like a curious neighbor peering over a backyard fence. It happened that there *was* a neighbor on the other side—one who could do more than hide.

From his crouch, The Shadow gave his hands an upward swoop. They plucked Salvo's neck in a tight double grasp that the fellow could not shake off. All that Salvo could do was flay about, swinging with both arms. Close to the inward curve of the half-lowered wall, The Shadow pulled away from every blow.

Salvo's struggle merely hastened the finish. Stretching too far in his desperate effort to fight free, he came half across the wall. Off balance, his weight no longer anchored him.

The Shadow gave a downward yank that teetered Salvo on the level. With a backward haul, he whipped the man into the cylinder, letting him hit the floor with an emphatic jolt.

Gloved fingers relaxed, but Salvo did not recuperate to renew the fight. Half choked, the wind knocked out of him, he could only groan and

The Shadow gave his hands an upward swoop ... plucked Salvo's neck in a tight double grasp that the fellow could not shake off.

reach his hands feebly toward his aching throat. Meanwhile, The Shadow vaulted the curved wall and reached the switch.

Upward pressure started the wall rising. It was Salvo's turn to occupy the cheese box, which had become a perfect prison. All his storming, when he recovered, would bring no aid, for he was trapped in a place that was almost soundproof.

The Shadow went forward, seeking others of the crew. He came upon one man standing at the door of a small bunk room. Things happened there, as they had with Salvo. The Shadow smashed forward like a battering ram, bowling the man back into his quarters. That crew member hardly knew what had struck him, except that it was something black and very powerful.

When The Shadow closed the door of the bunk room, his second prisoner was lying bound and gagged in a narrow berth.

Farther forward, The Shadow reached a tiny cabin that looked like an officer's quarters. Beyond it was a private stairway, a narrow, circular device that led somewhere below.

The Shadow descended the spiral stairs, doubled back along a passage. He believed that he would find the main control room farther aft, and he considered it to be his ultimate goal.

He came to a rounded bulkhead where the passage divided. It was the space into which the cylindrical lining of the conning tower could be lowered, and it also served another purpose. It contained a central submerging tank, which explained why The Shadow had so clearly heard the sound of entering water. Those gurglings had come almost below his feet.

The question of which passage to take seemed optional, until The Shadow caught the sound of footfalls from the other side. He waited in the dimness, until he made sure that they were approaching by the passage on his right.

Going to the left, The Shadow reached the other side of the tanklike bulkhead. He came into a brighter passage; at the end of it was the door to the control room, standing ajar.

Ready for a glide along the passage, The Shadow made a sudden turn. Two men had passed around that center tank, but one of them was coming back. He had returned so suddenly that there was no time for The Shadow to pick a hiding spot.

The fellow was a swarthy crew member; his voice raised an immediate shout. The Shadow was pulling an automatic from beneath his cloak, but he did not aim it. Instead, he took a backhand cut while the other was hauling a revolver from his hip.

The swarthy man couldn't ward off the blow one-handed. The Shadow's tight fist met him cleanly on the side of the jaw.

SWIFT though his swing was, The Shadow pulled the backhand punch as it landed. Weighted with the automatic, it did not need all the power. It dropped the swarthy man, but did not break his jaw. The clatter that the man made brought a running response from his pal who had gone forward.

The Shadow did not wait for the other to arrive. He sprang for the control room, slashed its door inward, spilling a man who was trying to close it. Slamming the door, The Shadow shoved home a bolt and swung about to aim his .45 for the man that he had floored.

He was clear across the control room, that final antagonist, huddled where he had landed against a small shelf that looked like a desk. He was moving one hand as if to steady himself; but that proved a ruse. When he swung suddenly about, the man flourished a .38 revolver that he had snatched from a drawer.

The Shadow was face to face with a man whom he instantly recognized from a portrait that he had seen. But it was not the picture that Claudette Marchand had shown him in the boathouse. The Shadow would have recognized the flattish, wide-jawed face of Felix Sergon from having seen it in life.

This face was different. It was long and tapering, with the expression of a dreamer, except for the fierce eyes that flashed complete defiance. Those were eyes that seemed to snap commands. They had a determination that almost matched The Shadow's hawklike gaze.

Gray hair topped the man's high forehead, adding dignity to his appearance, although he had cast aside all thoughts of everything except challenge to the black-cloaked intruder who had so suddenly appeared in his preserves.

Not only The Shadow, but anyone in San Francisco would have recognized those features, for they had been depicted on the front page of every newspaper within the past two days.

The occupant of the Z-boat's control room was Commander Rodney Prew!

HE and The Shadow were face to face, gun to gun. So quickly had the climax come, that it stood a stalemate. One might fire before the other, but no shot could stay an opponent's trigger finger. If one died, both would die. The Shadow knew it; so did Rodney Prew.

Men were hammering at the bolted door, proving that all escape was blocked. That merely brought a forward thrust of The Shadow's gun, a low-pitched laugh from lips that Prew could not see. The Shadow had accepted the stalemate: death for one, death for both.

He was moving forward, lessening the range. Those gun muzzles came side by side, each pointed toward a heart. Neither adversary cared about the banging on the door; but Prew was conscious of The Shadow's laugh. He heard a sibilant whisper almost in his ear, delivering terms that were unconditional. The Shadow was calling upon Prew to surrender.

The gray-haired commander balked. If there was a quiver to his gun hand, it was only because his trigger finger had begun to tighten. Then The Shadow's free hand was upon the revolver that Prew held, clamping it with a viselike grasp.

"You have yet to answer for murder," spoke The Shadow. "There are ways by which you may explain the past, but not the present. Remember: you are wanted by the law. My presence here is justified!"

Prew's hand went limp. The Shadow picked the revolver from his grasp, used it to gesture toward the door, as he commanded:

"Quiet them!"

Prew went mechanically to the door, answered the hammering with a sharp rap. The men outside heard his voice giving crisp orders for them to return to their quarters. There were mutters, as they hesitated. When Prew repeated his words, they went away.

Head bowed, Prew returned to the desk, sank to a chair beside it. He seemed in a quandary, regretful that he had accepted defeat, yet sadly resigned to whatever fate might come. He was wondering, too, now that it was over, why he had submitted to the dynamic influence of The Shadow.

In the center of a veritable underwater fortress, The Shadow, his exit blocked, had not become a prisoner. Instead, he had effected the capture of the man who controlled the Z-boat as his hidden domain!

Realization of all that struck home to Rodney Prew. With a lift of his head, the former naval officer said wearily:

"It is ended. You can take me away. I shall face whatever consequences—"

A strange laugh intervened. It carried no tone of triumph, no chill of further challenge. It held encouragement, that mirth that The Shadow uttered, for it seemed to betoken knowledge of long-hidden facts.

Amazement flickered over Prew's haggard features. A light came to his tired eyes. Next, eagerness seized him, inspired by his interpretation of the sibilant tone he heard.

Hope had replaced dejection. In The Shadow, Commander Rodney Prew realized that he had found a friend who would believe facts that no one else would credit!

CHAPTER XII
PREW MAKES PLANS

ANOTHER half hour found Commander Prew still seated at his desk, but he no longer faced the cloaked stranger who had captured him. Instead, he was studying the calm features of Lamont Cranston, a well-dressed gentleman listening quietly to everything that Prew told him.

"I still cannot realize it," declared the commander, after a momentary pause. "Circumstances were all against me; your finding of this ship was final evidence—"

"Not quite," interposed The Shadow. "You must remember that I saw the *Barracuda* that night when Sergon stole her—"

"But this ship, the *Lamprey*, is almost identical—"

"Except that she is not completely fitted for an undersea journey; nor is she manned by a full crew. In addition, Commander Prew, the one place where I knew you could not be found would be aboard the *Barracuda*.

"I was confident that this was a different Z-boat, the moment that I dropped from the dock. This ship's conning tower is much narrower than that of the *Barracuda*. I have a very definite recollection of how Felix Sergon bobbed about when he fired his farewell shots."

Commander Prew smiled. The Shadow had mentioned a very definite distinction between the *Lamprey* and the *Barracuda*. Prew realized that the matter of the conning towers should have occurred to him, since he had designed them.

"I constructed the *Lamprey* from my own funds," reviewed Prew, "but I ran out of resources. That was when I interested Carl Methron in the work. Since I had made important changes in the design, I started my new ship, the *Barracuda*.

"I had stored the *Lamprey* here. I never mentioned her to Methron, for he might have wanted me to complete her, instead of going ahead with the *Barracuda*. But I preferred to produce a better vessel, a ship that would truly be a speed submersible.

"Of course, Claudette knew about the *Lamprey*"—Prew's tone became bitter—"but I never thought that she would sell me out. You see, my first inkling of it came from Methron, when he began to receive those mysterious messages."

The Shadow nodded. Prew had been over that before, but it was well to let him repeat the story, in case he should recall some new detail.

"I had heard of Felix Sergon," declared Prew, "and when Methron told me that someone was trying to acquire the *Barracuda* through him, I warned him of the danger. That was why Methron took the apartment under the name of "J. H. Wiggin."

"But Sergon found him, even there"—Prew's fists were clenching tightly—"and murdered him! It must have happened before the *Barracuda* was stolen. And there was only one person"—the commander's voice had become emphatic—"who could have revealed where Methron was. That person was Claudette Marchand!"

THERE was a long pause, while Prew's eyes stared far away. He was chewing on the end of a half-smoked cigar, not realizing that it was out until The Shadow's hand approached with a lighted match.

"Thank you, Mr. Cranston," said Prew, methodically. "It is time I came back to myself. You can understand my actions, since you accept the fact that there are two Z-boats, something that no one else would do. You see, I was worried about the *Lamprey*. That was why I stayed in Frisco, sending Claudette to see that all was well with the *Barracuda*.

"The two ships were in contact by submarine wireless—something which only Claudette knew. I intended to come here and receive her report, but I was expecting a telephone call from Methron at the club. Then I heard the news by radio.

"There were only a few men aboard the *Barracuda*. I knew that they must have been overpowered by Sergon. I tried to signal the *Barracuda* after I had hurried here, but there was no response. I began to realize my own dilemma, when I read of how Sergon had gone in for piracy.

"I stayed here constantly, except when I went out to call Methron. There was never a response until you answered last night. I actually thought that you were Methron's servant; but today, I wondered, after I learned of Methron's death."

Prew's pause gave The Shadow a chance to put a question:

"The murder of Methron was your first proof of Claudette's treachery?"

Prew nodded.

"It meant an end to all my plans," he said, his tone dejected. "I have been equipping the *Lamprey* for a sea trip, hoping to ferret out the *Barracuda*. I believe that Claudette might be able to restore communication between the two ships."

"What is the range limit of such communication?"

"About fifty miles. But that means nothing. As I said before, Claudette's aid is needed. And she is not a prisoner, as I believed. She is hand in glove with Sergon!"

It was The Shadow's turn to become meditative. Prew thought that he could catch the thoughts behind the masklike face of Cranston.

"Tell me more about the Japanese," suggested Prew. "This chap Soyoto interests me because he is obviously behind Sergon's game. All his smooth talk, the gift he sent you, are merely a sham."

"That can be considered later," returned The Shadow, quietly. "I was not thinking about Soyoto."

"About Sergon, then?"

"No. About you."

Prew looked surprised.

"You were the victim of circumstantial evidence," declared The Shadow. "Not just chance evidence, for much of it was designed. Sergon expected you to be questioned, to your embarrassment. That was in case you should be found."

"But he hoped that I would disappear—"

"Yes. There were too many rumors to your discredit."

"I know." Prew was on his feet, pacing back and forth. "It began with those destroyer speed tests. I wanted to find out how fast they could really go, because I was already planning a speed submersible. But the intimation that I intended to keep my Z-boat for myself was an outrageous lie.

"You know the navy rule, Mr. Cranston—that any man, once an officer, shall always offer any new inventions to the government. Such has always been my code. I shall never depart from it. The implication hurt me—deeply. If—"

Someone was rapping at the door. The Shadow nodded. Prew stepped over to admit Salvo, who stated that Rusty had returned with the supplies.

"It does not matter," declared Prew. "I have only been keeping up the work because there was nothing else to do. I have found one friend, Salvo, and Mr. Cranston may influence others. I shall report to the authorities tomorrow."

"No, Commander," interposed The Shadow. "Proceed with the equipping of the *Lamprey*. Tell me; how soon can the work be completed?"

"Why... why"—Prew's stammer showed his amazement—"by tomorrow night! But we can never find the *Barracuda*—"

"I believe that we shall find her."

IN Cranston's style, The Shadow gestured for Prew to dismiss Salvo. The commander gave the order, adding that the crew was to proceed. Even when the door had closed, they could hear Salvo's excited voice giving the good news to the other members of the crew. Prew, when he turned about, still registered astonishment.

"I was thinking of you," reminded The Shadow, quietly. "How few facts were in your favor, yet how important they proved. First, why did you need Sergon, of all persons, as a go-between, if you intended to sell your new craft to the highest bidder? Again, if you had used Sergon, why was it necessary for you to disappear?

"Presuming, also, that you had murdered Methron, why should you have overlooked the envelope in his suitcase? Lastly, why should you have called his apartment and talked to a person pretending to be Methron's servant?

"I knew positively that if I found you hiding near the place from which you called, that you could not be Methron's murderer. That one point shattered, you became an innocent party, even though you were aboard a boat that would probably be identified as the *Barracuda*."

Prew nodded. He spoke thanks that he had expressed before. It was plain that he valued The Shadow's understanding. But the visitor who spoke so evenly had not yet finished.

"Consider Methron," suggested The Shadow. "What were the circumstances against him?"

"Why, none!" exclaimed Prew, indignantly. "He was honest from the start! He told me that he had been approached. He gave me clues to Sergon. He was forced to hiding; he was murdered for his loyalty!"

The smile on Cranston's lips was more than a faint one. It carried an expression of thoughts behind it, this time for Prew to understand; Prew's own lips trembled. He was horrified by the idea that gripped him.

"Again reverse the circumstantial case," suggested The Shadow. "Look at the facts the way you did not view them. Suppose that Sergon came to Methron and actually made a deal to acquire the *Barracuda*. What would Methron have done?"

"He would have tried to win me over," replied Prew, his voice hollow. "Yes, he would first have sounded me out—"

"Which is precisely what he did, and failed."

"But he practically identified Sergon—"

"To cover himself. Your fear for his safety forced him to take the apartment as Wiggin. That was to lull you, commander."

"But afterward—"

Prew's thoughts halted his own sentence. The whole chain was linking up, once The Shadow had begun it. Prew pictured Methron again in conference with Sergon, telling him that no deal could be made; that theft was the only way to seize the *Barracuda*.

That call that Methron had promised to make to Prew at the club—it loomed with singular importance. It was Methron's subterfuge to keep Prew away from Sausalito, where he believed that the commander intended to go. Even had he lived, Methron would not have made that call.

Then into Prew's mental picture moved the insidious force that The Shadow had already divined: the crafty hand of Felix Sergon. He had dealt with Methron only because he believed that the shrewd promoter might dupe Commander Prew. Having failed, Methron left Sergon's list of assets and became a liability.

Sergon had made sure that Methron would not telephone to Prew. The arch-crook had murdered the promoter, with a double consequence. He had disposed of a man no longer needed, a fool who might weaken; he had seen to it that evidence on the scene of the crime would incriminate Commander Rodney Prew!

Simple in every detail, that scheme compounded into a master stroke of evil genius that stunned the very man whom it had victimized. As he stared at the face of Cranston, still with its fixed smile, Commander Prew sank to the chair beside his desk and uttered the longest gasp that he had ever delivered.

"IT hurt you," remarked The Shadow, quietly, "to know that Methron was a traitor."

Prew nodded. His face was very sober.

"That should not be the case," added The Shadow. "I had hoped that my deductions would please you."

"Please me?" Prew became suddenly indignant. "Carl Methron was my friend!"

"A false friend," returned The Shadow, "and by exposing our false friends, we sometimes recognize our true ones."

"You are my friend."

"I am not referring to myself."

Prew didn't understand. He couldn't. His brain was in a whirl. He stared blankly, so The Shadow supplied a verbal clue.

"Consider this," he said. "Felix Sergon disposed of one accomplice. Therefore, he had no need for another."

Still Prew did not catch the inference.

"Put it this way," suggested The Shadow. "Someone betrayed your plans to Felix Sergon. Is that clear?"

"Of course!" replied Prew. "You have made it plain that the man was Carl Methron."

"In that case," completed The Shadow, "we have eliminated Claudette Marchand."

At last, Prew understood. This was good news that The Shadow had supplied. There was remorse, though, in Prew's distant gaze, when he remembered his false accusations. His eyes blurred so, he could scarcely discern the face of Cranston. But he heard the steady words that drilled home to his ears.

"Like yourself," The Shadow told Prew, "Claudette Marchand was victimized by false circumstance. She went to Sausalito, as you told her. But when she reached the boathouse, she sensed that something was wrong. She thought the trouble lay outside, where the Japanese were watching.

"That was why she hid, to see if anyone entered. I was the one who came, and she challenged me. Sergon's men had already captured the *Barracuda*; they were covering the boathouse with their guns. They waited to see what happened.

"When I shifted, Claudette saw the gun muzzles for the first time. Realizing that she was also covered, she wavered. That was my chance to make a break. I saved Claudette's life with my own, but the intervention of the Japanese prevented her escape. She went aboard the *Barracuda*, but not of her own will. She was thrust aboard, a prisoner."

That revelation of Claudette's plight brought sudden alarm to Prew. He was thinking only of the girl's safety, hoping that someday he would be able to repay her for the loyalty that she had shown. Then a new thought struck him, so forcefully that it made him forget all else.

Claudette was more than loyal. She was clever. She knew much about the *Barracuda* that would make her useful to Felix Sergon. She would certainly pretend to side with Sergon, if such a deed would serve a useful purpose. Of a sudden, Prew realized just why The Shadow had ordered the *Lamprey* to make ready for a trip to sea.

With Claudette aboard the *Barracuda,* the subsea contact could still be restored, if the *Lamprey* came within fifty miles of Sergon's pirate submarine!

One minute later, Lamont Cranston was alone in the control room listening to commands that came from far along the passage, where Commander Prew was barking new instructions to his crew, hurrying their work of fitting out the *Lamprey*.

A long-fingered hand drew a thin cigar from between the lips of Cranston. The low-toned mirth that issued from those same lips was the laugh of The Shadow.

CHAPTER XIII
PAST GOLDEN GATE

SPEEDED by The Shadow's assurance that the *Barracuda* might still be found, the work on the *Lamprey* was completed by noon the next day. It was highly fortunate that such was the case; otherwise the *Lamprey* would have lacked the advantage of a much needed element; namely, fog.

The misty shroud was thinning all that forenoon. To most navigators, the lifting of a fog was necessary before they could clear port; but the case was quite the opposite with Commander Rodney Prew.

He agreed with The Shadow that the *Lamprey* could not risk passage through the Golden Gate without some coverage. Once the fog was gone, she would have to wait for darkness, with the loss of many hours.

There was something weird in the way the *Lamprey* nosed out from beneath the waterlogged dock, to poke a periscope up through the fog-stilled waters of the harbor. Even that prying metal eye produced a wake that would have excited suspicion had it been seen.

Visibility was poor, yet sufficient to see the docks when more than a hundred feet from shore. On that account, the *Lamprey* circled out into the harbor. Through the periscope, Prew kept lookout for any other craft.

The Z-boat was progressing at the rate of a few knots, when something bulked from the mist. Prew's hand thrust a lever; the response of horizontal rudders drove the *Lamprey* toward the bay bottom.

When she arose again, the danger had passed. The bay was sloshing with the wake from a ponderous ferry that had plowed directly above the Z-boat's diving hull.

Thinner fog announced the Golden Gate. There, at Prew's suggestion, The Shadow looked through the periscope. Straight above, another mass was outlined in the haze. It was the Golden Gate Bridge.

The Shadow could glimpse the flicker of automobiles as they passed across the mammoth structure. Those cars were two hundred feet above the level of the channel, proof that the fog had lessened at the Gate and probably would be entirely cleared when the ship was well out to sea.

Reaching the open ocean, Prew turned the course southward, keeping close to the coast. He and his friend Cranston went into conference over a navigator's chart.

The Shadow had provided the subtle way to hunt the *Barracuda*. On the chart were colored pins that represented the positions of certain coastwise vessels, according to latest reports. The thing to do was pick the one that the *Barracuda* was most likely to attack and scour that vicinity. The logical ship was the steamship *Darien*, of the Panorama Line.

The *Darien* was a modern liner that plied from New York to Frisco by way of the Panama Canal. Yesterday, she had been off Mazatlan, the Mexican port just east of the tip of the Lower California peninsula. She was bound northward, for Frisco, and her passenger list was large. By all estimates, the *Darien* should promise Sergon a larger haul than he had gotten from the *Yukon*.

His attack would have to come after nightfall, for the coast was still patrolled by destroyers and airplanes. Lack of such searchers anywhere near Frisco was proof that the navy also believed that the *Darien* was threatened by the pirate *Barracuda*.

With slight mist still clinging to the coastal waters, Commander Prew was able to show The Shadow all that the *Lamprey* could do. His demonstration explained why the *Barracuda* had proven herself so highly elusive.

Bringing the *Lamprey* to the surface, Prew increased her speed. The indicator crept slowly upward until it was recording forty knots, an unheard-of speed for a subsea ship. On the surface, the *Lamprey* rivaled a destroyer, perhaps could outdistance one, for Prew was not pressing the Z-boat to its maximum.

Then came the great test. Without use of the submerging tanks, Prew adjusted the horizontal rudders. Like the wings of a plane in air, they met the water and drove the *Lamprey* downward. The speedometer began to waver; its pointer moved to the left, then steadied.

More phenomenal than her forty-knot surface speed was the ship's underwater pace of thirty!

COMMANDER PREW had made practical a theory which he briefly retold. He had designed the *Lamprey*, and later the *Barracuda*, as speedy surface craft, based on his study of destroyers. He had also planned them so that they could be driven beneath surface, retaining a good portion of their speed.

Tanks for submerging and for ballast were auxiliary devices. The ships used them only for special purposes. The real value of the Z-boat was the power that Prew had just demonstrated, and as he kept the *Lamprey* beneath the water level. Again on even keel, The Shadow noticed that the ship was actually showing an increase in its remarkable subsea speed.

"In the air," declared Prew, "man has managed to outspeed the flight of birds. I could never grant that it would not be possible to equal the speed of fish. Such creatures as the shark dash through the water at approximately sixty land miles an hour."

"Not only the shark," came Cranston's reminder. "You could also mention the barracuda."

"I know." Prew's tone was bitter. "That was why I named my second ship the *Barracuda*. She is speedier than the *Lamprey.* I overlooked the fact that the barracuda is also a killer fish. I did not realize that the name was a prophecy regarding the future of my own *Barracuda*."

By later afternoon, the *Lamprey* had sighted smoke on the horizon. Prew drove her deep, and slackened speed. It was time to seek contact with the *Barracuda*. Taking The Shadow forward, Prew stopped at the spiral staircase that led up to his own cabin. He opened a panel that was hidden beneath the bottom steps.

There, they watched a dim but steady-burning bulb, in hope that the light would give some indication. Dragging minutes made Prew nervous. He was about to close the panel, when The Shadow stopped him with the calm suggestion:

"Five minutes more."

Perhaps The Shadow had made some complex calculation regarding the probable location of the *Barracuda*. Possibly he had followed one of his inspired hunches. Which, did not matter. The thing that happened to the light was more important.

Its feeble glow suddenly brightened. The lamp shone with sparkling brightness.

"The *Barracuda*!" exclaimed Prew. "It means that we have come within fifty miles of her! If Claudette—"

He paused, wondering just what conclusion to form. The Shadow supplied one.

"Whatever has happened to Claudette," he said, "she has not told Sergon of this device. For the present, we must watch, and form our own conclusions."

Prew nodded. He drew a circle on a sheet of paper. Knowing the present speed of the *Lamprey*, he began to trace her possible course in reference to the *Barracuda*. One potential, however, was absent: the speed of the *Barracuda*.

The lamp went suddenly dim. Just how or why the *Lamprey* had lost the circle of the *Barracuda* looked like guesswork, until The Shadow suggested that they compare their own position with that of the steamship *Darien*, on the assumption that the *Barracuda* was headed her way.

Prew made a trip to the control room and changed the course. When he returned, The Shadow was still watching the dim light. Within ten minutes, it brightened again.

Then, with the same suddenness that had marked the lamp's first rising glow, came blinks in a quick succession of dots and dashes.

"It's Claudette!" exclaimed Prew. "She's safe! She's signaling us—giving the position of the *Barracuda*!"

FOR once, real elation showed on the maskish features of Cranston. Prew was right, and the flashes that came from Claudette were enough to show that they were headed directly along the trail of the *Barracuda*. If the other Z-boat loitered, as well it might, in seeking the *Darien*, the *Lamprey* soon would overtake her.

The blinks ended abruptly. Evidently Claudette had considered it unwise to signal further. Her flashes, though, might come again. It was Prew who suggested that The Shadow remain to take any new message. The plan was satisfactory, until they heard Salvo shout from along the passage.

Salvo thought that Prew had gone up to his cabin. Quickly, the commander closed the panel beneath the stairs and answered Salvo's call. Another shout brought bad news.

"Destroyer off the port bow!"

Prew rushed for the control room, The Shadow close behind him. As he stared through the periscope, the commander heard a question in his ear. The Shadow's tone was almost an accusation. Prew gulped a sincere apology.

"I thought more speed would help us," he began.

"So I brought the ship nearly to the surface, leveling her off just awash. There's a scouting plane above that destroyer. I'm afraid she's sighted us."

Prew reached for the lever that controlled the horizontal rudders. He intended again to shove the *Lamprey* down into the long swells, keeping her at high speed. His hand was stopped by a firm grip. Clamping Prew's shoulder, The Shadow urged him to the corner chair.

Taking over, The Shadow ignored the rudder lever. Instead, he drew back the rod that controlled the Z-boat's speed. The speedometer needle flopped to the left before Prew's astounded gaze. The Shadow had deliberately cut the *Lamprey* down to twenty knots!

"It's suicide!" Prew was on his feet. "If that plane has sighted us, it will inform the destroyer—"

"The plane has already done so," interposed The Shadow. Hand on the wheel, he was swinging the *Lamprey* about. "The destroyer is heading for us, and the plane"—his eye was tighter to the periscope sight—"is flying off to report to other vessels."

"More speed, then!" urged Prew. "The destroyer will overtake us!"

The Shadow stretched a hand to press Prew back. Crew members, congregated in the doorway, looked ready to seize the interloper who called himself Cranston. But Prew waved them away. He didn't understand, yet he trusted The Shadow.

Yet the situation still seemed suicidal. If anything, The Shadow was lessening speed as he curved the *Lamprey* northward. He was keeping her awash, unquestionably in plain sight of the destroyer that Prew knew was heading for the Z-boat at double the latter's speed.

The hand on the speed lever tightened; Prew knew that the destroyer was very close. He watched The Shadow reach for the rudder control, then gasped at what he thought was a mistake. The Shadow hadn't started the *Lamprey* on a dive; he was lifting her completely to the surface!

Prew thought the cause was doomed. He sagged back to the chair, motioned the crew to take their posts for the emergency soon to come. He knew that the *Lamprey* must have been mistaken for the *Barracuda*. That, plus The Shadow's action, seemed to seal the Z-boat's fate.

RIGHT then, the *Lamprey* took a forward lurch. The Shadow had yanked the speed lever to its limit. His other hand steadied, then reversed the rudder control. The horizontal fins reacted, tilting the *Lamprey* into a shallow, nose-end dive.

Despite what Prew thought was tardiness, the maneuver was perfect. With her surface lunge increasing the speed, the *Lamprey* had cut under, scarcely losing a knot.

Tense seconds went by, the speed dial roaming above thirty. Then came the thing that Prew had feared. A quiver shook the *Lamprey*; it came from a mighty concussion that affected all that stretch of sea. The destroyer had dropped a depth bomb.

Despite the blast, the *Lamprey* maintained her pace. Two minutes later, there was another tremor, but it was milder than the first. The third that arrived was scarcely noticeable. The Shadow had sent the *Lamprey* deeper, but still held her at top speed. In the quiet style of Cranston, his expression almost bored, he turned over the controls to Prew.

They were safe, and at last Prew understood The Shadow's strategy. Had he let Prew push the *Lamprey* at full speed along the surface, the destroyer would have kept right behind her, driving the Z-boat into the path of other ships summoned by the scouting plane. Even worse, the speed of the *Lamprey* would have been a giveaway of the Z-boat's incredible ability.

The Shadow had cut the speed to make the destroyer believe that the *Lamprey* was just another submarine. The final lurch along the surface, when the Z-boat gathered power, had been too short to reveal the submarine's real speed.

Timing its own calculations to suit an ordinary submarine, the destroyer had started dropping depth bombs just past the spot where the *Lamprey* had disappeared.

Hitting thirty knots, the *Lamprey* was by that time well away. Other destroyers, coming in to form a cordon, would calculate the Z-boat's speed as less than fifteen knots. The *Lamprey* would be gone from the circle when it closed in.

There was sure safety to the north, for it was dusk and night would cover Prew's undersea ship before it could again be sighted. To The Shadow went the credit for an escape that only his keen brain could have devised on such instant notice.

Yet escape, on this occasion, counted as defeat. Forced to reverse her course, the *Lamprey* had lost her chance to encounter the *Barracuda*.

Crime could proceed again tonight, despite the efforts of The Shadow.

CHAPTER XIV
THE SHADOW FORESEES

BRIDGE lights, twinkling above the Golden Gate, gave but cold welcome to the returning *Lamprey*. She had reached haven before dawn and could slip into San Francisco Bay unseen, but Prew and his loyal men were doubtful of the news that awaited them.

Though The Shadow believed that all could have gone well, Prew had definite doubts. It would be his fault, he felt, if Felix Sergon had succeeded in attacking the *Darien*. Conversely, if the *Barracuda* had been trapped, any harm to Claudette Marchand would be Prew's blame.

Once the *Lamprey* was moored in her hiding place beneath the old dock, The Shadow ventured ashore. He brought back news that he told Rusty to relay to Commander Prew. That news was good. It fitted with a possibility that The Shadow had outlined.

The *Barracuda* had attacked the *Darien*, but had met with stiff opposition. At Panama, the liner had been equipped with guns and taken on a quota of marines. Proceeding without convoy, she had baited Felix Sergon and had almost hooked him.

Like the *Yukon*, the *Darien* had traitors aboard. Sneaking up on her, the *Barracuda* had unloaded its masked leader with the iron jaw. Sergon and his crew had found themselves suddenly surrounded on the steamship's deck.

Only luck and colossal nerve had saved them. Ordering his men to scatter, Sergon had led one flight into the depths of the ship, while others had chosen varied routes. Having to protect passengers, the marines were handicapped.

Amid the scattered battle, Sergon and a few followers had actually reached the ship's strong-room, but had gathered only a small amount of swag when they were discovered.

Bursting through a gangway on the opposite side of the *Darien*, the invaders had reached the *Barracuda*, which had come underneath the steamship to receive them. Shells had been fired after the fleeing submarine, but she had dived in time to escape damage. Since then, she was unreported.

In return for several thousand dollars' worth of cash and valuables stolen, Felix Sergon had left a dozen of his followers dead aboard the *Darien*, shot down by the competent marines. About the same number of persons were missing from the liner; they were the deserters who had joined up with Sergon.

All that day, The Shadow remained away from the *Lamprey*, getting more news. When he visited Commander Prew that evening, he brought tidings that the *Barracuda* had made another complete disappearance.

Remembering their own difficulties in the open sea, The Shadow and Prew had a long conference upon the subject of that new evanishment.

It seemed to Prew that Cranston's face reflected bafflement; that The Shadow had at last met with a mystery that he could not explain. Later, though, Prew decided that he was mistaken. He realized that he could never hope to analyze The Shadow's thoughts from studying Cranston's expressions.

IT was possible that the *Barracuda* had slipped into some harbor as the *Lamprey* had worked into San Francisco Bay. Such harbors, however, had become places of intensive search. Navy planes had insisted upon bombing a thousand-foot lumber raft that was coming down the coast from Oregon, on the chances that the *Barracuda* was using the raft as cover.

Seagoing tugs had pulled away, to let the planes smash the raft to kindling. Tons of bombs, millions of feet of lumber, had been sacrificed, only to learn that the *Barracuda* was not underneath.

With that failure to bring the pirate ship to light, a new rumor arose. It was one that touched off a batch of international complications involving the Japanese. The whole situation could be summed in one word: Mazatlan.

The port of Mazatlan had long been a matter of controversy, since the Mexican government allowed use of it to the Japanese fishing fleet that operated off the coast of Lower California.

Charges had been made that Japanese funds were secretly being used to improve Mazatlan harbor; those charges, in turn, had been denied and ridiculed by persons who declared that the harbor was nothing more than an open road-stead, that could never be equipped for use by navy vessels.

The question of the *Barracuda*, however, awoke new references to Mazatlan. Perhaps the Z-boat was using that port as its base. Possibly the Japanese fishing fleet knew something about the *Barracuda*. Agents with that fleet might be negotiating for the purchase of the mystery ship.

When The Shadow visited Prew the next night, he found the commander studying a big map. Prew pointed to Mazatlan, shook his head; then he traced a line up into the Gulf of Lower California.

"There are islands in that gulf," declared Prew. "The *Barracuda* could have her base there. Sergon is clever—*very* clever!"

"Not clever enough to be in two places at once," objected The Shadow. "Hiding in the gulf and preying on coastwise shipping are two different propositions."

"Don't forget, Cranston, that he may be aided by the fishing fleet. Those Japs are frequently about the mouth of the gulf. They could act as Sergon's eyes."

"Since you are interested in the Japanese angle, commander, read this."

The late newspaper that Cranston produced was opened, as usual, to the financial page. But the column that The Shadow indicated had nothing to do with Wall Street. It spoke of a large transaction in international exchange.

For some months, exports to Japan had out-weighed imports from that country. The Japanese were settling up the difference. A shipment of gold, reputed to exceed five million dollars, was coming to San Francisco aboard a crack Japanese liner, the *Shinwi Maru*.

Prew read the news. His eyes took on their distant stare; a keenness tightened his features.

"It proves what I have said!" he snapped, suddenly. "This gold shipment, Cranston, is to cover the transaction with Sergon. He would be shrewd enough to demand gold for the sale of the *Barracuda*. A spare million would settle the deal."

"Do you believe, Commander, that a million dollars is all that Sergon would demand?"

"It might be all that the Japanese would pay. Perhaps your friend Soyoto"—Prew's tone had a trace of sarcasm—"could answer the question. Provided, of course, that Soyoto would actually tell all he knew."

"I have not seen Soyoto recently. There are other Japanese, though, who might be interviewed."

THE SHADOW pointed in the news account. In the final paragraph, it related that certain prominent Japanese officials were aboard the *Shinwi Maru*, en route to Washington to discuss international trade relations.

"There is the answer," insisted Prew. "Sergon has so definitely classed himself as a pirate that the way is now open for him to make a sale. Those men"—he tapped the paragraph—"are the ones who will treat with him.

"Sergon is pretending that he fears to attack any more vessels. A good enough bluff, since searchers are everywhere along the coast. But believe me, Cranston, after the *Shinwi Maru* touches at Honolulu, those Japs will begin to talk among themselves, deciding how much to offer Sergon."

The Shadow said nothing to indicate that he was influenced by Prew's opinion. His silence, however, made Prew believe that the argument had scored. At last, The Shadow declared, as though stating simple fact:

"Much might be learned by anyone aboard the *Shinwi Maru*. Provided, of course, that such a person had a purpose in mind."

Prew's eyes showed eagerness. He would have liked to listen in on those Japanese conferences that he had mentioned. Realizing that such work was not his specialty, he shook his head.

"I belong here," he declared, "on the *Lamprey*. I am ready to clear port whenever needed. Someone else—" He stopped, looked squarely at Cranston, who was smiling. Then Prew blurted: "You are going to Honolulu?"

The Shadow nodded. Prew reached out to grip his hand. He admired The Shadow's courage, but during that handshake Prew began to have qualms.

"You may accomplish something on the *Shinwi Maru*," he agreed, "but watch out for consequences. A misstep, you would be trapped. Much might happen to anyone alone among enemies on the high seas; even to The Shadow."

"I have foreseen that," declared The Shadow quietly, but in a tone that Prew did not quite understand. "Therefore, I intend to leave the *Shinwi Maru* before she reaches San Francisco."

"But how—"

"A ship will reach me at a time appointed."

"What ship?"

"*Your* ship, Commander," replied The Shadow, solemnly. "This ship—the *Lamprey*."

While Prew was recuperating from the new surprise, The Shadow traced a large half circle on the map. It represented the cruising range of the *Lamprey* between dusk and midnight. The Shadow brought a finger eastward from outside the circle, to represent the *Shinwi Maru* coming in from Honolulu.

"I shall send a radiogram from the liner," explained The Shadow, "to an agent here in San Francisco. He will contact one of your men, to relay the secret message. It will carry all the information that you need."

"Good!" decided Prew. "I shall tell my crew—"

"Tell them," interrupted The Shadow, "that you are starting out again to seek the *Barracuda*. Only that will be necessary."

CARRYING hat and coat across his arm, The Shadow ascended to the cramped conning tower. Prew followed; he was smiling in new anticipation, while he raised the Z-boat toward the dock. He watched The Shadow don cloak and hat for his journey to the shore.

Just before the trapdoor closed in the dock above, Commander Prew fancied that he caught the echo of a laugh. The tone was one of prophecy that pleased the gray-haired commander. Prew was sure he knew its full significance.

He was confident that The Shadow intended to balk the very factor upon which Felix Sergon depended, which—as Prew had analyzed it—was the sale of the *Barracuda*. If The Shadow could acquire real evidence against the Japanese while aboard the *Shinwi Maru*, the game would be won.

The *Lamprey*, returning at full speed, could bring documentary evidence ashore before the *Shinwi Maru* would arrive, and thus reveal full facts regarding any deal with Sergon.

That, in turn, would force the *Barracuda* to remain at large much longer, disowned even by the Japanese. With weeks, perhaps months, to go before Sergon could receive new offers, the *Lamprey* would have many opportunities to ferret out her stolen sister ship.

Thus did Commander Prew analyze The Shadow's purpose, believing that his mysterious friend could prepare for any future. In that latter supposition, Prew was very nearly correct. Nevertheless, he would not have credited it had he been informed of all that The Shadow had foreseen.

There were plans that The Shadow had wisely kept to himself, knowing that it would be better for Prew to learn them when the time came. Those plans were to reach their peak after The Shadow had verified conditions aboard the *Shinwi Maru*.

At dawn, the China clipper was scheduled for a flight to Honolulu. Aboard that multi-motored airliner would be an added passenger, The Shadow.

CHAPTER XV
THE MIDNIGHT STROKE

Six bells. It was eleven o'clock at night. The *Shinwi Maru* was knifing a sea track toward the dawn that would meet her just short of the Golden Gate.

Grueling work for the *Shinwi*'s captain, that little, weather-beaten Japanese who was up there on the liner's ample bridge. Not because of any roughness of the sea, for the Pacific was swayed by nothing more violent than long, slow heaves. The trouble was the driving rain that pelted the ship head on, cutting visibility down to guesswork.

How would it affect the *Lamprey*?

The Shadow considered that, as he sat in a corner of the smoking room puffing slow wreaths of tobacco smoke, to join the many blends already in the air. She would make the meeting, the *Lamprey* would, he finally decided.

That radiogram had told all that Commander Prew would have to know. In a way, the miserable weather was a help. The skipper of the *Shinwi Maru* was hanging to his course with true Japanese tenacity.

There would be delay, though. Prew would have to lay to, in order to make sure of the *Shinwi*'s approach. The mammoth searchlight of the liner didn't cut much of a path against the rain, but it would be a beacon for anyone who watched for it.

It would be some time after midnight.

Not long after, The Shadow hoped. His calculations had been excellent, at first. He had figured that the *Shinwi* would just about time her speed to reach the Gate at dawn. But that had been before the rain devils had broken loose, in a fashion as vicious as it was inopportune.

Most of the passengers had retired. They had found the voyage long enough to suit them, and the rain had dampened this last night's revelry, most of which had been scheduled for the open decks. But there was yet a group that interested The Shadow—that batch of poker players over in a corner of the smoking room.

They were making a lot of noise about it, but that was so their game would not look serious. They didn't want anyone to think that they were serious, which was one reason why The Shadow had kept tabs upon them.

They weren't Japanese, those five men. Two of them might be Americans, but the other three were of doubtful nationality—like many others aboard the *Shinwi*; but the officers of the Japanese liner were too polite to question passengers as to their ancestry.

Many people were leaving China these days. People who had originally expected to live there all their lives, but who were finally glad to get away from that war-torn country. Many of them had to come by way of Japan, where they blamed the Japanese for their troubles.

The Japanese politely accepted the blame, and with it the money for the steamship passage. Money counted in quaint old Nippon, where so much was going into the gold fund, to balance the American exchange.

In fact, ships like the *Shinwi* had carried so many doubtful passengers that the officers and crew had become used to them. Perhaps there were outcasts among the eastbound passengers, but so long as they behaved themselves, they were entitled to full courtesy.

Those aboard this trip—the poker players and others of their ilk—had behaved very nicely. That had suited the Japanese, but not The Shadow. He had been piecing together a lot of facts, since boarding the *Shinwi* at Honolulu. He knew of secret meetings, and what they meant.

He knew also that the men who met were troubled over some uncertainty. Apparently, they formed a group dependent upon one appointed man; but they didn't know which one he was, although he belonged to them. To The Shadow, that savored of a certain very crafty individual whose name he could have given.

There were others who met aboard the *Shinwi*—staid Japanese officials who had important matters to discuss. The Shadow had more or less ignored them, and that would have worried Commander Rodney Prew.

ONE of the poker players went out. Another man dropped in to take his place. With all their hilarity, tension was becoming high. Probably they were rushing things because they had nothing else to do. But they were glancing about the smoking room, casting suspicious eyes upon the few other people who remained.

On that account, The Shadow decided to advance his own move, for he was positive that he could lose nothing by such action.

Strolling from the smoking room, he took a passage to his stateroom. Arrived there, The Shadow seated himself before a mirror. He looked at a face quite different from that of Lamont Cranston. It was fuller; though maskish, it was less distinguished.

It was the face that he had used when he booked passage on the *Shinwi Maru*, because it went with the name that he had also adopted.

The Shadow was aboard the liner as a man named Henry Arnaud.

Steady smears with a towel would have obliterated the Arnaud disguise, but The Shadow had other plans. He worked deftly, smoothly, plucking here, molding there, until he literally removed a false layer from his face. The reason for this care became evident when the face of Cranston emerged.

As Arnaud, The Shadow had worn one disguise over another.

Curious that he should become Lamont Cranston again. That particular identity was one that had been guessed by certain Japanese, particularly Ishi Soyoto. There was a chance that every steward on the *Shinwi Maru* had a description of Lamont Cranston. For Ishi Soyoto had heard nothing more from Cranston since the time when the jiujitsu squad had brought back The Shadow's message.

The Shadow had done a favor for Soyoto that time; but somehow, he and Soyoto had begun a game of this for that. A good turn did not mean that another was to follow. In fact, the policy had been something of the reverse.

There was a way, however, to avoid all passing stewards. From a secret compartment of a special trunk that he had purchased in Hawaii, The Shadow produced his garb of black. Cloaked, hatted and gloved, he stole from his stateroom. His course led to B deck.

Few stewards were about. None saw the gliding thing of blackness that knew every cranny along those passages. When The Shadow finally stepped into a little side passage, he was past all chance of discovery.

The door that he tried was locked. But anyone inside could not have heard the turn of the handle. Nor did The Shadow's use of a special key give any inkling of his invasion. He opened the door so neatly that a glide into the cabin was a simple operation.

Across the cabin, a man was seated by a desk. His back was turned and his huddled position made it difficult to judge his height. The Shadow quietly closed the door, then took a chair of his own. From beneath his cloak, he drew an automatic; with the same move, he let his cloak slide from his shoulders. Peeling off his gloves, he removed his hat.

As Lamont Cranston, he sat with his .45 leveled right between the shoulder blades of the man by the desk.

The hardest part of The Shadow's whole endeavor was to attract the man's attention. He wanted to do it to a degree of nicety; to excite curiosity, rather than alarm. Slight scuffles, shifting of the chair—neither seemed to work. It was not until the tone of seven bells came vaguely to the cabin that The Shadow had the perfect opportunity.

The man in the chair looked up from his book. Momentarily diverted from his reading, he heard the slight stir that The Shadow made. The man looked about, came halfway from his chair in his surprise. He froze in that position when he saw the automatic.

A whispered laugh came from The Shadow's fixed lips. He relished this situation. It was a complete reversal of one that had been engineered at his own expense. He had not forgotten a certain night in San Francisco. Nor had the man from the chair.

That man was Ishi Soyoto.

AT first, Soyoto's eyes were disturbed; then his lips provided a wrinkly smile. He reached for his chair, turned it about. Folding his arms, he stared placidly at The Shadow.

"It is an honor," he said choppily, "to meet you here, Mr. Cranston. Especially since I have been to many pains to make sure you were not aboard the *Shinwi Maru*."

"I was not aboard," returned The Shadow, his words a monotone, "until a very short while ago."

"You mean, perhaps, that Mr. Cranston was not aboard?"

"That describes it."

Soyoto smiled wanly. He was looking very much at ease, and he decided to explain why.

"As I once told you, Mr. Cranston," he asserted, "my government is interested only in acquiring Felix Sergon; not anything that he may have stolen. Of course"—his smile ended, for he was becoming humorous—"no man should ever speak for a government. But I took that liberty.

"I made no mistake. When I was called to Honolulu, to meet officials from my country, they assured me that I was correct in all that I had said. As you probably know"—Soyoto showed his smile—"I have talked with them further, since we sailed from Hawaii."

The Shadow's silence was encouragement for Soyoto to continue. The Japanese proceeded.

"The one question," he assured, "was whether it

would be wise to tell your government what we know about Felix Sergon. That, we have decided, is the policy of friendship, and, therefore, the right thing to do.

"We shall insist, of course, that his name be kept a secret. We want Felix Sergon to believe that we shall give him welcome. That will bring him into our hands."

A singular tone chilled that cabin. It was The Shadow's laugh, sinister because it spoke of matters evil, to which its author was opposed.

Ishi Soyoto shifted uneasily, fearing that the tone was addressed to him. A moment later, he knew otherwise. The Shadow's mirth had ended. In the calm tone of Cranston, he inquired:

"Do you have a revolver?"

Soyoto nodded.

"Then get it."

Hopping to a suitcase, the Jap produced the gun. When he turned about, he saw The Shadow again enveloped in his cloak, only the burn of his eyes visible beneath the brim of his slouch hat.

Almost wonderingly, Soyoto followed The Shadow from the cabin. They neared the big stairway that led up to the strongroom. At the last turn, The Shadow halted.

"Felix Sergon does not believe you want him," he told Soyoto in a low whisper. "But even if he did, he would have no reason to care. Wherever he is, he has already found security, enough to suit his taste.

"You have counted upon Sergon's thirst for wealth. It has lulled you into believing that Japanese ships are secure from his attack, on the theory that he intends to treat with you. But what ship could be safe when it carries five million dollars?"

Across Soyoto's dryish features came the greatest alarm that he had ever shown. The Shadow's logic could not be disputed. Through Soyoto's mind flashed the fact that the *Shinwi Maru* was driving closer to the coast where Sergon had previously lurked. To his lips came the spoken thought:

"At dawn?"

"Or before," declared The Shadow. "This ship is peopled by the strongest array of accomplices that Sergon has as yet assembled. They are passengers, not crew members. We have time, however, to prepare for them—"

SCUFFLING noises interrupted from above. Soyoto sprang forward; The Shadow restrained him. Peering from a corner, The Shadow saw faces that looked down the stairway, then retired from sight. He motioned Soyoto forward. Side by side, they crept up the stairway.

At the top, they saw the Japanese purser and an assistant; both had lifted arms. Four masked men held them covered with revolvers, while another was using the purser's keys to enter the room across the way. Crouched low, The Shadow and Soyoto kept from sight.

Eight bells—midnight—had not yet struck. Events had begun far earlier than even The Shadow had anticipated. But this invasion of the strongroom might have been hurried because it was the most vital step. It had been accomplished with remarkable ease; but therein lay its weakness.

Thinking themselves undiscovered, the five men forced their prisoners into the strongroom, then followed, intending to close the door behind them. That was when The Shadow launched toward them, Soyoto at his elbow.

Before the crooks could swing the door, they heard The Shadow's laugh—a fierce, mocking taunt that brought a tremble even from his ally, Ishi Soyoto.

Swung about, Sergon's tools were covered by a brace of giant automatics held by a being that they recognized as crime's greatest foe!

The puny revolver that Soyoto aimed was unneeded as a backing to The Shadow's threat. Lips winced below masks, as the huddled invaders let their revolvers drop. They were trapped at the very goal they had conspired to reach, the strongroom where five million in gold had been within their very clutch!

As the echo of The Shadow's challenge faded, the solemn *clang* of eight bells sounded through the passages of the *Shinwi Maru*.

The stroke of midnight. The Shadow's hour!

Helpless crooks were filing from the strongroom, hopeful only that The Shadow would grant them life. Standing there with Soyoto, at the head of the wide stairway, The Shadow stood supreme. Nothing, it seemed, could shake him from his victory.

The next instant jarred The Shadow's triumph.

Out of that instant came a mighty blast, a message from the deep that almost hoisted the mighty liner from the waves. Steel plates quivered, bursting, as every light went black. Stopped by the compelling force of that explosion, the *Shinwi Maru* made puppets of all on board. All were flung forward by an irresistible impetus.

Headlong, The Shadow plunged to the bottom of the stairway, Soyoto with him. Both were still tumbling when flattened crooks began to reach their feet in the cross passage that fronted the opened strongroom.

Again the game was turned. Men of crime had not played their cards too soon. They had acted upon express orders of Felix Sergon, who had sprung the unexpected upon The Shadow, as well as the Japanese, by advancing his usual hour of attack.

The *Barracuda* had arrived ahead of the *Lamprey*, and had opened with a stroke well calculated to do away with any resistance aboard the *Shinwi Maru*.

The Z-boat had launched a torpedo that exploded the instant it struck the liner's hull!

CHAPTER XVI
SERGON'S TRIUMPH

IN the chaos aboard the *Shinwi Maru*, The Shadow lay forgotten. Crooks had last sighted him pitching down the stairway in a hapless, whirling, breakneck dive that promised his obliteration. That was almost enough to convince them that he was permanently out of combat.

They were shaken, too, by the shock that had shuddered the *Shinwi*, so that when they reached their feet, they reeled in darkness, unable to gather their senses. They had not expected the *Barracuda* to attack so early. They had counted upon holding the strongroom for at least an hour.

The crew had a leader—the man appointed by Sergon to start the shipboard crime in motion. His growl reached the ears of his confederates above the babble and confusion that had gripped the rainswept decks outside. Though his commands were almost incoherent, the leader managed to remind his men of their appointed task.

That was the removal of the gold.

It lay there, ready for them to take; but it weighed twelve thousand pounds, or more. A long and arduous task for the five men appointed, but the ingenuity of Felix Sergon lay in back of them. He had calculated well, that master of modern piracy.

Sergon had believed that when the *Shinwi* was torpedoed, the one place that would be neglected was the strongroom. Officers would be busy rallying the crew to aid the passengers. Human lives would be more important than the gold, which—like the average cargo of a stricken ship—seemed destined to share the fate of the *Shinwi*.

All happened as Sergon had designed.

Aboard the *Shinwi Maru*, one person alone had anticipated the secret seizure of the strongroom. That being was The Shadow, and ill chance had removed him from participation. True, The Shadow had taken one man into his confidence; but that one man, Ishi Soyoto, had also been wiped from combat.

As for the purser and his assistant, their rally was promptly suppressed. Struggling at the door of the strongroom, they were slugged and thrown back. That done, five crooks began to work like coal heavers, relaying the small crates of gold from the strongroom to the deck.

They were helped by the list of the *Shinwi*, which made their route downhill. They chose the lower side automatically, for they knew that the torpedo had come from that direction, and that the *Barracuda* would be waiting there. The deck that they reached was clear, thanks to the assistance of other accomplices.

Posing as passengers, the remaining crooks were adding to the confusion that swept the *Shinwi*. Whenever anyone came toward the strongroom, or the deck just outside it, blundering persons seemed to block the way.

Even ship's officers, when they came along, did not guess the reason for the interference. Rather than be delayed, they took other routes to wherever they were bound.

Soon, blockers were free to help the men inside. There were about sixty boxes weighing in the neighborhood of two hundred pounds apiece, but they were small and stacked easily against the stout rail along the slanted deck. The final test would come when the *Barracuda* hove alongside to receive the spoils. As yet, the pirate craft had not been sighted by those aboard the *Shinwi*.

Some lights were on again, but most of the illumination came from flashlights. Up in the wireless room, an S O S was crackling away; and that call would soon be answered. There were plenty of navy vessels near the coast, still keeping up the search for the *Barracuda*.

Of modern construction, the *Shinwi* had a double hull, as well as watertight compartments. The main force of the explosion had been spent in ripping her outer skin. Her list, though sudden, had ceased before it reached too dangerous an angle.

THE tilt of the ship, however, accounted for the curious position in which The Shadow found himself when he came back to consciousness. He was wedged against what seemed to be a doorway, in darkness that he could not remember. Someone was lying beside him, a man of frail build, who gave a roll when The Shadow pressed heavily against his shoulder.

Events began to replace themselves in The Shadow's memory.

This was the *Shinwi Maru*. He was at the bottom of the big stairway leading to the strongroom. The stunned man near him was Ishi Soyoto. Those above were crooks in the service of Felix Sergon, busy with the theft of Japanese gold.

Where was the *Lamprey*?

The Shadow was too dazed to calculate her probable position, but he kept thinking of Commander Prew and how surprised he would be when he learned that the *Barracuda* had tried to sink a Japanese ship. Perhaps Prew would realize how far The Shadow had seen ahead, beyond mere surface suspicions.

But that view of the future had not been complete. Certain lapses accounted for The Shadow's present plight. He had not expected that torpedo when it came.

It was not too late to make amends.

Perhaps a few strides upward would have convinced him that he was in no shape for battle. That discovery, however, was denied him. The last of the gold had been slid out to the deck. With the completion of the task, one smart thug had decided to take a look down the stairs below the strongroom.

A powerful flashlight cleaved downward. Into its focus lifted a wavery shape, a thing of blackness, formidable despite its slow movements. That cloaked figure was one that any crook would have recognized. There was a shout from the top of the stairs:

"The Shadow!"

Tilting his big automatics upward, The Shadow began to pump bullets toward the men above. They flattened, answering with wild revolver fire. If he had been in good form, The Shadow would have snagged those unwary battlers from spots where they crouched, to bring them toppling down the stairs.

As it happened, his shots were too high—as futile as the excited revolver stabs that crooks dispatched in his direction.

They were pouring down the stair now, and The Shadow, on his knees, was making himself a bulwark to protect Soyoto. Lifting his lone gun, he jabbed a last bullet at something lurching toward him. The thing flopped.

The Shadow had dropped the first comer. It was enough to halt the others, in momentary fear that they had met a snare. Then before they could guess that The Shadow was actually helpless, a wild shout ordered them back up the stairs.

As crooks scrambled, new gunfire reached The Shadow's ears. His wild barrage had attracted attention to the strongroom. Armed members of the Japanese crew had arrived from an upper deck, to begin a flank attack upon the pirate mobsters that they discovered.

Outnumbered, Sergon's men scrambled out to where the gold was placed, just as a signal flare was given from the rail. Stubbornly, the crooks held off the Japanese who were trying to cut through to reach them, while the *Barracuda* poked her cheese-box conning tower against the sleek side of the listing *Shinwi*.

While battle raged above, The Shadow found Soyoto crawling toward him. Helping the man to his feet, The Shadow sought an outlet other than the stairway. Fleeting through his brain was a vague plan of some flank entry into battle.

Laboriously, they reached a deck, came up through a hatchway. There, in the glare of reddish flare, they saw Felix Sergon, his mask discarded, pointing the last of the gold down into the *Barracuda*. Guns were peppering from higher decks.

Workers were floundering all about him, but Sergon stood unscathed. As the last box dropped aboard, he motioned two men below; then shoved away three crippled followers for whom he had no more use.

There were howls from the *Shinwi* as the half dome closed above Sergon's head. Men who had worked to steal the gold were begging Sergon not to desert them. Pressed by the Japanese, they flung themselves overboard, hoping to go with the *Barracuda*. Instead of reaching the Z-boat's roundish deck, they landed in the water.

His millions gained, Sergon no longer needed men who would claim a share of the profits. He had the gold; the Japanese could pay those fellows off with bullets.

In triumph, Felix Sergon had abandoned the stricken *Shinwi Maru*; and aboard her, helpless as those who fumed at the pirate's departure, was the only being who could have balked him.

The Shadow!

CHAPTER XVII
ABOARD AND BELOW

THE valiancy of The Shadow's thwarted struggle was proven by what followed it. Mentally numbed, he had brought every ounce of reserve energy into play; all during those last minutes of Sergon's escape, his trigger finger had been tugging at an empty gun.

With the *Barracuda* gone, The Shadow's effort ended in a natural collapse. He sank to the deck beside the obscure companionway, as inert as Soyoto, who had already given out from exhaustion.

Soaked by the drizzle, The Shadow's next waking sensation was a coldness.

Recollection reached The Shadow vaguely. He visualized a battle that had turned out properly, except for something that had happened afterward. Perhaps Soyoto would remember the details that The Shadow had forgotten.

Turning to the thin-haired Japanese, The Shadow lifted Soyoto's head and gradually brought him back to consciousness. Soyoto blinked, then squinted his eyes. He had lost his thick-lensed glasses and could not make out the face before him.

He tried to speak, to smile, which at least was helpful; but it wearied him. Soyoto closed his eyes and would have let his head thump the deck, if The Shadow had not caught it with his arm.

There was nothing to do, except revive Soyoto further. The Shadow was at that task again, when a long shout came from a Japanese lookout. In the dwindling rain, the man had seen searchlights swinging from the horizon, proof that swift destroyers were near. That was not all.

Another shout caused the *Shinwi* to sweep her own searchlight across closer waters. There, like a bobbing cork, floated something very much like the cheese-box conning tower of the *Barracuda*!

THIS time, The Shadow actually let Soyoto's head drop. The jar was slight; it aroused the thin-haired Jap. Sitting up, Soyoto squinted to see The Shadow, hatless, staring at the rail, toward something in the sea.

Again, The Shadow held exclusive knowledge.

The craft that the lookout had spied was not the *Barracuda*. It was the *Lamprey*, here for the meeting that The Shadow had ordered with the *Shinwi Maru*. Coming to the surface, Prew intended to cruise along and await developments. He probably had not noticed the list of the *Shinwi*, for the glare of the searchlight blanked the shape of the big liner.

There was no way whereby Prew could have learned of the attack that Sergon had made. From the *Shinwi*, word was going to the destroyers, telling them the wrong news. As on that earlier cruise, the *Lamprey* had been mistaken for the *Barracuda*.

Deep beneath his cloak, The Shadow carried a special flare, in case an emergency signal should be needed. He yanked the flare from his pocket, jabbed its spike into the rail. A few seconds more, he would have the cap away.

Three Japanese deckhands pounced upon him, yelling for more to assist them. Seeing his action with the flare, they wanted to stop the signal. One man introduced a gun into the struggle. That revolver looked like a toy, compared to The Shadow's automatics; but they were empty, this gun was not.

Snatching the weapon from its owner, The Shadow ripped away from grabbing hands. They clawed his cloak, tearing it from his shoulders, which left him garbed as Cranston, for he had dropped his hat before. But his gestures with the revolver needed no cloak to strengthen them. The three Japs scurried, bent for cover.

Guns began to bark from farther up the deck. Grimly, The Shadow ignored them, while he twisted off the flare cap and gave it a downward swing. A burst of purple light spat from the rail. To Prew, it would mean emergency if he saw it; The Shadow hoped only that the commander would understand that it applied to the *Lamprey*.

He wanted the Z-boat to dive while she still had time to avoid the destroyers. Afterward, The Shadow could explain matters; but it might take a while, considering the way that bullets were splintering the rail at his elbow.

To stay that fire, The Shadow faked a fall. Out bounced the three deckhands; he came up to grapple with them. Others couldn't fire at the mêlée, but they were running up to join it.

A steward saw The Shadow's face, recognized it from the description of Lamont Cranston, a man to be watched if on board. The fellow shouted for others to capture the lone battler at any cost.

Shoved against the rail, The Shadow saw the *Lamprey*, still on the surface. Her conning tower was open; a head was peering from it. The man was Prew, too far away to recognize, but he was trying to make out what was doing aboard the *Shinwi*. Dazzled by the liner's searchlight, Prew was oblivious to those other lights approaching from the horizon.

In that moment, The Shadow resolved upon one long hazard. The risk was worth its possible result. It meant a way out for himself; it would produce safety for Prew.

Even more, it offered a chance to deal with Felix Sergon, for in these minutes of recent mental clarity, The Shadow had found a likely answer to a long-perplexing riddle.

The Shadow took the risk.

GRIPPING the revolver, The Shadow fired rapid shots between the faces that bobbed about him. It took expert work to miss them, and the Japs, with lead searing past their cheeks and ears, did not recognize that The Shadow had ignored them as targets.

They flung themselves away from the fray, giving The Shadow a short respite while others along the deck were taking aim with guns. Vaulting to the rail, The Shadow took a long dive into the black water below.

Revolver crackles came with the bullets that zoomed above the rail. Those shots had missed, and marksmen could not spot The Shadow when they stared over the rail. His dive was long and deep; it was not until the searchlight picked him out that guns could begin anew.

By then, Soyoto was grabbing the hands that held revolvers, explaining that whatever the swimmer's purpose, he must not be molested. That news, unfortunately, could not reach the other decks the moment it was given. There, riflemen were spattering bullets along The Shadow's trail.

The Shadow had not attempted to elude the searchlight's path. He knew that it would swing with him, and he wanted it to stay as it was. That spreading glare ahead was his route to the *Lamprey*. His mind was centered on the hope that Prew had seen him.

Topping a swell, The Shadow spied the commander lowering himself from view. Flinging a long arm from the water, The Shadow gave a last-moment signal. Commander Prew hesitated, caught another lift of a long arm. He beckoned down into the conning tower.

Reaching the *Lamprey*, The Shadow slipped as he grabbed the smooth surface. Two of the crew bobbed out; forming a human chain, they hauled him aboard. Grabbing Prew, The Shadow pointed to the north. For the first time, the commander saw the spotting light of a vessel other than the *Shinwi Maru*.

Prew shouted an order below. The ship moved with a sudden jar. When The Shadow and Commander Prew reached the control room, the *Lamprey* was making close to forty knots. Prew gave an apologetic smile.

"Sorry, Cranston," he said. "There was no help for it this time. We had to get started. We're well ahead"—he was peering through the periscope, to sight lights upon the surface—"so we can dive. But they know our speed."

"Keep to the surface," advised The Shadow, "and head south."

"South? But you said the *Barracuda* had gone for haven."

"So she has, but to a port that we never suspected. Bring out the chart, Commander."

As Prew spread the chart, The Shadow added:

"Unfortunately, I had no chance to tell Soyoto about the *Lamprey*. The destroyers still take us for the *Barracuda*, and will not give up the chase just because Soyoto says that a friend is on board. His orders counted on the *Shinwi Maru*, but nowhere else; and especially not with vessels of the United States Navy."

Prew nodded, remembering his own distrust of Soyoto.

"So we shall lead the chase," concluded The Shadow. "They want the *Barracuda*. We can draw them to her."

"We had her signal a while ago," informed Prew, "but it ended. But why do you think she has gone south?"

The commander was spreading the chart as he spoke. The Shadow jabbed a pin into it, to indicate the spot where the *Shinwi Maru* had met the torpedo.

"Straight west of Frisco," declared The Shadow. "You started from there at dusk, commander, the earliest possible time. Yet Sergon arrived an hour sooner. We know, therefore, that he must have had a closer base, well west of the California coast."

Picking up a black pin to signify the *Barracuda*, The Shadow poised it above an irregular shape that showed in dotted lines on the chart, a location approximately one hundred and fifty miles to the south. Prew's jaw went downward.

"Maracoon Reef!" he exclaimed. "You're right, Cranston—the *Barracuda* could reach there before dawn! But that reef is entirely underwater!"

"And the *Barracuda*"—The Shadow's fingers jabbed the pin into the center of the dotted oval—"is underneath the reef!"

CHAPTER XVIII
MARACOON REEF

DESTROYERS were still hard upon the trail as the *Lamprey* neared Maracoon Reef. The speed of the Z-boat must have chafed the commanders of those trailing vessels, but there was nothing they could do about it, except cling on in pesky fashion.

Thirty miles north of Maracoon, The Shadow ordered a dive. Prew first provided a burst of speed that made the *Lamprey* quiver, chuckling as he did so.

Setting the *Lamprey* at a comfortable subsea speed of twenty-five knots, Prew went to the hidden wireless panel with The Shadow. The glowing light told that the *Barracuda* was within fifty miles. After approximately ten minutes, the light began to blink. It was Claudette Marchand's signal; she was giving explicit directions, and repeating them in methodical fashion.

She was merely repeating bearings that she had often noticed, along with depth measurements in fathoms. Those would be valuable when the *Lamprey* took soundings. There was more to tell, but Claudette suddenly was forced to sign off.

Daylight was on the water when the *Lamprey* reached the reef. Through the periscope, they saw a shelving rock above the vessel. Soon they were in darkness, using the tanks to raise and lower the ship, while Prew skillfully picked the unseen fissures in the rocks.

"I remember Maracoon Reef," declared The Shadow, "but from reputation, not by name. An eccentric millionaire once talked of creating an island kingdom by building an unnamed reef off California. He gave up the idea when he learned that the United States would claim it.

"The reef has been thoroughly surveyed. It must have been this reef, and the work unquestionably led to the finding of these channels. Sergon somehow acquired that information, and foresaw its value when he came to steal the *Barracuda*."

At times, as they probed deeper, the steel beak of the *Lamprey* scraped rock. Those jolts actually pleased Commander Prew.

SOME channels were wide; others narrow, until they came to the final stage mentioned in Claudette's instructions. There, the *Lamprey* poised, while Prew let water from the submerging tanks. As the *Lamprey* reached a fixed position, at a depth of ten fathoms, Prew peered through the periscope.

"Look, Cranston!"

The Shadow looked. Like Prew, he saw something else than water. Though the indicator showed them at a depth of sixty feet, the *Lamprey* was at the surface! The ship was resting in a low, wide grotto that covered several acres.

Phosphorescence from the water's surface provided a dim glow throughout the low-vaulted cavern, showing a low hulk moored five hundred feet away.

That hull was the *Barracuda*!

Only the periscope of the *Lamprey* was above the water. Prew drew it from sight and anxiously asked what step they should next take. After pondering, The Shadow discussed the matter of the grotto.

"An airtight cavern," he described it. "Whether natural or artificial, it forms a huge diving bell under the reef. Air pressure keeps the sea from reaching its right level, for the chamber is too low to be affected by the tide."

"If it were bombed from above," suggested Prew, "it would no longer be a refuge."

"The *Barracuda* could still lurk among those lower channels," reminded The Shadow. "There is something about the grotto, though, that should interest us. It is a place where Sergon and his crew can go ashore."

"To what purpose?"

"To unload their swag, as they have probably already done. To leave extra men who may be wounded, or unneeded on an expedition. A place, too, to keep prisoners—your men, commander, who were captured with the *Barracuda*."

An idea struck Prew.

"If we could lure the *Barracuda* out! Without the swag, without the prisoners! While someone remained here, and the *Lamprey* lurked below! It would mean—"

Prew stopped, realizing that The Shadow was ahead on every point. With a slight smile, The Shadow added in Cranston's quiet tone:

"It would mean, moreover, that by this time the *Barracuda* would find a fleet surrounding Maracoon Reef. Ships prepared to welcome her, ready to give proper chase, since they have learned the speed of which a Z-boat is capable."

There was a nod from Prew, but his face showed doubt. He could not figure just what lure would bring the *Barracuda* from her lair. Wild schemes flashed to his mind; all were preposterous. Then he heard the steady voice of Cranston.

Step by step, The Shadow was detailing a method by which the deed could be accomplished. It meant that Prew would remain aboard the *Lamprey* with his entire crew, for only one person would have to be landed in the grotto.

That one venturer would be The Shadow.

SETTLING a few fathoms deeper, the *Lamprey* worked forward. By the time Prew was inching her upward, The Shadow was in the circular conning tower. He signaled to Salvo. The cylindrical wall raised, the cap above unclamped.

Squeezing out, The Shadow stretched his hands to a line of rivets. Dragging his legs in the water, he worked his way to the rounded surface of the other ship. Waiting there, he watched the cap clamp tight above the conning tower of the *Lamprey*.

Allowing for a proper time interval, Salvo had pulled the lever. The *Lamprey* went from sight.

Glow was very slight above the water level. Moving carefully along the sloping side of the *Barracuda*, The Shadow reached a runway. He could hear voices coming from a ledge among the rocks; he saw the glow of flashlights. But they were going in the opposite direction, into caverns above the waterline.

Then darkness. The Shadow was about to follow the runway to the shore, when a light came moving back toward him. Only a few feet distant was the wide conning tower of the *Barracuda*, its half dome open. Calculating that the inner cylinder would be lowered, he dropped aboard.

Down the spiral stairway, The Shadow started toward the control room. He met the circular bulkhead, much wider in diameter than the one on the *Lamprey*. Rounding it, he saw that the door of the control room was open. Drunken voices came from there.

Across the way was a storeroom, so filled with junk that no one could have squeezed inside it. Everything from old clothes to parts of torpedoes had been piled there. The passage, however, was dark enough. Hearing footsteps from the stairway, The Shadow waited where he was.

Into the dim light came Claudette Marchand.

The girl stooped to open the hidden panel to communicate with Commander Prew. Silently, The Shadow drew close behind her. He watched while she made contact, saw the blinks of the message that came promptly from Prew.

A gasp left Claudette's lips. In that message, she was learning facts that pertained to The Shadow. She remembered the battler at the boathouse. Perhaps it was such recollection that caused her to stare up suddenly from the floor.

Claudette saw The Shadow.

She knew who he must be, although he was no longer a being clad in black. Instead, she saw a man, Lamont Cranston, whose features were strangely masklike. His face, though disguised, was the sort that she had pictured as belonging to The Shadow. That, however, was probably because of its expression, rather than its mold.

FROM that moment, Claudette Marchand realized that she would have needed no instructions to make her trust The Shadow. She had been too tense when she had met him at the boathouse. Claudette had been through many perils since then, had used her wits so often that they were remarkably sharpened.

As The Shadow supposed, Claudette had gotten the full confidence of Sergon and his crew. She had done that by revealing facts about the *Barracuda* that they would have learned anyway.

With a final whisper, The Shadow went up the spiral stairs. Claudette waited, counting off the minutes. After five of them, she was to follow. Her duty was to talk to Sergon, to suggest a further search of the *Barracuda*, in hope of finding concealed equipment.

She was sure that she could manage that game; but even if the bluff weakened, The Shadow would be near. Claudette gave a satisfied smile as she reached down to close the stairway panel. Her five minutes were ended.

So were her hopes, as a harsh chuckle made her turn. Staring from the spiral steps was the very man that she intended to trick. His face hard and evil, Felix Sergon gave a sneer that marked an end to all his trust.

Claudette was trapped, caught in a secret task; and The Shadow was no longer standing by!

CHAPTER XIX
CRIME'S LAST STROKE

CLAMPING a big hand on Claudette's arm, Sergon spun the girl away from the open panel. He studied the bright light that he saw there, then snapped the question:

"What's this for?"

"I don't know." Claudette tried to make the lie sound truthful. "I just discovered it by accident."

She could have added that Sergon would soon have "discovered" the panel himself; for her move, as detailed by The Shadow, was to suggest a search that would have eventually uncovered the subsea wireless device.

Such a result would have brought her commendation, and with it, the only privilege she intended to ask: that of remaining ashore. But present circumstances eliminated all such prospects.

Sergon was working on the light, unscrewing it, tightening it again. That action, Claudette knew, would be noted aboard the *Lamprey*. She began to talk fast.

"I had a suggestion," she began. "I thought it would be wise to search this ship, just on the chance that we would find something new. I came aboard to talk to you—"

Sergon's interrupting laugh was raspy. He was positive that Claudette knew he was on shore. The excuse was to him another proof that Claudette had double-crossed him.

The light from below the steps began to blink.

"*Attention*," it said, in Morse. "*This is Commander Rodney Prew. I offer a reward to any loyal man. Attention—*"

Sergon released Claudette's arm. He backed her to a corner by brandishing a gun. The signal was flashing its previous announcement. Sergon snorted.

"Any loyal man," he sneered. "He's thinking of you! He says 'man' so we won't suspect. But he knows you're for him. Lucky you didn't find this thing before."

That last remark was Claudette's one glimpse of hope. She was granting her own death as a certainty; but she saw a chance that might at least bring success to the all-important cause. Sergon had seen through her loyalty, but he did not realize its past importance. He was taking the very bait that The Shadow had prepared.

There was a switch just below the blinking bulb. Sergon began to tap it. The light flashed a question:

"*Who are you?*"

Sergon gave a deep, ugly chuckle, as he tapped back:

"*Claudette Marchand. I am loyal. State how I can aid.*"

Eyeing Claudette, Sergon observed that she had read the coded taps. It pleased him to think how cleverly he had seized upon her name as the one that Prew hoped to hear.

A longer message came from Prew. In it, the commander stated that he was aboard another ship, the *Lamprey*, a Z-boat like the *Barracuda*. From the way Prew put it, Sergon was sure that Claudette had never heard of the other ship before. As he looked toward the girl, she feigned a surprised expression and managed it to perfection.

"*We are near Maracoon Reef*," stated the light, in conclusion. "*State how we can reach you.*"

Sergon stroked his chin. He was scheming something, and Claudette hoped that his ingenious brain would jump to the very idea that The Shadow wanted him to hold. At last, Sergon tapped. Again, he had taken the bait!

"*State your position*," he ordered. "*I can then inform you later.*"

Prew's blinks located the *Lamprey* as two miles east of Maracoon Reef. Sergon signed off. He kicked the panel shut. With the gun, he forced Claudette toward the control room.

"You'll see what we'll do to Prew," he told her. "So he's got another Z-boat? He won't have, very long!"

THE drunks in the control room came to their feet when Sergon arrived there. He shoved Claudette toward them, told them to keep her under guard.

"Ashore?" asked one man, thickly. "With the rest of 'em?"

"No. On board," retorted Sergon. "She's going to see the fun. She'd better enjoy it"—he slanted a look at Claudette—"because it's the last fun she'll have!"

Stamping out to the passage, Sergon bellowed orders. By the end of ten minutes, all was ready. Her conning tower closed, the *Barracuda* began to sink under the grotto.

Sergon knew the passages beneath the rocks; he avoided blind channels that had troubled the *Lamprey*. As they came out into the open sea, he began to sight through the periscope. He had kept Claudette in the control room; his remarks were for her benefit.

"We'll fix that fool Prew," he growled. "Likely enough, he'll have his ship up on the surface, because he won't know we're coming."

He paused as he viewed the surface through the periscope. His hands gripped the controls.

With a swift oath, Sergon fixed the levers. He turned about, not merely to address Claudette but all the others present. At first, his face showed anger; then over it spread a knowing leer.

"That Z-boat talk sounded phony," he declared. "Smart of Prew, making up a name for a ship he hasn't got. All he has is a subsea wireless. Do you know what's waiting off this reef?"

Men shook their heads.

"A cruiser," chuckled Sergon. "Say—those torpedoes of ours will cut a cruiser's armor like cheese! She's a pretty old baby"—he was looking through the periscope—"and if one don't sink her, we'll send another. If she's got destroyers hiding in back of her, we'll shake those buzzards like we always have!"

The door of the overfilled storeroom was open. Sergon didn't like its looks; he turned on a light and glared about suspiciously. Satisfied that Claudette had released no prisoners, to make them stowaways, he pointed to the torpedo room.

Two men entered; they lifted the top torpedo from the stack. Lugging the fifteen-foot cylinder, they pointed it toward a torpedo tube. As they shifted the fat torpedo, it toppled, off balance.

"Look out!" bawled Sergon. "Hang on to it!"

They couldn't hold on. Nose end, the torpedo hit the floor. Its head bashed loose, the main cylinder rolled sideward. Sergon, dropping back along the passage, had expected a disaster; he gruffed his relief when he thought the danger past.

There was a yell from the men in the torpedo room. With it, the sharp bark of a gun. Sergon bounded forward as another shot was fired. He saw his men sprawling to the floor. Then, he spied the torpedo aiming for himself!

That, at least, was the illusion that Sergon gained. Where the torpedo head had been, a face was peering forth; below it, a shoulder; then a hand with a smoking revolver. For a moment, the thing on the floor was half torpedo, half man; then Sergon realized that it was a man inside of a torpedo shell.

The laugh that rang through the torpedo room left no doubt regarding the identity of that fighter who had stowed himself inside the cramped container. Sergon recognized the avenger as quickly as did Claudette.

The Shadow!

TO Sergon, The Shadow's arrival was incredible, even though he wore a torpedo instead of a black cloak. To Claudette, realization was immediate. The Shadow had seen Sergon pass. Instead of remaining in the grotto, he had doubled back into the *Barracuda* to share Claudette's own danger.

Again, flame spat from The Shadow's gun. The weapon was Prew's .38 revolver, and with The Shadow's aim, the borrowed firearm should have proven as deadly as a .45 automatic. All that saved Sergon was a roll of the torpedo.

The shot went wide. Backing along the passage, Sergon whipped out a gun himself. By that time, The Shadow had grabbed the doorway, to haul his body from the cylinder that held it. Two guns spoke at once; Sergon's shot was badly aimed, while The Shadow's missed only because Claudette's captors were lunging toward him.

The girl was grabbing at their gun hands, when The Shadow dropped one with an upward shot. On his feet, he downed the other while the fellow fumbled. Sergon was gone, dashing toward the control room. Snatching up unfired guns, The Shadow kept one, gave the other to Claudette.

The light by the stairway was blinking: "*Ready... ready... ready*—"

The Shadow ignored it. The signal was from Prew, to be understood and answered by The Shadow or Claudette, if either were aboard. But The Shadow preferred any risk rather than stop the final stroke that he had ordered, and he knew that Claudette felt the same way.

At a pace that Sergon had not expected, The Shadow reached the control room. He was blasting shots as he came, his bullets stabbing the guards who tried to stop him. Sergon was trying to yank the rudder lever, to send the ship into a dive, when The Shadow grappled with him.

Guns were lost in that hand-to-hand fray. The final weapon that staggered Sergon was the rudder lever, ripped from its place by The Shadow. Flooring Sergon with a hard swing, The Shadow was away again, to rejoin Claudette.

The girl was cowing crew members with her gun. They ducked as The Shadow swung the lever toward them. When they came about, they saw The Shadow and Claudette upon the stairs. The pair reached the top ahead of followers; there, The Shadow shoved the controls that raised the cylindrical wall and opened the top of the conning tower.

He shoved Claudette over the rising wall and sprang after her. A man had followed them, was aiming from the passage, but The Shadow snatched Claudette's gun and beat the fellow to the shot. Two seconds later, the slowly rising cylinder had closed. The Shadow was urging Claudette up the ladder.

The *Barracuda* was riding the sea awash. That opening above still afforded a chance for escape. They were almost to the top when the Z-boat jumped forward, signifying that Sergon had managed to yank the speed lever, as a last resort. But that lunge was not the only one the *Barracuda* took.

Just as The Shadow rolled Claudette from the conning tower, the Z-boat heaved into the air. Something had driven up beneath it, to prod it with a mighty slice that ripped half the bottom from the craft.

Claudette was hurled far clear; as she struck the water, she saw The Shadow take a sidewise dive from the tilted conning tower.

Reeling like some sea monster wounded in a fray, the *Barracuda* wallowed away along the surface. She was stricken beyond repair, succumbing to the gash that was pouring water into her hull. That was recognized by the waiting cruiser. Her guns were already opening fire.

The Shadow and Claudette were safely out of range, for the *Barracuda* still had speed. They saw the shells explode about her; then one struck the conning tower when she was a quarter mile away. When that happened, they were swimming no longer.

Up from the sea beneath them had come a rounded platform: the deck of the *Lamprey*. Prew's ship was intact, except for a battered prow. The *Lamprey* was the monster that had doomed the *Barracuda*. From a hidden channel, she had sneaked along beneath the pirate submarine, then driven up to rip her.

Safe were The Shadow and Claudette—the only two who would ever again be seen of those who had been with the *Barracuda*. Thrust from the water, a half mile out to sea, was the stern of the other Z-boat, ready to follow her prow in a final dive.

They glimpsed the wide slash that the *Lamprey* had made along the keel, then that sight was obliterated, not by a dive but by an eight-inch shell that struck the tail fins, just ahead of the racing propellers. In a flash, the last trace of the *Barracuda* was obliterated.

She was gone, that submarine menace of the sea, and with her the pirate master, Felix Sergon, and with his picked crew of rascals.

THE rest of Sergon's tribe capitulated when the *Lamprey* returned to the hidden grotto. By taking The Shadow and Claudette rapidly aboard, Commander Prew had escaped observation from the ships that were settling the *Barracuda*.

Reaching the grotto, the *Lamprey* rose to the surface, to be mistaken for the *Barracuda* by the men who greeted her.

Unarmed, fearing no attack, they were rendered helpless by the guns that jutted from the Z-boat's opened conning tower. The half dozen that were still at large soon surrendered when they realized that, otherwise, they could never leave these caverns.

With Sergon's men as prisoners, and Prew's own loyal men released, the boxes of gold were carried aboard, along with the other valuables that were stored in the pirate's nest.

By afternoon, the *Lamprey* was headed northeast, away from Maracoon Reef, toward the Golden Gate of San Francisco Bay, where the glow of sunset would again be tinting the sea when she arrived.

With the *Barracuda* sunk, all searchers had put into port. Along the surface, gliding at forty knots, the *Lamprey* was coming home unchallenged, to tell her story when she arrived. A welcome would await her when she put into Mare Island; for there, Commander Prew would keep his promise of delivering a Z-boat to the government he served.

Atop the ladder of the conning tower, a lone figure was leaning upon the raised side of the half-domed shield, watching the Pacific's surface wash past the speeding *Lamprey*. Into the sweeping air there passed a chilling tone, strange in that placid daylight setting, for it was a taunt that belonged to darkest night.

The laugh of The Shadow!

THE END

INTERLUDE by Will Murray

We take a serious departure from the usual run of Shadow stories in this volume. The Shadow was a mystery character who sometimes became embroiled in espionage. Although the character's origins lay in World War I, the Second World War seldom crept into the pages of his civilian exploits.

Here, however, The Shadow battles Japanese militarists in one form or another in two change-of-pace suspense stories.

Our first effort is *Death Ship,* dating from 1939. Written the previous May, it first appeared in the April 1, 1939 issue of *The Shadow*. For reasons still unexplained, Walter Gibson took an unusual three-month sabbatical from chronicling The Shadow's exploits after turning in *Shadow over Alcatraz* in February. Here, he picks up the action with the Master of Darkness still in San Francisco, including a rare reference to the previous exploit. The two stories were printed months apart.

Gibson submitted this manuscript under the title "Ship of Doom." This perfectly purple pulp title was changed to the somewhat flatter *Death Ship*. Coincidentally or not, exactly a year later, Walter wrote another Shadow story he entitled "Ships of Doom." That title stood. Go figure.

San Francisco and its Chinatown was one of Walter's favorite settings for a Shadow story. As with the previous entry, Chinatown is de-emphasized. In *Death Ship*, Ying Ko—as the Dark Avenger was called by his Chinese allies—does enter the Oriental quarter, only to find it changed in a sinister way. None of his usual Chinese contacts are present in this tale. The influence of the expanding empire of Japan is showing itself.

Editor John L. Nanovic first teased this novel as an action tale:

> The Shadow novel will be "Death Ship," a fast-paced, mystery-packed tale with the Pacific coast as its locale, and with all the threatening danger of the Orient overshadowing its action. A clever, diabolical scheme? A master criminal? Well, master enough to be able to pierce The Shadow's disguise; clever enough to put The Shadow in the toughest spot he has ever been in, and clever enough to make you get a great kick out of this marvelous story.
>
> It seems that these novels are coming along better and better each issue, even beyond our own expectations, which are set very high. Your enthusiasm cannot help but imbue Maxwell Grant with even more enthusiasm to do a better job, and that's what we all wish to see continued.

By the time the issue rolled around, Nanovic's tone darkened. In the year since Gibson had written "Death Ship," the world had become a gloomier place. The shadow of World War II was falling over Europe, while in Asia, the growing power of Imperial Japan was extending her voracious influence.

> Most of the talk about war that you hear nowadays is about war in the air. However, military experts have not forgotten war on land, or war on the sea—and "Death Ship," the novel in this issue, treats a phase of war on the sea that is as interesting as it is vital. The last war taught us many things, one of the best of which is to be prepared for the worst. The nation that has the best means of defense as well as offense is the one that will fare best when attacked, or when it attacks others. To that point, not even the smallest item must be overlooked. You'll find "Death Ship" not only filled with the usual sparkle and excitement that fills every Shadow novel, but also containing a great deal for every American citizen to think about for a good many days.

This issue of *The Shadow* marked the debut of a new cover artist, replacing the departing George Rozen. His full name was James Francis Graves Gladney, but he invariably signed his covers, Graves Gladney.

"You have to realize that when I got the Shadow contract it was almost like stepping into financial heaven," Gladney later recalled. "It meant that I would earn $5,000 or more a year, which in 1938 was a considerable amount of money."

Taking over for George Rozen, Gladney reached

Graves Gladney

out to the model Rozen had been using for many years for The Shadow and his other faces, William Magner. A former Silent Screen actor, Magner was an extremely popular artist's model, both for the pulps and the slick magazines. With his strong mature features, hooded eyes and and hawklike nose, he was perfect for The Shadow.

For this cover, Gladney chose the unusual scene in which the Master Avenger confronted his Japanese antagonists with his Shadow regalia casually worn, revealing Lamont Cranston beneath. This striking display was part of Walter Gibson's change in portraying The Shadow, now that readers knew that his true identity was really World War I aviator, Kent Allard. As a way of deflecting any suspicion that Allard was The Shadow, the Dark Avenger began flaunting his Cranston disguise.

His first time painting The Shadow, Gladney showed the unmasked face of Cranston—or should we say William Magner? Gladney soon realized that his own sharp features resembled The Shadow's so much that he dropped Magner and posed for his own covers, thus saving the modeling fee. Gladney sported a pencil mustache, but since The Shadow's red collar usually obscured his mouth, this presented no problem.

Occasionally, Gladney appeared on his *Shadow* covers as a mustached bad guy, also posing for similar situations on the *Doc Savage* covers by his friend, Emery Clarke. When he took over *The Avenger*, Gladney also modeled for that hero, Richard Henry Benson—sans mustache, of course!

As for William Magner, he got a lucky break. Six months after Rafael DeSoto took over painting the covers for Popular Publications' *The Spider.* He needed a model.

William Magner fit the bill perfectly. And so, the face of The Shadow became the visage of his chief rival, the *Spider!*

We jump ahead four years to our second selection. It is a very different world now. *The Black Dragon* was written in October, 1942, and printed in the March 1, 1943 issue. Pearl Harbor was less than a year in the past, but since it was a mystery-crime magazine, *The Shadow* was slow to deal with the war. This is one of those rare exceptions. Here, the vague threat that Japan represented in *Death Ship* has come to full fruition.

Again, John Nanovic sets the stage:

> "The Black Dragon" is our next great novel—a novel which will make you realize to what lengths our enemies can go. The evil schemes of Japan can penetrate far if we are not careful. How the cult of the dragon built its snare in the very heart of Chinatown, trying to masquerade its viciousness under the covering of our Chinese friends and allies, makes a thrilling story. The Shadow, who has many friends in Chinatown, is called by these to help fight an influence which is threatening to destroy every good thing that the leaders of Chinatown have built up; indeed, is a menace to our war effort.
>
> You'll get many a thrill out of this coming novel, complete in our next issue. "The Black Dragon" has mystery and action, and a plot that is extremely clever. It will baffle your ability to pick out the villain, unless you are specially expert at deducing these things. Don't miss it.

Nanovic's jingoistic editorial in the issue containing the novel displays the wartime hatred for Japan that infused American culture after the attack on Pearl Harbor.

> "The Black Dragon"... will give you plenty of thrills. From the land of treachery—Japan—comes an evil hand to strike its vicious blow in our own country. What better place for it to hide than in Chinatown, where it takes every opportunity to use as a front the established reputations of our Chinese friends and allies. It makes the task of uncovering the master behind the treachery that much harder, and that much more exciting.

This story marks the final series entry set in Chinatown for a very long time. Apparently the string of editors who replaced John Nanovic after 1943 shied away from approving tales laid against this quasi-exotic backdrop. For it would be nearly six years before Gibson produced another—a very long time considering that Chinatown intrigue was a Shadow staple going back to his debut novel.

The Black Dragon features the last appearance of Dr. Roy Tam, who became Ying Ko's Chinatown ally in the 1935 novel, *The Fate Joss*. Dr. Tam had taken up residence in San Francisco with the 1941 story, *The Chinese Primrose*. Here he's back in New York for this case. Also, Myra Reldon, alias Ming Dwan, who got her start as an agent of The Shadow back in 1937's *Teeth of the Dragon,* bows out for a very long time. Myra would return for another adventure in 1946, but her Asian alter ego would not. Fortunately, when Walter Gibson returned to the Shadow series after a two-year absence in 1948, his first contribution would be *Jade Dragon*, with Myra Reldon playing a huge role.

This issue is also the beginning of Modest Stein's long run as cover artist. He had been the main cover artist for Street & Smith's *Love Story Magazine* for a long time. Most of his Shadow covers de-emphasized the Dark Avenger. This is one of the rare ones that didn't. •

A Complete Book-length Novel from the Private Annals of The Shadow, as told to

MAXWELL GRANT

CHAPTER I
BLACK MADNESS

STEVE TRASK stared at the carved dragon that squatted in the shop window. It was a tiny object, not more than four inches high. Carved from solid jet, the dragon was a glossy black, save for two dots of jade that gave it the look of a green-eyed monster in miniature.

It might even be Miljohn's dragon!

Singular, how Steve had scoured Manhattan's Chinatown in vain, looking for just such a dragon, only to find one in the window of this obscure shop which bore no name and looked as though it was no longer doing business!

Black Dragon

The Shadow strikes back—at a devil god that symbolizes all the hate and menace and trickery of the Japs!

As Steve stared, something more singular happened. A saffron hand came through the curtain that backed the show window, gripped the jet dragon in its fist and disappeared as rapidly as it had arrived.

Springing to the door of the shop, Steve pounded with one hand, while using the other to grip the stubby revolver that he carried in his pocket. Shuffly footsteps answered from within; the door opened a crack, and Steve received a minute inspection from a slanted eye.

Then the door went wide and a yellow-faced man bowed Steve to a counter. Seeing Steve's eye upon his fist, the man inquired:

"You wantee buy dragon?"

As Steve nodded, a telephone bell rang. The shopkeeper answered, all the while keeping a wary eye upon the door. Across the wire, Steve heard a sharp voice that inquired:

"You, Sujan?"

The shopkeeper muttered quick words that ended the call. Turning to Steve, he spread his hand twice to indicate the price of the dragon as ten dollars, absurdly low for such a rare curio. With his free hand, Steve produced the money and pocketed the jet ornament, but he still gripped his gun as he stepped outdoors.

That ten-dollar price was proof that something was wrong in this shop. But it simply clinched an impression that Steve had gained earlier. It wasn't until the door slammed shut and bolts slid home that Steve put facts together.

The shopkeeper hadn't said "dlagon" as most Chinese would. He had correctly pronounced the word "dragon." Also, the name that had been spoken over the wire, Sujan, was distinctly not Chinese.

The man was a Japanese!

No wonder the shop bore no name and looked closed. It was a hideaway for Sujan and perhaps for other Japs.

Steve started to dismiss the thought as preposterous, until he reasoned how shrewd the game could be. Chinatown was the one place where Japanese could risk being seen by Americans, because there they could be mistaken for Chinese.

Naturally, they'd have to make sure that the Chinese did not spot them, but Sujan's actions proved that he was following just such a policy. He'd taken a chance when he saw that Steve was an American. But Steve had guessed the truth and maybe Sujan knew it. If so, there could be trouble!

THIS dimmed street was sinister. Looking about, Steve saw a mass of basement entries, so dark they looked like foxholes. The only place that promised Steve safety was a doorway across the street. It was deep, even though it ended in a door of heavy bronze, so formidable that quick entrance would prove impossible.

To the right of the house with the bronze door was an alley; on the far side, Steve saw a higher structure that looked like an old apartment building. Its second floor was fronted by a balcony with bulky ornamental posts.

Odd how the nearest of those posts looked like a huddled figure watching for some prey!

Shaking off the illusion, Steve glanced elsewhere. His eyes narrowed as they covered the cornice of the house roof above the bronze door. Even more ominous than the apartment balcony, that cornice jutted like something carved from blackness, yet with a clinging effect that reminded Steve of a living creature.

Turning his gaze across the narrow alley, Steve looked higher to the projecting eaves of the apartment building, four floors up. If he'd wanted to let his fancy get the better of him, Steve could have imagined a stir beneath those eaves.

But Steve wasn't letting himself be deceived by shadows that looked like things alive!

Dimmed lights were coming along this forgotten street. They marked an arriving taxicab, its driver looking for some address. As the cab pulled in front of the house with the bronzed door, Steve saw that it had a passenger who was about to get out.

This was real opportunity. All Steve had to do was get into the vacated cab and ride from this weird neighborhood. Once away, he could examine the black dragon and figure out what it meant. Probably owners of black dragons were regarded as members of a secret fraternity, something that Miljohn hadn't known. Those thoughts were flashing to Steve as he crossed the street, wisely going in back of the cab so that its dimmed headlights would not disclose him. But as he rounded the rear of the cab, Steve stopped short, face to face with the passenger who had just stepped to the sidewalk.

Fierce eyes met Steve's, ugly eyes that flared narrowly beneath bushy brows. He saw a sharp nose; beneath it yellow teeth that gritted from the sudden thrust of a heavy jaw that poked from a muffling overcoat collar. The man was an American, of tawny visage, but he wasn't welcoming Steve as a compatriot. An instant's glance at Steve, then those narrowed eyes tilted upward. With a half snarl, the tawny man swung his arm wide, as if in a signal. Steve didn't lunge, because the man was springing back into the cab. What Steve did was swing about, following the direction of the tawny man's gaze.

Shadows had come to life!

THE balcony post across the alley was lunging into human shape, if its grotesque lurch could be called human. Steve saw a saffron Japanese face push forward from the rail; with it came a clawed hand that furnished a downward whip. From those fingers came the glint of a knife that the creature was releasing —with Steve as the only target in its path!

Nothing could stop that hand of death, for its fling was complete. The intervention that saved Steve was of a more amazing sort.

A gun tongued from the cornice on Steve's side of the alley. Straight as the knife-fling and far swifter was the bullet that intercepted the blade of death. Literally, that leaden slug plucked the knife

★ ★

Whenever fliers gather together, whenever the public talks of aviation, the name of Kent Allard is one of the first to be mentioned. World-famous aviator, Allard is a public hero. But what no one knows—save his two Xinca Indian servitors—is that Allard is the real identity of The Shadow!

Assisting The Shadow in his perpetual battle with the underworld is a retinue of aides—men who owe their lives to The Shadow and for whom they gladly do his slightest bidding.

Burbank is the contact man between The Shadow and his aides; through him go all orders and information. Rutledge Mann gives invaluable service to the Master of Darkness through his "front" of investment broker. Harry Vincent is very close to The Shadow, and acts in many cases as his advance man. To Moe Shrevnitz goes the honor of transporting the crimefighter to battle—in his taxicab. Clyde Burke, reporter on the *Classic*, furnishes The Shadow with inside information and advance news.

Cliff Marsland and Hawkeye are purported tough underworld characters; but, in reality, they are aides of The Shadow. When physical strength is needed the Master of Darkness calls on Jericho, giant African, whose muscular power is equaled only by his willingness to fight crime.

These, then, are the aides of The Shadow, characters who are willing to subject themselves to the Master of Darkness because they realize in him a superior force counteractant to crime.

The Shadow knows!

from the hand that hurled it. Steve heard the sharp *ping* and saw the knife go flying out into the street, while the clawing hand whipped back as though stung by the force that shivered the deadly dirk!

Steve's rescuer was the black shape that he had mistaken for a segment of the cornice. Timed to the recoil of its gun, that figure was rising to reveal itself as a cloaked form. Shadows had truly came to life.

This one was The Shadow!

Cloaked fighter who battled men of crime, The Shadow wasn't stopping with his first endeavor. He was swinging from the cornice to take another gun stab at the foiled assassin on the balcony across the alley. And Steve, knowing that this cloaked being must be a friend, was wheeling about to handle the glaring man who had sprung back into the cab.

That man was gone; so was the cab. Steve's hearty lunge carried him out into the street, where he sprawled. He heard the staccato punches of The Shadow's gun, saw the knifeless assassin scrambling along the balcony to avoid the fire. Then, rolling on both elbows, Steve was staring straight up, to witness something truly amazing.

Both sides could boast rescuers in this combat!

TWO floors above The Shadow's head, a mere dozen feet across the alley, the eaves were disgorging another Japanese assassin who traveled along with the murderous stroke he hoped to deliver. This creature was swinging a weapon shaped like a cleaver, and the drive of the chopping blade was carrying it to its mark!

Before Steve could aim his gun, the cleaver man landed.

Weird was the laugh from the cornice. Steve's revolver was talking into the darkness. The Shadow had heard the clatter of the eaves and had literally rolled across the edge of the cornice to avoid the cleaver stroke. By a quick clutch back across the brink, The Shadow was hauling himself back to solid footing by seizing the scrawny opponent whose cleaver slash had gone wide!

His shots not being needed, Steve sprang across the street to see what happened next. As he reached the front of Sujan's shop, guns jabbed from all about. The basement doorways on this side of the street were alive with marksmen shooting at The Shadow!

On the cornice, The Shadow twisted his scrawny opponent as a shield against the gunfire. They twirled back across the roof, where the scrawny man wrenched free and scrambled to a higher ledge.

With a howl of indescribable glee, the wiry Jap jabbed his hands to The Shadow's throat!

Another defiant laugh resounded as The Shadow sprang after his slippery enemy, to regain him as a shield.

With a howl of indescribable glee, the wiry Jap jabbed his hands to The Shadow's throat. They twisted like a windmill painted black and yellow. Amid the kaleidoscopic spin, the human whirligig disappeared over the rear of the higher roof. Clutched by a tenacious strangler, The Shadow was bound on a three-story plunge to a solid courtyard behind the house with the bronze door!

Black madness gripped Steve Trask. He wanted the quickest route to reach The Shadow and wreak vengeance on the strangler who had gained the upper hand in the fatal plunge.

Steve's dash stopped as suddenly as it began. It stopped when he drove through the opposite doorway and met the bronze barrier shoulder-first. Grabbing the big door latch, Steve found it wouldn't yield. There wasn't any chance to pound the door; others were doing it for him.

They were pounding it with bullets, those marksmen from the basement foxholes. Having settled The Shadow, they were giving Steve their attention. Escaping the first wild shots, Steve at least had sense enough to respond with his own gun, but to even less avail than his enemies.

Steve's bullets might as well have been blanks, considering the way his adversaries ducked to shelter. Besides, his fire was rapidly exhausted. Steve was simply clicking a hammer on empty chambers. Why he kept tugging the useless revolver trigger, Steve didn't know, any more than why he should be keeping his other hand in his pocket, clutching the black dragon as a lucky token, but this was one spot where luck looked sure to fail.

Back against the bronze door, Steve braced as he saw revolvers thrust. Then came the jabs of flame accompanied by a unanimous roar. With it Steve caved; but he was pitching backward, not forward, a thing that he couldn't understand until he saw that the bronze door was swinging shut above him, echoing from the clang of bullets.

The barrier had yielded at the crucial instant, gulping the victim whose death had seemed so imminent. But Steve wasn't stopping just across the threshold; he was going down through a space where there wasn't any floor, into an abyss of engulfing blackness!

The bronze door slammed with a mighty clangor. Tuned to that strident clash, Steve struck the bottom of the pit below. He saw sunbursts outmatching the gun spurts that he had so luckily escaped. Then, as though jarred into oblivion by the brazen echoes, Steve's senses vanished.

Black madness had overwhelmed Steve Trask, just as it had taken his rescuer, The Shadow!

CHAPTER II
THE HOUSE OF LI HUANG

THE sound was sharp. *Click!* So close that it seemed to snap exactly in Steve's ear.

Coming to one elbow, he took his head between his hands. While his brain still swam, he realized that it wasn't the clicking sound that had roused him.

There were other sounds, very distant —the shrills of police whistles, the wails of sirens. They came from the street, a place Steve couldn't reach, for there was more than a brass door barring his exit from this pit. When Steve came to his feet and struck a match, he saw that a solid floor had closed above his head.

The match flame wavered along with Steve. It reached his fingers and he opened them suddenly. The match struck a stone floor and went out. Sagging to his knees, Steve struck another match and looked along the floor.

Something glittered in the corner; it was Steve's revolver. Clutching the gun with his left hand, Steve shook out the match flame with his right.

The moment he gripped the revolver, Steve remembered the *click* that he had heard. The walls about him seemed solid, like the floor; still, it was from one of those walls that the sound had come. Steve didn't light another match. Instead, he swung to his feet again, shoved his back against the wall and found the nearest corner. He was forgetting that his gun was empty as he gestured it in the pitch darkness. At least he preferred darkness, since it enabled him to stay from sight.

Then, in a hoarse whisper, Steve demanded:

"Who's there?"

The question came back, hollow, like a sneer. Its repetition marked it as an echo, but Steve wasn't sure. It certainly didn't resemble his own voice. Still, the confines of this narrow pit could probably produce vocal illusions.

After listening for several seconds, Steve began to creep along the wall. He could hear other footfalls, timed to his own. Again, they seemed echoes, but of a distorted sort. Steve halted his caged pacing. When he did, the other sounds stopped, too.

The *click* hadn't been an echo. So Steve waited, hoping it would sound again. If it did, it would mean that his unseen companion was going out. So Steve was reasoning—when the sharp sound came straight across the pit. Gun ahead of him, Steve lunged.

There wasn't any wall when Steve arrived. He went right through, swinging his gun, hoping to overtake the person who was darting out ahead of him. Only nobody was going out, except Steve, and he didn't travel far.

What Steve met were men coming in. They stopped his gun swing, along with his surge, hurled him back and pinned him helpless against the far wall that he had left. A flashlight suddenly appeared and Steve found himself confronted by a yellow-brown face, flanked by two others belonging to the men who clutched him.

All three belonged to the group that stopped Steve's drive. Except for them, the pit was empty. Completely flabbergasted by the way his imagination had tricked him, Steve subsided without further resistance. His captors took his gun away and marched him out through the open wall, clicking it shut behind them.

THE brief parade ended in an upstairs room, where a thin-faced Chinaman was seated behind a teakwood desk. Though shrewd, the eyes that greeted Steve were somewhat friendly. The man, himself, looked Chinese, though the three servants did not.

They seemed more Mongolian, those three, when Steve gave them side glances. However, he wasn't well enough versed in Oriental nationalities to be sure of anything, except that the trio looked ugly and dumb—two points that did not apply to their thin-faced master.

The man behind the desk spoke first. "I am Li Huang," he declared in precise English. "This is my house. I am glad to receive you"—the lips gave a twitch which Steve decided was a smile—"but I regret the sudden method that necessity impelled. Perhaps Ming Dwan should explain the situation, since she was the person responsible."

Li Huang gestured toward the door of a room, and Steve turned to see a Chinese girl enter. She was dark-haired, petite, more typically a native of Cathay than Li Huang himself. In what seemed a correct Chinese fashion, Ming Dwan looked straight past Steve and answered Li Huang directly.

"It was right that I should allow a friend to enter," declared Ming Dwan. "But it would have been wrong to let an enemy reach you, Li Huang. Not knowing which was outside our portal, I treated this stranger as both.

"I opened the door as to a friend. I pressed the switch that let the floor fall, that I might trap a foe." Li Huang actually smiled as Ming Dwan bowed. Crossing the room, the Chinese girl stopped beside the desk, folded her arms and turned toward Steve. Words of gratitude stopped on Steve's lips as his eyes met Ming Dwan's.

This Chinese girl was utterly impersonal. Her expression showed no interest in the man whose life she had saved. Rather, Ming Dwan regarded Steve coldly, as though no thanks on his part could make amends for the inconvenience he had caused.

At least Li Huang proved more affable.

"I have introduced myself," stated Li Huang blandly, "because I have nothing to conceal. My doorway was a trap, yes, but it is lawful for a man to protect his own premises, particularly when he is a retired merchant known to possess wealth.

"Your situation may be different." Li Huang fixed his eyes steadily, on Steve. "Therefore, I do not ask you to declare your name. It is but fair, however, that you should detail the events that occurred outdoors and give me some token of your circumstance."

Fairly spoken, those words of Li Huang. They stirred Steve's mind to a logical chain of thoughts. He remembered the events that brought him here.

THE chain began with the death of Steve's friend, Rufus Miljohn, once the owner of a black dragon carved from jet—a death that the police termed suicide, but which Steve classified as murder for the Black Dragon. It was on Miljohn's account that Steve had scoured Chinatown for a jet dragon like Miljohn's, and had finally found one in the shop of Sujan.

Men of evil had sought to murder Steve. Therefore, the little black dragon could only represent a clan that favored justice. Looming in Steve's memory was the picture of a black-clad fighter who had saved him from doom, only to receive death's burden. The Shadow, cloaked master of justice, somehow symbolized the black dragon token that Steve himself had acquired.

Li Huang was a just man, too. More than that, he understood. His words proved it, those final words that were still chiming through Steve's brain. He could almost hear those words again:

"Give me some token of your circumstance—" Steve saw the bland face of Li Huang, awaiting his reply. A friendly face, with sympathetic eyes that formed a counterpart of Li Huang's patient smile.

All Li Huang wanted was to hear the truth.

Steve opened his lips to speak the facts. It wasn't the gaze of Li Huang that stopped him. The stare that caught Steve's attention came from Ming Dwan.

No longer did the girl's face lack expression. She was putting contempt and more into the glare that accompanied the twist of her lips.

It wasn't that Ming Dwan would doubt whatever Steve might say. It went deeper than that; she wanted to hear his story. Behind that wish was nothing friendly, judging from the girl's expression. She was in a different camp than Li Huang; her very purpose in this house was to betray the placid Chinaman who owned it! That Ming Dwan represented the wrong people seemed clear enough to Steve from the girl's expectant gloat. That was Ming Dwan's one mistake; she'd given herself away too soon. It was up to Steve to play the smarter hand, in a way that would satisfy his friend, Li Huang, yet keep Ming Dwan totally at sea.

There was a perfect way to do it.

Silence was the answer; absolute silence, so far as Steve's name and mission were concerned. Yet with such silence he could declare himself. All he had to do was show Li Huang the dragon token, thus proving that he, Steve Trask, was a worthy guest, so worthy that there would be no need to know his name.

That was what Li Huang expected, and Ming Dwan, too. But the girl wanted the embellishments that Li Huang would not demand. So, in one stroke, Steve could handle both situations, winning the confidence of the honorable Li Huang and keeping the treacherous Ming Dwan baffled.

With a smile of his own, Steve Trask slid his hand into his coat pocket, intending to produce the jet dragon and place it on the desk in front of Li Huang. But Steve wasn't watching Li Huang; he was looking at Ming Dwan.

Steve's triumph never came. Astonishment swept him as his hand reappeared as of its own accord, bringing the lining of the pocket with it. Steve's hand was empty, and the pocket—turned inside out—was obviously empty too!

Somehow, somewhere, the jet dragon, token of security, had gone from Steve Trask's possession!

CHAPTER III
DEN OF DISASTER

LEANING forward on his desk, Li Huang lifted his eyes inquiringly toward Steve Trask. Though his lips were moving, Steve couldn't stammer the things he wanted to say. He was trying to tell Li Huang that he was a friend and could prove it, but he didn't want to commit himself to facts that would have to remain unsubstantiated.

To claim that he carried a black dragon then fail to produce one would be the worst step Steve could take. It was the sort of trick that an impostor would try. A name sprang to Steve's mind.

The Shadow!

It was a term that fitted the cloaked fighter on the roof, the rescuer whose efforts had plunged him to an undue disaster. But should Steve mention the friend whom he classified by that appropriate name, The Shadow?

It might help him with Li Huang. Of that, Steve felt sure as he studied the friendly, patient eyes across the desk. Li Huang, in his green, gold-braided robe, looked the part of a retired Oriental merchant, who had won his wealth through honesty.

But the eyes of Ming Dwan were different.

Stiff, prim, in a high-collared jacket of black and silver, the girl's poise resembled the poker-faced expression that she had renewed. But her eyes were eager with their narrowed gloat; they were watching for any betrayal on Steve's part. It struck Steve that such betrayal might apply to others than himself. For instance, The Shadow, who if not dead, was certainly lying helpless—a fatal thing if enemies should find him!

Li Huang was placidly watching Steve, glancing at the empty pocket as though wondering why his visitor had turned it inside out. Steve shot a defiant glare at Ming Dwan, then gave the first excuse that popped to mind.

"It's about my gun." Steve gestured toward the desk, where one of Li Huang's servants had laid the revolver. "I thought I had the permit with me." Pausing, Steve flipped his empty pocket and pushed it back where it belonged. "But I guess I forgot it."

Picking up Steve's revolver, Li Huang toyed with it. All the while a smile kept creeping to the Oriental lips, only to dwindle before it was half formed.

"Ah, yes, this gun," spoke Li Huang. "It is most embarrassing for both of us. It would not be wise for you to carry it without your permit." Li Huang's slow headshake was a tribute to Steve's honesty as well as his own. The merchant was taking the attitude that Steve would be honor bound to truthfully answer any questions that the police might put. Stroking his chin, Li Huang found the answer for the dilemma. Rising, he approached Steve, placed a friendly hand on his shoulder and said:

"Come!"

INSTEAD of going to the front door, they arrived at a side portal, which was equally well-barred. One of the servants unbolted the door, and Li Huang gestured through a passage, which ended in a gate.

"My servants will conduct you to a house on the next street," explained Li Huang. "I advise you to remain there about half an hour. You will have no trouble leaving if you are discreet."

The arrangement suited Steve as well as Li Huang. Shaking hands, Steve then turned and followed the two servants, who led the way. Hearing footsteps behind him, Steve looked about and gave an annoyed glare.

Those footsteps were Ming Dwan's.

Why the Chinese girl was trailing along, seemed much too obvious to Steve. Ming Dwan wasn't interested in merely speeding the departing guest, as was Li Huang. But if she thought she could keep further tabs on Steve, she'd be mistaken. Steve felt he could personally attend to that when the time came.

Then the grating of the iron gate jarred Steve's thoughts to a case more pressing than his own. The gates that the servants were swinging, opened into a courtyard, the very space where The Shadow had made that farewell dive in the clutch of a merciless strangler!

Without ado, Steve pushed right through, as

though anxious to reach his own destination, wherever it might be. Actually, he was taking this chance to scan the courtyard, and what he saw stiffened him.

At the very spot where he expected, Steve saw the crumpled figure of The Shadow heaped beneath its outspread cloak. The twist of the black-covered body was a worse token than its lack of motion. The Shadow wasn't merely stunned; he was practically mangled. If life still remained in that hulk of an intrepid fighter, it could be no more than a feeble spark.

What little Steve could do, he did. Turning, he caught the attention of Li Huang's servants before they looked toward The Shadow's body. It wasn't that the servants mattered; Steve was particularly anxious that Ming Dwan wouldn't spot the obscured huddle of immobile blackness. She'd be the sort to tell the wrong people of The Shadow's plight, the kind who would come here to destroy the cloaked fighter's last glimmer of survival.

Blocking Ming Dwan, Steve gave a shrug as though asking where he was to go next. The girl pointed to another gate across the courtyard, fortunately away from The Shadow's direction.

Past the gate were other passages that led, at length, to a basement stairs. Underground, Li Huang's servants seemed to be conducting a house-to-house canvass by the cellar route, until they stopped at a door they recognized. Opening it, they ushered Steve up a few stone steps into a narrow bunk room, with curtained booths on both sides.

THE place was smoke-filled, and one whiff of the sweetish aroma told Steve that he had arrived in an opium den. One servant found an empty bunk for Steve; the other provided him with a lighted pipe, at the same time informing him that it was free of opium.

As they left, the first Mongol paused to whisper that Steve was to go out the front way, when he finished the half-hour spell that no one would disturb. With that, the flap of the bunk fell, cutting off the outer world completely. It was then that Steve Trask remembered Ming Dwan.

After a few more puffs at the pipe, Steve poked back a corner of the curtain to see if the girl had left with the servants. His glance was timely. It gave him a flash of Ming Dwan in her silver-decorated costume. She was turning to follow others out through the rear door, but as the girl went, something flapped behind her.

It was the curtain of the last bunk in the row. Ming Dwan had tarried to speak to someone lurking in that booth, without the knowledge of Li Huang's servants!

This opium den had become a trap!

Not a trap of Li Huang's making, but of Ming Dwan's device. Back in his own bunk, savagely puffing the harmless pipe, Steve wondered how he'd make his safe exit now. The den was gloomy, but its two ceiling lights, spaced well apart, were sufficient to reveal the corridor between the rows of bunks.

To start out through the front, Steve would have to make himself an open target for a watcher from the rear booth. The thought was disconcerting, until it suddenly became an inspiration.

The front way wasn't the route that Steve should take.

This was his opportunity to go back to the courtyard, to give aid to his friend, The Shadow—or what was left of him. Provided, of course, that Ming Dwan hadn't seen the huddled shape in the court and passed the word along. Even if she had, so much the better. Such was the final thought that drilled home to Steve.

For if Ming Dwan had passed the word along to anyone, the receiver must be the lurker in the rear booth, the very man who was posted to stop Steve's departure first!

A fighting spirit swept Steve. Here was his chance to deal a double blow. He'd crack that lurker in the other bunk and thereby clear a route to aid The Shadow. Even while the idea gripped him, Steve found himself acting upon it. He was out of his own bunk, letting the curtain flap behind him, and moving with long, loping paces toward the booth at the rear.

It was odd how those motions blended, how fast Steve was moving and yet so slow. The sickly opium odor no longer tanged his nostrils, but Steve didn't connect that fact with his dreamlike locomotion. He was feeling the effect of the drug that filled the atmosphere of this bunk-lined den, but it was giving him a false sense of energy, rather than producing stupor.

As Steve reached the curtain, its flap stirred before his hands could touch it. While Steve puzzled over that curious occurrence, a jarring clatter crashed through to his inner senses, causing him to turn so suddenly that he surprised himself.

The commotion was coming from the front of the opium den. There, Steve saw an arriving figure who stopped beyond the pair of low ceiling lights and darted a look between the rows of dingy bunks. Steve recognized the newcomer like a hideous monstrosity left over from a nightmare.

The den's new customer was Sujan!

OBVIOUSLY, the Japanese shopkeeper had come here by some underground route. That Sujan recognized Steve was evident by the shout the Jap gave. Like an "Open Sesame," it spread wide the mouths of caverns as represented by the bunks between Steve and the front door.

They were like things from under stones, these slimy Nipponese whose faces matched Sujan's. No mistaking their race when they arrived in a group. This opium den was a nest of Japanese, probably their chief lair.

These were the assassins that Steve had eluded by his precipitous trip into the house of Li Huang. The denizens of this place had returned to make it a den of disaster, with Steve as their victim. They had waited only for Sujan to identify the man they wanted!

In this new swirl of madness, Steve groped for the nearest refuge—the curtained bunk beside his shoulder. He was forgetting that it had an occupant, an unknown person who already rated as an enemy. It was simply that Steve's whirling senses were turning everything about, even to the mad belief that he could conjure up a rescuer from nowhere.

The rescuer arrived. Amazingly, he sprang from the very bunk that Steve had thought the lurking place of a foe. With one huge lunge, a tall figure unlimbered from behind the curtain, caught Steve as he was turning in that direction, and flung him into the security of the bunk.

Steve hadn't time to glimpse his rescuer's face, as the man of the moment completed his spin so rapidly that a pair of hands came flinging into sight, each carrying an automatic. So swiftly was it all accomplished, that those big guns roared before a single revolver spoke or any knife was hurled.

But all this was mild, compared with the incredible challenge that the lone fighter added to his actions. Strident was the laugh that pealed through the opium den, promising disaster to those who expected to deliver it.

The same mirth that Steve had heard uttered from the rooftop, but which he believed was silenced forever:

The laugh of The Shadow!

CHAPTER IV
THE SHADOW'S GIFT

BEWILDERING was The Shadow's self-transformation from a crumpled, lifeless figure in a forgotten courtyard to a master fighter ridding a notorious opium den of the human scum that infested it.

More astonishing, however, was the way in which The Shadow transformed the setting itself. He changed it from a lighted scene into the element that was his favorite fighting ground: darkness!

Two shots did it.

One from each gun, the jabs were aimed at the two ceiling bulbs that illuminated the den. Each roar was followed by an echoing explosion and a clatter of glass. Pitch-darkness followed, cloaking The Shadow with surrounding blackness.

Then stabs of flame were knifing the gloom. They counted no more than the real knives that flew with them. Gunshots and blades were missing The Shadow, a fact that his repeated laugh proclaimed. The location of The Shadow's weird challenge told why the opposing thrusts had failed.

The Shadow was delivering that laugh from the very midst of his startled antagonists!

He'd made a forward dive beneath the level of the barrage. Wildly, savagely, men wheeled and sledged the darkness with their guns.

This wasn't empty darkness!

Hard-dealt blows met receiving heads. Other swinging guns clashed with steel. The heads belonged to the very foemen who were trying to slug The Shadow. Killers were bludgeoning their own ilk in the darkness. The steel represented The Shadow's guns, swinging wide and hard, warding off any blows that came his way, directing them to the skulls that deserved such strokes.

Doubled in The Shadow's bunk, Steve heard the clash of battle and saw a few gun spurts that accompanied it. Whenever a frenzied assassin let go with his trigger, he made himself a target for The Shadow's prompt reply. It didn't do the others any good to use The Shadow's gun jabs as a target, the way he was picking out theirs. He was no longer there by the time they aimed and fired!

Bunks were crashing under the sprawl of bodies as The Shadow, totally invisible in the darkness, pitched his staggered foemen from his path. Shrieks, groans, thuds, other evidences of a complete rout, were tribute to The Shadow's skill. And Steve was wondering what it would be like to run up against The Shadow in the dark, or vice versa, when he gained the experience.

Out of nowhere came a hand that hauled Steve from his lodging place. With it a whispered voice commanded "Come!"

Brought to his feet, Steve was traveling along the very route that he had originally planned—that cellar trail to the courtyard where he had hoped that he could render some assistance to The Shadow!

WHEN they reached the courtyard, Steve gained his first real look at his companion. For one thing, The Shadow wasn't cloaked, a thing that Steve had realized when his tall rescuer whirled from the bunk in the opium den. But at that time, Steve hadn't even gained a real impression of The Shadow's attire.

Now Steve saw, and gaped.

This fighter par excellence was wearing evening clothes! More than that, his flawless attire was scarcely ruffled. Momentarily, Steve saw The Shadow's face, but had no time to check its features. The visage impressed him as immobile, masklike, with a trace of a hawk's profile. Then The Shadow

Gunshots and blades were missing The Shadow.

had turned away and was stopping above a huddled shape beside the wall.

For a moment, the impression of unreality chilled Steve. This man in evening clothes had demonstrated that he must be The Shadow. Yet the form toward which he stooped was the same cloaked figure that Steve had observed earlier and was certain was The Shadow.

Was The Shadow a ghost, returning in another guise to gaze upon the remains of his own human form?

It wasn't the effect of the opium that threw this thought into Steve's mind. Steve's senses had cleared, so fully that he was dealing in cold facts; The Shadow, alive, was plucking the cloak from The Shadow, dead. That was fact—or seemed so—until the cloak was lifted.

The shape beneath told its own story. Upturned from the twisted shoulders of a grotesquely distorted figure, Steve saw the ugly face of the scrawny Japanese strangler who had tried to throttle The Shadow during the death plunge from the roof!

Whether through luck, skill or some uncanny power, The Shadow had settled that question of supremacy by landing uppermost. His Jap foeman had taken the brunt of the blow with the natural results attending a thirty-foot dive to a bed of cement. Sole survivor of the plunge, The Shadow had used his cloak to cover the remains of his deceased antagonist.

Steve felt he could congratulate himself on having aided The Shadow to a slight degree. Steve had helped with the cover-up, by diverting attention from the huddled thing that The Shadow wanted to conceal.

Ming Dwan hadn't learned the secret of the courtyard!

That thought was merely a preliminary satisfaction. More things were due to happen, of a sort that pleased Steve. The Shadow was putting on the cloak and slouch hat that he had regained. He merged with the semi-darkness and was invisible, then his hand plucked Steve's arm.

Willingly, Steve went along, back through the house of Li Huang!

It was a wise choice on The Shadow's part, for a din was coming from the direction of the opium den, indicating that reserves were picking up the trail. The Shadow's low laugh indicated that he'd welcome them in a way they wouldn't like, but it also expressed some concern that Steve felt was meant for himself.

The Shadow wanted to take Steve to safety by the shortest route, and Li Huang's afforded it.

AS they reached the side door, Steve remembered that Li Huang kept it bolted. That meant nothing to The Shadow. He simply opened the door, drew Steve through and promptly barred the door behind him. So far, so easy, until a sharp voice offered challenge.

Steve turned and saw Ming Dwan.

The girl's face showed no trace of pallor. Rather, it displayed a creamy flush above the stubby, shiny revolver that matched the silver braid of her pajama costume. The words that Ming Dwan spoke were in Chinese, which The Shadow evidently understood.

No laugh came from The Shadow's hidden lips. Instead, Steve saw the glint of burning eyes beneath the slouch hatbrim. Those eyes, the only visible portion of The Shadow's countenance, were fixed directly on Ming Dwan, the frail, delicate creature who dared to block the fighter who had trampled a dozen assassins from his path!

The Shadow recognized Ming Dwan's determination. He moved slowly, not rapidly, as he drew Steve along. Steve found himself wishing that The Shadow would wither this lotus flower with a scorch from one of those deadly automatics. The trouble seemed that The Shadow hadn't a chance to draw one, so sharp was Ming Dwan's watch.

Then they were stock-still, The Shadow and Steve Trask, their very motion hinging on Ming Dwan's bidding. Steve was looking for the triumphant gloat to end the girl's fixed expression, when one of Li Huang's servants shuffled into sight.

It was the very break that The Shadow awaited!

As Ming Dwan gestured, the servant lunged. But in gesturing, the girl let her gaze rove from The Shadow, who sprang into instant action. Before Ming Dwan could turn to aim anew, The Shadow caught the lunging Mongol, spun him like a toy top and flung him at Ming Dwan, who was forced to duck aside.

Next, The Shadow was thrusting Steve along a passage in a mad race toward the front door. From behind them came the flashes of Ming Dwan's gun, but a corner intervened. Then, as the girl reappeared to open direct fire, The Shadow hurled Steve ahead, right to the front door itself, giving the two-word command: "Unbolt it!"

Complying, Steve wondered why Ming Dwan was no longer shooting. Hearing commotion, he turned and saw the answer. Li Huang's other servants had arrived. One from each side, they were flinging themselves upon The Shadow, slashing knives at the cloaked fighter. At least, they were blocking Ming Dwan's aim; but to Steve, the knives were a greater menace.

Not so to The Shadow.

WITH a spin he let the blades slash his cloak as it fluttered in their paths. By then, Steve had the door unbarred and The Shadow was springing toward him with a forward gesture. Steve didn't accept the hint, because the Mongols were after The Shadow, poising their knives for a fling, and Steve wanted to help out.

The Shadow aided Steve, instead, with a shoulder lunge that spilled him right through the door. Sprawling, Steve saw The Shadow coming with him, only a few feet ahead of the deadly knives. But as he came, The Shadow flung a hand to the inside of the doorway and pressed a switch located there.

A clatter followed The Shadow's arrival on the sidewalk. Steve saw Li Huang's servants disappearing, knives with them. They were dropping right through the floor into the same pit that Steve had earlier tested. Clutching Steve's arm, The Shadow whipped him away from the open door just in time to avoid the shots that Ming Dwan fired from beyond the open floor. The trap was closing, but the girl wasn't taking chances with it while The Shadow was still close by. Then The Shadow was gone, and Steve with him, around the corner of Li Huang's house and through the narrow alley between that building and the eaved apartment.

As they went, they heard the bronze door clang, slammed shut by Ming Dwan. The Shadow added a whispered laugh to the brazen echoes, but kept Steve on a steady dash through the alley. Police whistles were shrilling from the front street.

How The Shadow would manage an escape was a puzzle to Steve, until the answer cropped up just when wanted. The answer was a taxicab that didn't have to be summoned. It was wheeling to the curb, its door wide open. The Shadow thrust Steve inside, then joined him.

Out from the streets of Chinatown, into a quiet area where gunfire and excitement were very far behind; there, The Shadow opened the door as the cab paused for a traffic light. The Shadow didn't have to state his purpose. It was obvious. He was going his own way, leaving this cab for Steve to do with as he chose.

It seemed that there should be some parting token, though Steve didn't quite know how to introduce the subject. Shaking hands with a friend who might vanish in the middle of the clasp was just a bit too eerie. Still, The Shadow's hand was coming toward Steve, so he reached out to accept it.

What the Shadow did was place an object

squarely in Steve's hand. Then, as the cab started forward, the cloaked being whirled suddenly through the door, disappearing.

Squatting in Steve's palm was the miniature dragon carved from solid jet, the black talisman with green jade eyes that had so mysteriously disappeared from Steve's possession—to be returned by that incredible master of things unknown:

The Shadow!

CHAPTER V
THE LAW DECIDES

CLYDE BURKE waited until Steve Trask filled his pipe and lighted it. While Steve was drawing a long breath of smoke, Clyde said:

"Go on."

"That's about all there is," returned Steve. "I'll admit that my adventures sound fabulous, particularly when related in the broad daylight of this hotel room, but last night they were real enough."

Clyde shook his head. "The part about the opium den queers it, Trask. People would class it as a pipe dream."

"There's the jet dragon." Steve gestured toward the object. It was on a writing table in the corner. "It should prove something."

"It might prove that you went Sujan's shop, if he would admit selling you the thing. But Sujan won't do any talking. The police loaded him with lead when they were mopping up the hop joint."

"But the fact that Sujan was in the opium den! With other Japanese!"

"That's all been covered," argued Clyde. "The police have rounded up a lot of Japs in other places, and this makes just one more. The fact that they were hopheads makes this bunch look like a lot of no-accounts. Sorry, Trask, but your yarn won't make news, not even in a scandal-loving tabloid like the *Classic*, for which I work."

Steve was glad Burke wouldn't print his story. In fact, Clyde's decision gave Steve a deeper inkling into the real purpose of the reporter's visit.

It struck Steve that Clyde Burke was working for The Shadow rather than for the New York *Classic*. At least, the reporter's arrival at the hotel formed a connected chain. Having come from Chinatown in the cab supplied by The Shadow, Steve assumed that the driver of that cab had checked his identity and informed his cloaked chief. Today, The Shadow doubtless learned that Steve Trask was acquainted with Rufus Miljohn, whose recent death was marked as suicide.

For Clyde Burke, by way of introduction, had mentioned that the *Classic* was looking into the Miljohn case. The reporter hoped that Steve could shed some light on it; and Steve had, by recounting the whole story of the jet dragon, along with describing such participants as Sujan, Li Huang, Ming Dwan, and most important of all—The Shadow.

Now Clyde, in his casual reporter's style, was picking up the tiny black dragon and examining it. Reverting to their initial premise, Clyde queried:

"You saw a dragon like this in Miljohn's apartment?"

"I did," replied Steve. "Only an hour before Miljohn was found with a bullet through his brain and a gun in his fist!"

"And Miljohn had no reason for suicide?"

"None at all. He told me he'd cleaned up plenty while he was in the Orient."

Clyde produced a clipping and handed it to Steve, who read it between pipe puffs. The clipping classed Miljohn as a refugee who had lost an entire fortune when the Japanese invaded Hong Kong. Steve shook his head.

"That was Miljohn's bluff," he declared. "He was smart enough to pretend he'd lost everything, because he didn't want the wrong people on his neck. Trouble was, they guessed the truth, so they murdered Miljohn and framed it to look like suicide."

SO confident was Steve regarding his theory that he went further with it. Picking up the jet dragon, Steve tapped it with his pipe stem.

"Miljohn counted on one of these to protect him," argued Steve. "I'd say this token must represent some secret group that aided Miljohn's escape. Whoever carries one of these will find friends when he needs them. Maybe it slipped with Miljohn, but the rule worked with me. The person who proved it was The Shadow."

Clyde's lips straightened, suppressing a smile. Bluntly, the reporter inquired:

"Would you like to test the dragon further?"

Steve sucked deeply at his pipe, comparing the pleasant aroma of this afternoon's tobacco with the sickening smell of last night's opium. Somehow, the taste of the pipe gave Steve new confidence.

He nodded. Whereupon Clyde drew an afternoon newspaper from his pocket and unfolded it on the writing desk, beside the jet-black dragon.

"This happened last night," declared Clyde, "about the time when you were in Chinatown. Only they didn't discover it until this noon."

The newspaper account shrieked murder. The victim was Lewis Pendleton, a wealthy publisher just returned from the Orient. His case couldn't be suicide, for three bullets of varying caliber had been extracted from Pendleton's brain, after the police discovered him dead in his hotel room. Nor were any guns found on the premises.

"Why, this ties in with Miljohn's death!" exclaimed Steve. "Only, this time, the police know that it was murder."

"There's another difference," put in Clyde, referring to the newspaper. "Pendleton really suffered heavy financial losses, because his publishing plants were destroyed."

"Maybe he'd written off the costs," remarked Steve cagily. "From what Miljohn told me, smart men in the Orient saw things coming a long while before they happened."

Clyde pointed to another paragraph.

"It doesn't apply to Pendleton," the reporter stated. "He was going to start all over. He'd found a million-dollar backer, whose name is given right here—Miles Fenmore, one of New York's biggest financiers."

The mere name of Miles Fenmore was enough to take Steve's breath away, but the thing that Clyde suggested was even more gasp-producing. Picking up the carved dragon, Clyde plunked it in Steve's palm and queried:

"Why don't you take this to Miles Fenmore? Show him the dragon and tell him about Miljohn. Fenmore wants to find the men who murdered Pendleton. He'd listen to your story."

At first, the proposition staggered Steve, but gradually he regained his mental balance. Knocking the ashes from his pipe, he dropped the brier in one pocket and placed the carved dragon in the other.

"All right, Burke," Steve decided firmly. "I'll go."

DUSK was settling over the Fenmore mansion when Steve knocked at the front door. Admitted to the house that rated as one of Manhattan's showplaces, Steve stated bluntly that he wanted to see Miles Fenmore. To his surprise, his request was promptly granted.

There was some red tape along the way, the footman passing Steve to a secretary, who turned him over to another at the top of a grand staircase. Then there was a private secretary who wanted to know something about Steve's business, but this caused little delay. The moment Steve said that it concerned the Pendleton murder, the secretary spoke to Fenmore by telephone. Immediately, Steve was ushered through a final door into Fenmore's own study.

Broad-shouldered, with a face proportionally wide, Fenmore gazed at Steve with sharp, appraising eyes that flanked an aristocratic nose. Below that high-bridged centerpiece were wide lips, firm and tight, that showed neither smile nor greeting. The proof that Fenmore had weighed Steve satisfactorily came when the financier raised one hand and brushed back his short-clipped hair, as though to cover its streaks of gray.

Then, in blunt tone, Fenmore spoke. "Good afternoon, Mr. Trask. You have something to tell me about my friend Pendleton. Let me hear it."

Inasmuch as Steve's story began with Miljohn and wouldn't really include Pendleton, Steve started proceedings by producing the jet dragon and sliding it across Fenmore's glass-topped desk.

Immediately, Fenmore's eyes showed curiosity. He picked up the miniature dragon and proceeded to examine it while Steve talked.

Steve found himself contrasting this interview with the one he had held with Li Huang. Of course, the circumstances were different; still, the contrast held good. With Li Huang, Steve had found it difficult to choose his words under the steady gaze of the merchant's eyes. In Fenmore's case, it was a case of telling everything to even gain the man's attention.

Indeed, Steve felt that Fenmore hadn't heard a tenth of what he said, until it was all finished. Then Fenmore laid the little dragon aside and looked up with that same sharp gaze. Aloud, he repeated the high spots of Steve's story practically word for word, to prove how completely they had registered.

Nodding his corroboration, Steve brought out his pipe and tobacco pouch. Finding the pouch almost empty, he produced a flat tin of smoking mixture. Then, fearing that he might be offending Fenmore, Steve laid the tin on the desk and started to put his pipe away.

At that point, Fenmore actually smiled, and his lips were very genial. Opening a square ebony box that rested on the desk, he pushed it Steve's way, displaying a full supply of rich tobacco.

"Try my blend," suggested Fenmore. "Fill your pouch, too, Trask. My friends all like this special mixture."

Having thus classed Steve as a friend, Fenmore went further. He produced a meerschaum pipe and filled it after Steve had finished packing brier and pouch. They were both smoking away when Fenmore completed his summary and inquired:

"Am I correct on all the details?"

When Steve nodded, Fenmore asked if he would like to dictate the whole account to one of the secretaries. Steve agreed that he would, so Fenmore ushered him into a little room off the study.

When the secretary arrived, Fenmore left, closing the door behind him. Choosing his words carefully, Steve repeated his account as nearly verbatim as he could remember it.

AT the end of ten minutes, Steve returned to the study. From behind the desk, Fenmore gestured him to a chair. Picking up his tobacco tin, Steve dropped it in his pocket and brought out the pouch, to load his pipe for another smoke. He was reaching for the jet dragon when Fenmore stopped him.

"Inspector Cardona is outside," stated Fenmore. "He is the police official who is handling the Pendleton case."

Steve decided that the law could know the facts, so far as he'd dictated them. He'd left out the little matter of his revolver, now in the possession of Li Huang, whose whole behavior he had commended.

Pressing a buzzer, Fenmore smiled dryly and gestured toward the carved dragon.

"We'll let the inspector see this," said Fenmore. "If it excites his curiosity as it did mine, it will keep him occupied until the secretary finishes typing your statement."

Inspector Cardona entered. He was a stocky individual with a swarthy face that formed a perfect deadpan. But his eyes couldn't restrain their sudden interest when they lighted on the jet dragon. While Steve and Fenmore were exchanging smiles, Cardona pounced upon the object as though intending to swallow it.

Turning the dragon from hand to hand, Cardona stopped abruptly and looked from Fenmore to Steve. Maybe the inspector detected the pride of ownership in Steve's expression, for he quickly demanded:

"Did you bring this here?"

Steve nodded, whereupon Cardona promptly tendered him the tiny dragon, gesturing for him to put it away. Steve was dropping it in his empty coat pocket, when he noted that Cardona was rubbing his hands as though they were sticky. Muttering something about a handkerchief, Cardona was reaching in his own hip pocket, when he added:

"Funny, the way that black polish comes off! Leaves your hands looking like a coal-heaver's!"

Steve brought his own hands palms upward and stared at them. He couldn't see any traces of the black stain that Cardona mentioned. Still staring, Steve exclaimed:

"Why, I didn't get any of it, Inspector—"

CARDONA'S hand was slashing forward with a glitter. Cold metal cracked against Steve's wrists and clamped there! Before Steve could realize that he was solidly handcuffed, Cardona was hauling him to his feet. Turning his prisoner toward the desk, the swarthy inspector displayed him like an exhibit. Staring in amazement, Miles Fenmore couldn't seem to understand the sudden turn of things any more than Steve.

Then came Cardona's gruff explanation, if it could be called such.

"Lucky I came along, Mr. Fenmore," announced the inspector. "Whoever the fellow is, he's dangerous. We want him for the murder of Lewis Pendleton!"

CHAPTER VI
WHOLESALE MYSTERY

THINGS looked very black for Steve Trask; blacker, even, than the jet-hued dragon that nestled deep in the pocket from which it had once vanished—something that Steve wished it would do again. For the tiny dragon was looming more and more as an incriminating factor.

According to Cardona, Lewis Pendleton had owned just such a souvenir, because hotel employees had seen it in his room. With Pendleton's death the black dragon had vanished, exactly as Steve claimed it had in Miljohn's case.

Far from clearing Steve, that link only deepened the accusations against him. Cardona shot the question:

"Do you know what the black dragon represents?"

"It must stand for some organization," replied Steve. "The members carry black dragons as tokens, I suppose. Somebody is preying on them—"

As nearly as it could, Cardona's face formed an interrupting sneer. Steve stopped talking, puzzled.

"You *would* play innocent!" scoffed Cardona. "You'll be telling me next that the Black Dragon crowd is made up of Chinese."

"Isn't it?" Steve asked.

"Hear that?" Cardona turned to put his question to Fenmore. Then, seeing that the financier looked really puzzled, the inspector said: "Sorry, Mr. Fenmore. Naturally, you wouldn't know. The Black Dragon Society is made up of Oriental thugs who are Japanese-controlled. There are mighty few Chinese who belong to it, and these are renegades."

"Then why would Miljohn and Pendleton have Dragon tokens?" demanded Fenmore. "They must have suffered at the hands of that organization."

"They were murdered by it!" expressed Cardona, "Don't you get it yet, Mr. Fenmore? Those carved dragons aren't membership badges, not by a long shot, They're death certificates. Whoever gets one is marked for murder, unless he delivers whatever the Black Dragon wants!"

Steve's thoughts exploded.

So that was why Miljohn had been murdered! He'd ignored the warning from the Black Dragon. The same applied to Pendleton, and even Steve's own case was covered. The Dragon Clan hadn't come after him; he'd gone after it, and gained a due reward. Sujan, planted in Chinatown for just such a purpose, had given Steve a jet dragon when he'd asked for one.

Therefore, Steve had been tagged for death, from which The Shadow saved him!

THE trouble was, Cardona didn't see it that way. The ace police inspector was figuring things to his own convenience. He thought that Steve had murdered both Miljohn and Pendleton, each time picking up the dragon token that the victim hadn't heeded. The clincher in Cardona's estimate was Steve's absurd alibi of a fantastic Chinatown adventure at the very hour of Pendleton's death.

"Smart stuff, Trask," jabbed Cardona, "coming here with the dragon you brought from Pendleton's and saying Miljohn had one like it! You wanted us to know that Miljohn's death was murder, instead of suicide; you thought we'd never accuse you of the very thing you so obligingly revealed!"

He added:

"You figured, too, that by chattering about one crime, you could dodge questions on another. We'd just ride over the Pendleton case and forget it, where you were concerned—at least, that's how you doped it. But we've tagged you for both jobs, and what's more, today you were delivering another death threat. "That's what you did when you handed the black dragon to Mr. Fenmore."

Steve was sweating under the third degree. A light blinded his eyes.

Then came a welcome pause, produced by new arrivals, persons who stopped beyond the light. Whoever they were, Cardona saw fit to greet them; and Steve, given a chance to speak for himself, made the most of it.

"Call Li Huang!" blurted Steve. "He'll tell you that I was in his house."

Paper crinkled beyond the glaring light. It was Steve's typewritten statement, being passed from hand to hand. Then Cardona's voice:

"All right. We'll phone Li Huang."

Steve heard Cardona make the call, and though he couldn't see the telephone, he took it for granted that the inspector wasn't faking. Finishing, Cardona gave a short, harsh laugh.

"Li Huang never heard of you!" the inspector sneered.

Steve broke into a frenzied protest. Of course Li Huang wouldn't know who Steve was, because Steve hadn't identified himself. Cardona's whole handling of the matter was unfair, done in a manner that Li Huang would mistake for a trick. If they'd take Steve to Li Huang's, the Chinaman would remember him.

Cardona extinguished the glaring light. After a minute of blinking Steve made out other faces. One that wore a military mustache belonged to Police Commissioner Ralph Weston. Steve heard Cardona address the commissioner by his title.

Accompanying Weston was a man named Cranston, whose face was dignified, reserved and quite impassive. Indeed, Steve might have identified Cranston with The Shadow, but for the fact that the commissioner's companion was leisurely in action and utterly indifferent to the business under discussion. Every time Weston addressed him, Cranston appeared bored.

"Trask admits knowing Miljohn," asserted Weston brusquely. "The question now is whether he knew Pendleton, which is something that he won't admit. Perhaps some of Pendleton's friends can tell us."

"Pendleton just returned from the Orient," objected Fenmore. "He has very few friends in New York. Even I knew him only by reputation."

"What about Sauber, the importer?" queried Weston. "His business with the Orient was huge. He must have advertised in some of Pendleton's journals. They should have known each other quite well."

Steve saw Fenmore shake his head.

"I am afraid Pendleton knew Sauber too well," said Fenmore. "Two years ago, Pendleton canceled Sauber's advertising because it was misrepresented. Nevertheless, Sauber might be the very man to supply information concerning an insidious organization like the Dragon Clan."

MARCHED from Fenmore's mansion, Steve found himself planted between Cardona and Weston in the commissioner's official car.

Cranston wasn't accompanying them. Either he felt that the trip would bore him, or people like Sauber didn't belong in Cranston's social set. Then, as the car rolled away from Fenmore's, Steve had a hunch. Maybe the choosy Mr. Cranston didn't care to ride in a car that contained a common criminal like Steve!

That was enough for Steve to dismiss Cranston completely and think of what Sauber might be like. Steve was left to his own conjectures, for Weston and Cardona were remaining strictly silent.

The big, official car was nosing its way through a slum area, which struck Steve as an odd district for a wealthy importer's residence. Then Steve noted that large warehouses, sprouting up among the squatty tenements, were largely occupied by importing concerns.

Swinging a corner, the car stopped near an archway that opened into a secluded court, a short street of its own. There were trees as well as houses beyond the archway, marking the court as an exclusive residential sector.

One of the houses was Sauber's, because Weston and Cardona alighted, drawing Steve with them. Passing through the archway, Steve looked to his right and saw a similar arch, leading to another street. It was very dark, that archway, like the boxes surrounding the trees and the narrow cul-de-sacs that flanked the houses.

A servant answered Cardona's ring, but it was Weston who introduced himself and asked for Sauber. Before the servant could summon the importer, a querulous voice arrived, followed by

Sauber himself. At first, the importer was just a blocky figure, but when he reached the vestibule, his face showed plainly, as though a veil had been swept from it.

The reason, of course, was the light in the vestibule. Sauber had stepped right into its focus. But that only made the thing the more startling to Steve. It was like something snatched from a forgotten dream and brought into reality.

Beady eyes, bushy brows, sharp nose above yellowed teeth—those features, and the thrust of the jaw beneath them, jabbed Steve's memory like a pin puncturing a balloon.

Sauber was the man that Steve had met outside of Li Huang's, the figure who had arrived by cab only to dart away when shadows came to life!

If the evil Dragon Clan owned a local chief, Carlton Sauber was a logical candidate for the insidious title of Black Dragon!

Briefly stating the object of the visit, Cardona asked if Sauber could identify Steve as a person who had known Pendleton. Briefly, those beady eyes showed recognition; then, with a sudden head-shake, Sauber drew back into the vestibule.

"No, no!" began Sauber hoarsely. "I never saw this man before. I never met Miljohn or Pendleton. I know nothing about the Black Dragon, except that it should be avoided. I am an importer. At least, I used to be until the business closed, but I have never been to China, nor any part of the Orient—"

"Except Chinatown!" With that interruption, Steve shoved his handcuffed fists toward Sauber. "You were there last night, outside of Li Huang's, and you're going to tell us why!"

Madly, Sauber was trying to thrust Steve back and slam the door in his face. Weston and Cardona aided by hauling their prisoner down the steps. They were at the bottom, Steve halfway up, and Sauber at the top, all etched against the light, when Sauber gave a warding gesture in his wide-arm fashion of the night before.

The signal that had unleashed a horde of villainous fighters, followers of the notorious Black Dragon!

Steve was lunging for a grab at Sauber's arm when the door slammed hard. But it wasn't the combined pull of Weston and Cardona that brought Steve down. Instead, the force was living blackness that swooped from nowhere up between the two men whose clutches couldn't hold Steve back.

Again, The Shadow!

SOMERSAULTING as the black swirl swept him, Steve heard whizzing sounds above him. Those whirs ended in thuds as a pair of knives drove deep into Sauber's door and stopped there, quivering. There were startled shouts from Weston and Cardona as they sprang off to the sides of the steps, pulling their police revolvers.

Finishing against a tree, Steve was hauled to his feet by the human tornado that had swept him from murder's path. Next, he was reeling through the side arch leading from the court. Guided by The Shadow, Steve could feel sudden jolts along the route. They were produced by the recoils from the gun with which The Shadow was jabbing shots at seemingly invisible foemen.

Steve's whirl increased as he landed in a waiting cab, the same timely vehicle as the night before. The door slammed and Steve was spinning away.

Back in the double-arched court, Weston and Cardona were making for the commissioner's car, jabbing useless shots at hidden lurkers who were beginning to respond with guns. Seeing his chauffeur, Weston yelled for the fellow to summon assistance, and the big car sped away to its assignment.

Then new guns were talking from the very center of the court. The Shadow was back again, revolving like a battle turret, tuning his evasive laugh to the stabs of his deadly automatics. Each .45 seemed to snatch lurkers from their hiding spots. Tonight, they preferred flight to mortal combat with The Shadow.

Four were coming straight for Weston, when Cardona hauled him around the outer corner of the archway and down into a basement entry. Whistling knives went past and clattered across the street; then motley men were scattering away from the shots that The Shadow was free to fire, since Weston and Cardona were out of the way.

Coming up from cover, Cardona glimpsed The Shadow wheeling back into the court. Then he was gone, that shape of blackness, pursuing a pair of stragglers who were making for the other archway. It seemed a sure finish for the Dragon Clan despite their mad flight, for The Shadow was scattering the human chaff where the police could gather it.

From various directions, Cardona heard the shrill of whistles, the blare of sirens, and finally the roaring motors of patrol cars. Weston's official car was back, speeding from one street to another, to summon more reserves. The glare of searchlights spotted in from every street, picking out every niche and cranny along the house walls, blocking off all escape.

And in the middle stood Inspector Joe Cardona, more astonished than he had ever been before. Steve Trask was gone: that was bad enough. The Shadow had disappeared: that was to be expected.

But along with The Shadow, master of invisible methods, had vanished the entire tribe that served the Black Dragon, producing utter mystery on a wholesale scale!

CHAPTER VII
THE DRAGON IN BLACK

THE same thing was happening on two streets in Manhattan. That was, a unique event was occurring in two separate places, which was really extraordinary!

One thing involved Commissioner Weston's official car. It was coming back from its task. Patrol cars swung to the curb to let it pass. There wasn't a cop in town who didn't know the commissioner's oversized crate by sight. Indeed, that was the reason why the roving chauffeur had been able to gather so many police in so short a time.

When the big car pulled up in front of Gotham Court, where Carlton Sauber was a resident, Commissioner Weston stepped forward to congratulate the chauffeur. But Weston's tone of commendation changed when Inspector Cardona arrived to report the wholesale disappearance of at least a half dozen unidentified thugs, who by this time might be east of Suez for all Cardona knew.

"Find them!" bawled Weston. "Search everywhere! Hunt through the court!"

"That's one place they can't be!" insisted Cardona. "The Shadow drove them out."

"Search, anyway, to make sure that Sauber is safe. Those killers were trying to get him. The moment Trask attacked Sauber, the whole tribe popped out!"

Weston still had the wrong slant on Steve. In fact, the commissioner wasn't really certain of anything except that his car had returned and was parked outside Gotham Court.

Curious, therefore, that the big vehicle should also be rolling along a side street, outward bound, a dozen blocks from the commissioner's present base! However, it was—and patrol cars were making way for it. The same thing, in the shape of Weston's car, was in two different places!

Nobody realized that two editions of that vehicle were at large: the genuine and this counterfeit.

No one except The Shadow.

He was a passenger on board the duplicate car. Actually "on board" because he wasn't inside it. The Shadow was stretched on the top, his presence unsuspected by the huddled men who crammed the interior. This was the getaway car for the Black Dragon's six-man crew!

Clever of the Black Dragon to have a replica of the commissioner's well-known car outside of Sauber's. It had literally whisked his assorted followers from the vortex of the converging police. In planning crime, the Black Dragon could launch it best wherever the commissioner might be. Whoever he was, the Black Dragon was surely endowed with foresight.

HOWEVER, the Black Dragon hadn't made allowance for the unpredictable methods of The Shadow. In choosing this car for his own travel, The Shadow was running little risk of discovery. The driver was following dark, secluded streets.

The motley mob disembarked in a gloomy, blind alley behind an old loft building. The place was midway between Sauber's and Chinatown, convenient to both.

When the varied sextet poured from the fake official car, The Shadow noted limping members of the group, proof that he had winged a few targets. The limpers huddled by an obscure door leading into the building, while the rest made a brief inspection tour to make sure they hadn't been followed.

They were thinking in terms of The Shadow, probing every cranny for traces of their cloaked foe, and all the while he was perched in their very midst on top of the car that they were using as the base from which they made their search!

There was one rule that The Shadow had never known to fail. It was the axiom that confidence would produce carelessness. So sure were these Orientals that The Shadow couldn't be anywhere about, that the way was paved for an even bolder course.

Easing down from the car top, The Shadow actually joined his recent enemies as they moved in through the doorway. The shrouding blackness hid him perfectly, and he knew this tribe wouldn't be using lights. Keeping with the tribe, The Shadow went right past the guards.

The loose-knit crew climbed a flight of stairs, reached a door that opened to receive them. The room beyond was lighted, but its glow came from past some concrete pillars of the bulky sort so common in loft buildings. Shielded by the advancing dragon men themselves, The Shadow followed them into the meeting place, then side-stepped to a pillar as they continued onward.

At least two dozen of the Dragon Clan were already assembled, but their total was unimportant. Numbers dwindled when compared to the individual who presided over this meeting. This wasn't just a batch of underlings, holding a get-together.

Seated on a raised throne near the far wall, directly facing the assembled throng, was the master of the show:

The Black Dragon!

LONG had The Shadow sought the human monstrosity who represented the insidious Japanese clan. Finding him, The Shadow saw that the Black Dragon was indulging in suitable theatricals. Sinister though the Dragon's followers considered themselves, they shrank to pitiful proportions in the presence of their powerful leader.

The Black Dragon saw to that. It fitted his style

to play the role of an Oriental potentate, before whom his creatures could grovel. Likewise his identity was concealed; not merely as a precaution—a thing which he might be expected to disdain—but because the very title of the Black Dragon constituted a personality in itself, and therefore should be kept as such.

All that was manifested by the device which kept the Black Dragon unknown. He was attired in a Japanese robe, its jacket golden, its sleeves silver. Circling upward from the hem of the robe was an embroidered dragon, so huge, so fanciful, that it was forced to coil several times around the costume.

The embroidered dragon was jet-black, and everytime its wearer moved, the coils produced a writhing effect. But that was not the most remarkable feature of the costume, nor the most lifelike. It happened that the robe wasn't large enough to include the entire dragon, so it had an extension in the form of a hood, which made the dragon's head.

Coming up from the back, the embroidered head was artfully arranged to show a yawning mouth with jagged black teeth fronting its golden throat. There were green eyes, of course, but they were atop the hood. The eyeholes, through which the Black Dragon peered, were fangs belonging to the embroidered dragon's mouth.

Squatting deep in his gilded throne, the Black Dragon might have been anyone. Since the hood hid his face, it was impossible to discern whether his complexion was the yellow that belonged to Li Huang or the tawny color so conspicuous in Sauber's countenance.

The Dragon's hands were no clue. They were doubled idly on the throne arms, and the fingers were encrusted with rings that gave off a jeweled glitter. The Dragon's voice was forced, like the restless undulation of his body, a motion which he continued mechanically in order to preserve the living illusion of the dragon coils that encircled him.

The tilts and turns of the Dragon's head added to the weird effect of a living monster. If the Black Dragon had suddenly gone lashing all about the meeting room, it would have been a logical climax to his serpentine act.

INSTEAD, the Black Dragon contented himself with hissing epithets at the men who had just arrived. From the wounded among them, he knew that they had failed in their recent mission.

"Twice you have failed!" accused the Black Dragon. "Last night you saw the man who carried the death token when Sujan pointed him out. Instead of settling the score, you left members of your own band dying on the scene, Sujan among them!"

The Dragon was speaking in English, but interspersing his terms with Japanese words.

"Another opportunity!" The Dragon raised his doubled fists, letting their gems strike the light. As the embroidered coils writhed, from the fangs of the dragon head came the repeated accusation: "Again you failed!"

There was a thud as one of the crippled murder crew sagged to the floor. The Dragon's head bobbed like a cobra's as his fang-eyes looked at the sprawled follower whose strength had given out. Meanwhile, The Shadow was studying other faces.

A mixed lot, these, but in nearly every visage The Shadow could detect Nipponese traces. Obviously these men had been sent from the Orient to serve the Black Dragon while posing as something other than Japanese. Only a few, who looked something like dead Sujan, had faces that gave them completely away.

Now the Black Dragon was proving something by his stare. He was proving that he was not Li Huang. For the Dragon's eyes were fixed upon a cringing member of the throng, beckoning him into the light. As the cowering man advanced, he proved to be Li Huang!

"You, too, have failed!" stormed the Black Dragon. "Years ago, Li Huang, we brought you from Manchukuo to live in Chinatown and be ready when we needed you. We even provided you with servants"—the Dragon gestured toward the three Mongols who stood behind Li Huang—"in the hope that you could deceive the local Chinese into thinking they could trust you. Last night, you failed when needed!"

"Only because my visitor did not produce the death token," pleaded Li Huang. "However, because of my suspicions, I placed him where Sujan could identify him. Tonight the police phoned me to say that they are holding a suspect named Trask, unquestionably the man I interviewed. He expects me to support his alibi."

"Which you will not do, Li Huang!"

"I have already disclaimed it, master," assured Li Huang. "But, from now on, my house cannot serve as a meeting place, the way we originally intended. Even my membership in this organization may endanger others. Therefore, I beseech that you dispense with my future services, since the police may be watching me."

"Your apprehension seems well-founded," decided the Black Dragon. "Your request is granted—with one condition. I shall give you a final task, the delivery of a death token to a person whose name will be stated at the proper time."

Li Huang bowed, greatly relieved. The Black Dragon placed a doubled hand into a pocket formed by a dragon coil. Promptly, The Shadow's hand slid beneath his cloak. Returning ahead of the Dragon's move, The Shadow's fist leveled an automatic past the edge of the concrete pillar, straight for the monstrous creature in the throne.

The Shadow was waiting to see the jeweled fist open wide to reveal a tiny dragon carved of jet. That would be the timely moment for a shot that would bring the Black Dragon sprawling from the throne with one of his own death tokens in his clutch. Such a climax would mark The Shadow as the real master of this show, with due effect upon the superstitious members of the clan.

The wait was costly. It spoiled The Shadow's chance for an immediate triumph. Instead of opening his hand palm upward, the Black Dragon gave a downward fling. Something left his fist and struck the floor. The object wasn't a miniature dragon token.

It was a missile that exploded instantly, with a sharp puff that produced a bursting cloud of smoke that enveloped the throne completely. The white swirl writhed as though the dragon coils had stirred it, and during those brief moments The Shadow kept steady aim, waiting to sight his target.

Then, as the vapor filtered itself away, The Shadow found himself staring at an empty throne. Amid the puff of smoke, the Black Dragon had completely vanished!

CHAPTER VIII
TRAILS CROSS

IT wasn't in The Shadow's nature to be startled by sudden disappearances. The art of vanishing on instant's notice was one of his own specialties; hence he wasn't even surprised to witness the result of the Black Dragon's puffball.

The Shadow looked for visible effects, as evidenced by the Dragon Clan. They took it as a matter of course, proving that the vanish was their master's usual routine. One man had pitched forward on the floor, as though overcome by the startling sight, but The Shadow discerned that he was merely another gun-fray victim, succumbing like a previous companion.

Lifting the collapsed pair, the rest of the dragon men carried them from the meeting room, passing right between the concrete pillars. The Shadow remained unnoticed by the simple expedient of stepping to the far side of his pillar, but it was doubtful that he would have been detected.

Blended with the pillar's blackness, The Shadow was indeed invisible. After the procession passed, the space behind the pillar was vacant. Somehow, The Shadow had followed in the wake, for his gliding form appeared briefly in the outside corridor, then faded from all chance of view.

The Shadow was picking one figure among the departing throng—that of Li Huang. Lacking traces of the Black Dragon, The Shadow was concerned with the treacherous merchant as the next best choice. Only if something better should show up, would The Shadow change that course.

Something better did appear, coincident with The Shadow's thought on the subject.

The person in question was Ming Dwan. The Chinese girl should have been back in Li Huang's house, but she wasn't. Hardly had the motley dragon tribe gone down the stairs before Ming Dwan came darting from a side hall. She made directly toward the stairs, then hearing footsteps coming up, turned and hurried in The Shadow's direction.

Ming Dwan wasn't treacherous, as Steve had supposed, unless spying on the Dragon Clan came under that head. But the girl was running into serious difficulty, through having followed Li Huang here. Guards were coming back to close the meeting room. Flashlights gleaming ahead of them, they'd be sure spot Ming Dwan.

Just as the revealing beams stabbed the hallway, Ming Dwan was enveloped in darkness, so swiftly that she couldn't even gasp. Lost in the folds of a sweeping cloak, the girl was whirled into the meeting room itself, since it formed the only outlet close at hand. The girl saw the swirl of blackness that represented The Shadow, but it seem to dissolve under the light of the flashlights.

Still, they were coming toward the meeting room. A clash seemed imminent, considering that The Shadow couldn't keep Ming Dwan obscured in a room well filled with light. Battle would not be wise under present circumstances, when the first crack of guns would bring back the entire Dragon Clan.

Only The Shadow could have nullified that dilemma, by a surprising course that his foresight could connect with quick results.

SWEEPING Ming Dwan toward the deep end of the meeting room, The Shadow halted with a sudden spin. Launching the girl in a similar twirl, he sent her into the lap of the golden throne, where Ming Dwan landed, very surprised, her head jouncing backward and her feet flying in the air.

Less than a second later, The Shadow was in the darkness of a pillar, beating the arrival of the incoming guards. As he looked toward the throne, The Shadow tightened his hidden lips, repressing the laugh of satisfaction that he should have uttered.

The Shadow had called the trick to perfection.

Ming Dwan was no longer in the glided throne. She had vanished as instantly as the Black Dragon!

The guards turned out the lights and closed the meeting room. As soon as they were gone, The Shadow approached the throne and examined it with a tiny flashlight that cast a concentrated beam. Focused to silver-dollar proportions, the disk of light revealed a narrow slit in the back of the throne. Pressing one arm, then the other, finally jogging both, The Shadow gained results.

An edge slid downward from the slit. It was a sheet of glass that formed a long angle to the throne's front. The glass reflected the flashlight, giving the throne an empty appearance. Since nothing further happened, The Shadow pushed the glass up into its slit and seated himself in the throne.

When The Shadow jogged the throne arms with his elbows, the glass came down again. Boxed in the angled compartment, The Shadow delivered a low, reflective laugh. He should have fired immediately after the Black Dragon vanished, for one shot would have shattered the glass, and the next could have drilled the Black Dragon. Crime's vanished ringleader had still been close at hand after his disappearance!

Obviously, the Black Dragon hadn't remained there very long. So, to test the next stage of the journey, The Shadow leaned back in the throne. There was a sharp *click*, well muffled by the glass. The back of the throne revolved, carrying The Shadow through the wall, where he dropped off to let the thing ride back again.

As the panel completed its circuit, The Shadow gained a rear view of the glass sheet sliding up through his side of the wall. Neat, this delayed vanish, where the glass worked as a mirror to make the first stage quick, then remained in position until the mechanics of an actual departure could be completed.

Ming Dwan was awaiting The Shadow in the little room where they had both arrived. A door marked the exit that the Black Dragon had taken earlier. Removing his hat, dropping his cloak collar, The Shadow revealed the features of Lamont Cranston and gave Ming Dwan a slight smile which the girl returned.

"That was close, Myra," observed The Shadow, in Cranston's leisurely tone.* "But it wasn't the closest I've seen tonight. I had to pull our favorite chestnut from the fire again."

Ming Dwan raised her thin eyebrows.

"Steve Trask?"

"None other," replied The Shadow. "What's more, he may be heading for further trouble, once he's on his own. I see the Black Dragon has provided a convenient telephone. I'll handle Steve's situation while you're getting back to Li Huang's."

*Myra Reldon (Ming Dwan) is an American girl who was born in China. She has acted as one of The Shadow's agents at various times, including *The Golden Pagoda* (*The Shadow* Volume 17) and *The Devil Master* (*The Shadow* Volume 29).

The Shadow was picking up the telephone when Ming Dwan reached the door. The girl paused as The Shadow added a detail that belonged to her department.

"Watch for a dragon token," The Shadow stated. "Li Huang is to receive one and deliver it as bidden. Find out where it is to go."

With a confident nod, Ming Dwan left.

THUS far, Steve Trask hadn't encountered trouble, because he was still riding in The Shadow's cab. Its driver evidently knew Manhattan well, for he was covering a multitude of streets that Steve had never seen before.

All this was necessary to avoid questioning by patrol cars that seemed to be everywhere tonight. It wouldn't do for Steve to meet up with unobliging officers who would insist upon looking at his wrists. But he felt safe while in the cab, The Shadow's driver at the wheel.

Who the driver was, Steve didn't know, because the cab lacked the usual identification card that bore the cabby's name and photograph.

The ride continued for another fifteen minutes, until the cab halted in a very quiet neighborhood where the only visible lights showed from an old pawnshop.

The cabby thrust his face through the connecting window. Steve noted that the fellow had a pointed face, with quick eyes, but the cab was too dark to reveal his features clearly.

"Slide into the hockshop," said the cabby. "Tell old uncle to unclamp the jewelry. Say that Shrevvy sent you. I'll be waiting."

Alighting, Steve entered the shop and found the pawnbroker. Mention of "Shrevvy" produced immediate service, but Steve expected the process to be prolonged. Instead, it took less than five minutes. It seemed that handcuffs weren't like ordinary locks. Each brand of cuff had its own interchangeable key. As soon as the old pawnbroker had satisfied himself as to the make and model, he unlocked the handcuffs and handed them to Steve.

"Keep them for your trouble," remarked Steve with a grin. Then looking about, he added: "Is there a back door out of this place? I don't want Shrevvy to put himself in a jam on my account."

The pawnbroker showed Steve through the back door which led into a darkened alley. Going out, Steve decided that he'd done the right thing. After all, he was making it easier for the cabby, and therefore for The Shadow. Maybe The Shadow wouldn't want it that way but Steve did. He was an independent sort, Steve was, and though he owed much to The Shadow, he preferred to operate on his own.

Hand in his pocket, Steve clutched the jet

dragon, glad that it was still there. Pausing at the outlet of the alley, Steve took a long look, just to make sure. In gazing along the street, he didn't bother to probe the darkness around him. The alley was its own security, helpful with its thick darkness.

More helpful to others than to Steve.

One step toward the street, and Steve was clamped from both flanks by a pair of brawny men who knew their business. His arms were pinned behind him so firmly that the handcuff treatment reminded Steve of putty. So expert were these captors that they bent Steve right back to his heels, which enabled them to clamp their free hands over his mouth.

Then Steve's captors were carrying him, still doubled, into a sedan, where they planted him without relieving pressure.

What added to Steve's bitter defeat was the course that the sedan took. It swung around the block and rolled right past Shrevvy's cab, which was still waiting in front of the pawnshop!

As the sedan rolled along, Steve kept staring upward through the window, unable to fight against the pressure that held him muscle-bound. There was no comfort in what Steve saw. He recognized buildings that the car was passing and knew that they were on the fringe of Chinatown. Steve was going right back to the ominous quarter of Manhattan where his strange adventures had begun, but this time he wasn't traveling in quest of a miniature dragon carved from jet.

Steve Trask already owned such a curio. He was carrying it in his pocket, and he could feel its bulge—like the pressure of a gun, applied muzzle-first. For that black talisman meant death to its carrier!

Twice The Shadow had frustrated doom intended for Steve Trask. If the cloaked stranger from nowhere could miraculously appear to stay the present threat, Steve would be willing to believe anything. For Steve had deliberately put himself beyond The Shadow's protection, only to meet up with this.

Stolid faces, peering down at Steve's, seemed by their very lack of expression to taunt him concerning the death he knew must come!

CHAPTER IX
DEEP IN CHINATOWN

EFFICIENCY was the watchword of Steve's new captors. When their car pulled into Chinatown, they didn't park it on one of the narrow streets. Instead, Steve felt the sedan swerve, take a slight jolt over a low curb and roll in through a narrow opening, where a well-oiled door slithered shut behind the car.

Immediately, the stopping place became an elevator, its open platform descending to a stone-walled cellar. The car rolled forward, curved between two pillars and stopped beside a narrow door that showed a gloomy passage leading underneath a street. Brought from the car by his two captors, Steve began to learn what underground Chinatown could really be like.

Steve was marched through what seemed an array of catacombs, some of the passages looking more like pipes than tunnels. Always there were turns and devious angles, until Steve hadn't a glimmer of the direction that they followed. The trip ended in a steel door that slid aside to show a small elevator into which Steve was pressed.

Unable to determine the speed of the elevator's rise, Steve couldn't tell how many floors they covered. However, the ride marked journey's end, for when Steve was shoved from the elevator, he promptly arrived in a small room furnished like an office, where an Oriental was seated at a desk. The seated man gave a dismissing gesture, and Steve's captors retired.

For the moment, Steve thought that he was back in Li Huang's presence, but in a different setting. There was nothing Oriental about these surroundings. The man at the desk was wearing American attire, instead of a robe. This might be a trick of Li Huang's, though curiously, Steve didn't entirely mistrust Li Huang. Steve's deductions were still persistently blaming the girl, Ming Dwan, for most of his trouble.

Then Steve saw that the seated man was not Li Huang. Though Oriental, this man had an American manner; his face was rounded, with an owlish expression so utterly devoid of challenge that Steve felt he could handle this situation with ease. Instead of waiting for the man to speak, Steve lunged forward, intending to clear the desk and overwhelm the trivial man into submission.

Blackness met Steve halfway. A flood of it, that seemed like the engulfing depths of Li Huang's pit. Then he was whirling, faster than his brain could twirl, under the manipulation of something that could be described as a human tornado. When Steve did finish his spin, he was deep in a chair that seemed to be prolonging the merry-go-round ride.

THE blackness that had done it all assumed a human shape—that of a cloaked figure, which Steve didn't see, because it stood behind his chair. Having come from nowhere, first as a living whirl, then a cloaked form, The Shadow carried the transformation still further. He removed his cloak and hat to become the complacent Mr. Cranston.

As Cranston, The Shadow was placing his black garments in a closet while Steve, slowly recuperating from his bewilderment, began to stare at the innocent Chinaman beyond the desk, wondering what kind of buttons had been pressed to produce the miniature earthquake. Then, in between stepped Cranston, idly tendering Steve an open cigarette case.

"A smoke, Trask?" queried Cranston in an even tone. "You could use one, considering the strain your nerves have been under."

Steve started to accept a cigarette, then shook his head. Reaching in his pocket, he brought out his pipe and pouch. Lighting a cigarette himself, Cranston finished by extending the lighter to Steve's pipe bowl. Taking a few draws of Fenmore's special smoking mixture, Steve looked squarely at Cranston and said:

"Your name is Cranston. I saw you up at Fenmore's house."

"Quite right," Cranston acknowledged. He gestured toward the desk. "And this is Doctor Roy Tam, a Chinese friend of mine who is very desirous of curbing the activities of the Black Dragon."

Dr. Tam leaned forward on his folded arms.

"We regret the measures necessary to bring you here," spoke Tam in precise English. "The Shadow would have preferred that you remain in the cab which he provided. Fortunately, the driver foresaw that you might not—"

"So he notified Dr. Tam to intercept you," put in Cranston. "It would be dangerous for you to remain at large, Trask."

Steve didn't see it that way, and said so, adding that he could have dodged the police indefinitely, if necessary.

"We were not speaking of the police," put in Tam, politely. "Your danger lay from the Dragon Clan. My men kept you from falling into the hands of your former friend, Li Huang."

Steve turned a startled glance to Cranston, who nodded calmly and gestured back to Dr. Tam, who said:

"The Shadow informs us that Li Huang attended a meeting of the Dragon Clan this evening and was deputed to deliver the next death token, by order of the Black Dragon. Fortunately, Ming Dwan will inform us of Li Huang's moves."

Steve's thoughts whirled anew, only to arrive on an absolute balance. It was as though his spinning recollections focused upon a single tangible fact that proved the truth of Tam's words. Indeed, the thing was so tangible that Steve could actually grip it—the tiny jet dragon, in the pocket where he had just shoved his tobacco pouch!

The Shadow had returned that token, and The Shadow was certainly Steve's friend. But, so far, Steve had overlooked the mechanics of the operation, taking it that The Shadow had simply plucked the dragon from thin air. It was hearing Ming Dwan classed as an ally that made the truth strike home.

Assuming Ming Dwan to be a friend, facts fell into a new line. It was the girl who had dropped Steve to a rough but ready safety. The click he'd heard while waking in the pit must have been caused by Ming Dwan leaving after a preliminary visit, carrying the black dragon found in Steve's pocket so that Li Huang would not find it!

Those warning glances from Ming Dwan had stopped Steve from giving himself away. Later, her shots at The Shadow and Steve had been purposely wide. She was merely preserving her status with Li Huang in pretending to stop the fugitives. The proof of all this, the one point that Steve had so blindly overlooked, was the incident in the opium den.

There, Ming Dwan had stopped at the booth from which The Shadow later emerged to Steve's rescue. Then, only then, could the missing dragon token have reached The Shadow, delivered by Ming Dwan!

"You spoke of the police," remarked Cranston, his calm tone chiming with Steve's sudden vindication of Ming Dwan. "Suppose we let the police speak for themselves."

Tuning in a radio that stood on Tam's desk, Cranston picked up a garble of police reports to which Steve listened, horrified. The manhunt was on in full, its object Steve Trask! Not only was Steve wanted for the murders of Miljohn and Pendleton; the law had added another charge.

Boldly, Steve had summoned unknown killers to an attempt upon the life of Carlton Sauber, on the threshold of the importer's own home, with the police actually on the scene. Failing in the murder thrust, Steve had escaped with the aid of the assassin crew that served him. When last seen, he'd been wearing handcuffs that might still mark him as the wanted killer.

Sagging back in his chair, Steve rubbed the wrists that still ached from the manacles he'd worn. He looked helplessly from Tam to Cranston, and received calm glances in return. As he turned off the radio, Cranston casually remarked:

"I think that Trask would like to be your guest a while, Dr. Tam. Meanwhile, I can use my influence with the police commissioner to straighten matters as they should be. I am sure The Shadow would approve."

Dr. Tam bowed profoundly as he pressed a button, summoning servants to show Steve to his quarters in this safe refuge deep in Chinatown.

THE swiftness with which the Dragon Clan could move was proven when The Shadow left Tam's stronghold. Moving through dark alleys, The Shadow was quite unseen, for he had once more obliterated the identity of Cranston under the cloak and hat that blended with the shrouding night. But The Shadow could see skulking creatures in the darkness which he navigated so invisibly.

Bold skulkers, servers of the Black Dragon!

Police cars were about, their searchlights appearing suddenly to cut unexpected swaths along the narrow streets. Always the skulkers tumbled like phantom tenpins into alleys, doorways, or basements, to avoid those revealing beams.

The Shadow, too, was shifting away from each sudden glow. In avoiding one sweeping searchlight, The Shadow suddenly thrust himself into an unprepared snare.

Side-stepping into an alley as a police car wheeled past, The Shadow came right into the midst of some dragon lurkers who were about to issue forth. This time, half a dozen hands were upon him, all sensing the texture of the black cloak that they could not see. Not for an instant did they hesitate.

Like goblin claws, half of those hands clung to The Shadow as he tried to wheel away. Even as he whipped guns from beneath his cloak, free hands were swinging knives at the blackened mass that represented The Shadow.

Only the circling stroke of The Shadow's gun hand prevented the blades from driving home. But in the whirl, The Shadow lost his footing. Knives went clattering as The Shadow sprawled, but other attackers were pouncing on their prey, slugging hard with revolvers. The Shadow's only respite was the lack of gunfire. The Dragon Clan were fearful of clipping one another; likewise, they knew that shots would bring police.

Few fighters other than The Shadow could have risen amid such a slugging hail. He managed it, but could only partially ward off the gun swings. Reeling out into the street, The Shadow was blindly seeking a wall against which he could brace his back. Hard after him came the murderous pack.

Grabbing at a corner, The Shadow missed. He stumbled across a curb, but turned his stagger into a lurch across the street to a big car parked there. The pack overtook him as he wrenched the door open. Twisting about, The Shadow did a backward drop to avoid the pounding weapons; at the same time, he used his other hand to stab shots with an automatic.

Spurting upward, those shots found no human targets, but they made assailants dodge. Moreover, they were the summons that the Dragon Clan had restrained themselves from giving, the thing that would bring the patrol cars. His senses slipping, The Shadow had scored a last moment stroke. Weakly, his lips throbbed a laugh.

FEEBLE was that laugh compared to the glee of the Dragon Clan. Half a dozen hands slammed the door shut to hide the flopped form of The Shadow. Like a thing released, the big car roared away through the narrow streets, unstopped by the converging police.

For the officers in the squad cars identified that long-built vehicle as the commissioner's own official car! They did not know, as did the Dragon Clan, that two such machines were roaming Manhattan this night. No wonder scattering assailants were gleeful. This murderous tribe had dispatched The Shadow, half stunned and helpless, straight to their master, the Black Dragon!

It seemed an inglorious finish to the saga of The Shadow, this choosing of a way out that enemies took as a play into their own hands. But the sequel produced a different story.

The real climax was when Commissioner Ralph Weston arrived at his unofficial headquarters, the exclusive Cobalt Club. Alighting from a cab, Weston saw his official car parked by the curb. Purple-faced, the commissioner approached the chauffeur.

"So!" stormed Weston. "This is where you came! I don't blame you for leaving Chinatown when the gunfire started, but why didn't you wait when I shouted after you?"

The chauffeur blinked, bewildered. At that moment the rear door opened and Lamont Cranston, pale but composed, stepped to the curb.

"My fault, Commissioner," said Cranston. "I was looking for you in Chinatown when the trouble started, so I commandeered your official car and had the chauffeur bring me here."

Mollified, Weston went into the club with Cranston, whose wan lips showed the traces of a smile. Well did The Shadow know why a certain car hadn't stopped at the commissioner's shout. The commissioner had seen the wrong vehicle, the imitation of his own official car.

As for the Dragon Clan, they'd made the opposite mistake. They'd packed off The Shadow as a gift to the Black Dragon, not in the replica official car, but in the original that belonged to Commissioner Weston.

Even in sagging state, The Shadow had seen the difference and made the most of it. Like his rival, the Black Dragon, The Shadow was skilled at taking a quick way out when occasion demanded. Now they were due to meet again on equal terms:

The Shadow versus the Black Dragon!

CHAPTER X
DEATH'S REAL TOKEN

SAVAGELY, Steve Trask flung the newspaper upon Tam's desk and glared at the placid Chinese doctor. Tam's quiet eyes invited comment, so Steve gave it.

"Still they're hounding me!" Steve yelled. "Can't they get it through their heads that I didn't murder Miljohn or Pendleton—that one was my best friend, the other a man I never saw?"

"Time will bring your vindication," replied Tam. "The Black Dragon has composed a noose of his own coils. The Shadow is waiting for it to tighten."

Steve's glower lessened; his eyes showed interest.

"You have forgotten that Li Huang is to deliver a death token," reminded Tam. "When that happens, The Shadow will know the identity of the Black Dragon's next victim, and will move to prevent crime."

"I haven't forgotten Li Huang," retorted Steve, with a new surge of impatience. "He's only an intermediary anyway. He won't take a hand in murder."

"Others will," assured Tam complacently. "At least, they will attempt it. Whoever their victim, The Shadow will protect him and deliver them to the law. From the lips of such culprits, the police will gain clues to the Black Dragon himself."

"And if they won't talk?"

"The Shadow will personally provide the needed clue. Such is the way of Ying Ko, The Shadow."

Tam's solid confidence took effect on Steve. After all, Tam had as much at stake as Steve himself, and Tam had been fighting the Black Dragon a long while. Though passive, rather than active like The Shadow, Tam had been equally successful.

Every time that the Black Dragon had tried to gain a foothold in Chinatown, Tam had stopped him. Tam's system was to warn important Chinese whenever the Dragon sought to dupe them. As a loyal, solid race, none could match the Chinese. The Black Dragon hadn't been able to influence a single important citizen of Chinatown.

That was why the Black Dragon had planted Li Huang to pose as a retired Chinese merchant. But Li Huang hadn't fooled Tam nor anyone else. They knew he was an import from Manchukuo, long a sphere of Japanese influence.

Dr. Tam had let Li Huang stay in Chinatown, so that he could be watched as an index to the coming moves of the Black Dragon; and so far Li Huang had been deceived by that policy. By fooling Li Huang, Dr. Tam had likewise kept the Black Dragon unaware of the true situation.

Steve was rising and turning toward the door, when another thought struck him. Turning, he questioned:

"How is Cranston making out with the commissioner?"

"Very well, I understand," replied Tam. "He just phoned me from Fenmore's. They expect Sauber there to discuss the Black Dragon question. Cranston may learn much of value to our other friend, The Shadow."

That sounded good to Steve as he returned to his room in a corner of Tam's commodious house. Steve would have liked to attend that conference. He wanted to press the claim that Sauber had called the Dragon Clan to the attack, with Steve as the intended victim, instead of matters being the other way about. Steve felt that Fenmore would believe him.

With that thought, Steve started to fill his pipe, only to find that he'd used up all of Fenmore's tobacco. So Steve opened the tin of his own, which he still carried in his other pocket.

THE conference at Fenmore's was producing some results. Behind his big desk, Fenmore was receiving papers that his secretaries handed him and was passing them alternately to Commissioner Weston and Inspector Cardona, for comparison with their own reports.

Beside the desk, Sauber was watching, chin in hand, his quick eyes darting glances from beneath their bushy brows. At times, Sauber beckoned to a dapper man seated near him. In an undertone, Sauber asked for the papers which the dapper man supplied from a briefcase.

"I have inquired among friends who know the Orient," declared Fenmore. "These letters constitute their confidential replies. They all agree that the Black Dragon is the title given the leader of a clan that bears the same name. It is an organization of many heads; each chapter of the insidious clan has its own Black Dragon."

"That tallies with our reports," put in Cardona. "There's a Black Dragon right here in New York, running the local outfit. What puzzles me is why the outfit is only picking on people who have come back from the Orient?"

"These letters explain that point, Inspector," declared Weston, referring to some of Fenmore's correspondence. "When a marked man leaves the jurisdiction of one Black Dragon, he becomes the property, so to speak, of the next."

"Now we're getting somewhere!" enthused Cardona. "Fellows like Miljohn and Pendleton landed back here with a lot of dough from the Orient. Miljohn admitted it, but Pendleton pretended to be broke. It made no difference; the Black Dragon was ahead of them. The boss of the New York bunch told them to deliver—or else!"

"It was 'or else' with Miljohn and Pendleton," agreed Weston. "But there must be a lot of cases where frightened men delivered, perhaps to the extent of millions. How about it, Sauber?"

Jerkily, Sauber thrust his own batch of letters into Weston's hands. They were old letters from Sauber's former correspondents in the Far East.

"Read those," suggested Sauber. "You'll find complaints about a lot of things, but no mention of a Black Dragon."

"But surely, Sauber, you must have heard—"

"I've never been in the Orient, I tell you!" Sauber's tone became an excited pitch. "Why should I know anything about the Black Dragon, if there is such a thing—or person?"

Sauber's half-scream awoke Cranston, who was deep in one of Fenmore's comfortable chairs. Opening his eyes lazily, Cranston saw Weston impatiently thrust the letters back at Sauber, who took the gesture as an insult and flung the papers in a fluttering stream across the floor. Cardona came to his feet and thrust himself between the two men, whereupon Sauber's frenzy ceased.

Turning to his dapper secretary, Sauber gestured at the scattered papers.

"Gather those, Pelly," Sauber ordered. "Bring them home with you. I am leaving now." Swinging to Weston, Sauber added: "After tonight, I won't need any of your protection, Commissioner. Why should I be afraid of things that don't exist—like Black Dragons?"

The conference ended with Sauber's sudden walkout. Leaving with Weston and Cardona, Cranston declined the commissioner's offer to ride in the official car, saying he preferred a stroll in the fresh air, to awaken from his recent doze. Cranston's stroll ended in the shadows just around the corner. As the commissioner's car rolled away, the corner gloom stirred to life.

Keenly, The Shadow had foreseen that Sauber's erratic behavior might be the forerunner of something deeper and more purposeful. At least, it allowed for certain opportunities that were not apparent on the surface. It had certainly paved the way for one man to go his way unsuspected; namely, Sauber's secretary, Pelly.

Soon, the dapper man appeared from Fenmore's front door. Still poking gathered papers in the briefcase, Pelly glanced up and down the street. Seeing no one watching, he threw a suspicious look back at Fenmore's front windows, then moved along at a quick but shifty pace past the spot where The Shadow watched unseen.

Pelly's first stop was at a small cigar store a few blocks away. Still having trouble with his brief case, he unpacked some papers and laid them on the counter. Buying some cigarettes, he pocketed them, put away the papers and left. From the blackness that fringed the store window, The Shadow still watched the counter.

There, Pelly had left a square package, placed under cover of the papers. The cigar clerk scooped up the package and went through a rear door of the shop. Circling to the next street, The Shadow saw the man from the shop step out, to be promptly accosted by a slouchy panhandler.

What the clerk gave the panhandler wasn't a dime for coffee. It was Pelly's package, obviously for delivery to someone else. Instead of following along the trail, The Shadow faded into thick darkness with a whispered laugh.

IT was Ming Dwan who answered the tinkly ring at Li Huang's front door. No longer was Li Huang keeping that portal guarded. He no longer had his brawny servants, and Ming Dwan knew why, though she hadn't been informed—at least, not by Li Huang. Those vanished servants were members of the Dragon Clan, who had actually kept Li Huang under a form of surveillance after he had sold out to the Black Dragon—for a price.

As an employer of traitors, the Black Dragon probably knew how untrustworthy they could prove. However, Li Huang's stint was through, or would be, after he went through with the delivery of a death token to some victim as yet unnamed. The Black Dragon had probably sized Li Huang as willing to do that final task in return for freedom. Hence, the removal of the servants in advance was a form of encouragement.

But Li Huang was restless. Ming Dwan could hear his quick footsteps approaching as she opened the front door. Outside was a laundry man with a sizable bundle. Ming Dwan knew him for an honest Chinese. But she knew him to be careless, too, for she'd visited his little one-man shop. Someone could easily have stowed something in this bundle along with Li Huang's laundry.

The proof was the way in which Li Huang snatched the bundle the moment that Ming Dwan closed the door. The girl was almost tempted to press the switch controlling the floor, when Li Huang turned to hurry back to his den. A tumble into the pit, and Li Huang would still be dazed while Ming Dwan joined him and searched the laundry package.

Still, Li Huang would guess things afterward, and that would injure The Shadow's plans. So, instead of using the floor trap, Ming Dwan let Li Huang go his way, while she made a detour past the side door and drew the bolt. Then stealthily the girl went to Li Huang's own door and listened.

Prolonged silence caused Mint Dwan to worry. She'd always been suspicious of Li Huang's paneled room, where he liked to drowse over a pipe containing a dash of opium, until a small alarm gong awakened him. Li Huang's frequent naps might be faked. If he had a secret route from the room, he could use it and return before the time at which he had set the gong. Tonight would certainly be an occasion for secrecy on Li Huang's part.

Slowly, carefully, Ming Dwan turned the handle of the door, ready to give a sudden knock and act surprised when the door went inward, as it sometimes did. Pausing as she gained a view of the room, Ming Dwan was relieved to see Li Huang, in his chair, leaning forward, head on arm, as he always napped. Beside him was the alarm gong; near it the inevitable pipe.

More important, the laundry package lay open on a chair, its contents rumpled. Li Huang had found what he wanted. It was on the desk in front of him—a little jewel box, its deep lid hinged wide, revealing a curved, jet dragon with tiny eyes of jade!

Step by step, Ming Dwan moved inward, breathing the air cautiously to detect the degree of opium that Li Huang had used, and therefore gauge the depth of his sleep. Reaching the desk, she saw a slip of paper projecting from beneath the carved dragon. Ming Dwan's confidence became complete.

Li Huang must have read the instructions on the folded paper, telling him to whom the dragon was to be delivered, and stating the hour at which he was to go. So Li Huang, to soothe his nerves, had set the little gong and taken some long drags at his pipe.

Still, this drowse might be feigned. The thought worried Ming Dwan until her gaze moved from Li Huang's fingers to his wrist. There she saw the telltale marks of a needle's jab. Evidently, Li Huang had been finding the pipe too slow of late, and had resorted to a quicker way of absorbing dope. So his sleep was deep enough.

Ming Dwan crept a slender, cream-yellow hand toward the jet-hued dragon. She intended to remove the token from the jewel case and read the folded note that lay beneath it. Li Huang could then fare forth upon his evil mission, only to have The Shadow reach the goal ahead of him. Just as those delicate fingers of Ming Dwan had saved the life of Steve Trask, so could they provide rescue for another threatened man.

A life was hanging in the balance! Such was Ming Dwan's thought, without the realization that the life was her own.

The truth came with a hiss, delivered by the death token that the girl thought was a carved dragon.

With a writhe, the creature came to life. No dragon, this, but a poison lizard that had already left its mark of death upon Li Huang! Again disturbed, the venomous reptilian darted its green-eyed head at the wrist of Ming Dwan!

Stabbing ahead, faster than any human hand could move, was a long, forked fang, thrusting its fatal stroke upon the girl who served The Shadow!

CHAPTER XI
THE DRAGON'S MESSENGER

THE anguished shriek that started from Ming Dwan's lips was interrupted on the instant. So suddenly did death jab home that it was done and over before the echoes of the broken cry had faded. The stroke itself was merciless, but the swift result was merciful.

Crumpling forward, Ming Dwan's frail form sagged across the desktop. Her hand gave a lifeless slither away from the spot where death had struck. There, where a carved, jet dragon had reared itself into a living instrument of murder, lay a plasmic mass of blackness dyed with crimson. From the gel, the redness began to ooze into a slanted furrow that had plowed the teak of Li Huang's desk.

Strange how the echoes of Ming Dwan's cry followed the roar that suppressed the scream itself!

Perhaps it was because the shriek was piercing, voiced in a moment of mortal agony; whereas the roar, though louder, had come with the burst of a thunderclap, an appropriate accompaniment for the flash of flame that produced it.

Yes, death had been swift and merciful, to a creature that deserved death yet could not appreciate mercy—the poison lizard!

His gun still smoking in his fist, The Shadow sprang in from the doorway and caught Ming Dwan as her sliding arm carried her body across the far corner of the desk. Brushing the tumbled laundry from the handy chair, he rested the girl there and tilted her chin upward. Ming Dwan's breath came back with a gasp, as her eyes opened wide.

The opium-tainted air, the lizard's hissing death jab, the sudden explosion of The Shadow's gun—any of those could have been enough to throw a person into a faint. Not such a person as Ming Dwan. It had taken all three—and more—to overwhelm this stout-hearted girl.

The more was represented by the bullet from The Shadow's gun. The lizard's darting fang, too fast for a hand to escape, could not outmatch the instantaneous action of a single finger pulling a hair-trigger. The Shadow had proven this with a timely shot that blasted the living trip-hammer midway in its errand of doom.

It was The Shadow's bullet that gave the death jab, reducing the lizard to the gelatin now on the desk. Ming Dwan had felt the quiver of the woodwork as the continuing slug grooved its downward path beneath her frozen hand, forming the channel through which the lizard's life blood now trickled.

Her eyes meeting The Shadow's, Ming Dwan stared, unbelieving. Following his gesture toward the desk, the girl looked in that direction. Her lips formed for another startled cry that her throat failed to voice. Knowing that the lizard's pulp wasn't enough to so startle Ming Dwan, The Shadow turned.

The thing to which Ming Dwan pointed was Li Huang. His body was showing grotesque signs of life, as its arm slithered sideways, under the pressure

Ming Dwan intended to remove the token from the jewel case....

of a tilting head that turned a bloated, sightless face toward the persons by the desk.

Having witnessed Ming Dwan's slide across the polished surface, The Shadow defined Li Huang's motion properly. The bullet's impact against the desk had jogged the dead man from his balance point. His arm, brushing pipe and gong ahead of it, was definitely lifeless, as Li Huang's hideous face proclaimed.

WITH The Shadow's hands bracing her shoulders, Ming Dwan steadied as she saw the corpse of Li Huang complete its slide and disappear with its frozen leer in a toppling slump beyond the desk. Her eyes again meeting The Shadow's, Ming Dwan found her voice and began to detail all that had occurred, prior to The Shadow's timely appearance.

What interested The Shadow most was the paper that Ming Dwan mentioned. It was intact, for The Shadow's shot had literally plucked the lizard from the jewel case. Yet there was something strangely grim in The Shadow's mirth as he reached for the folded note. He knew the paper couldn't contain the Black Dragon's instructions to Li Huang.

As good as dead when he received the package with the living death token, Li Huang, a traitor no longer useful, would need no further orders. Already, The Shadow could sense evil omen in that folded slip of paper.

Opening the sheet, The Shadow read its contents and passed the paper to Ming Dwan. The girl's expression changed from horror to anger, as she read:

To The Shadow:

Greetings, Ying Ko, when you find this message. Alive, Li Huang could have told you much. Dead, he is as useless to you as he already was to me. If you suspected that Li Huang was to deliver a death token to my next victim, you were wrong. I have already provided another messenger.

THE BLACK DRAGON

The Shadow was clicking a telephone on Li Huang's desk. The action proved useless, for the line was disconnected—more forethought to the Black Dragon's credit. Clutching Ming Dwan's arm, The Shadow spoke in a tone much like Cranston's, except that it was quicker:

"Come, Myra. There's not a moment to lose!"

"You mean the messenger?" queried the girl as they were hurrying toward the side door. "You know who he is?"

"Too well," returned The Shadow grimly. "The Black Dragon slipped in writing that message. The word 'provided' is our clue. It seems impossible, yet stranger things have happened—"

NOTHING could have seemed stranger to Steve Trask as he sat in the quiet security of his room at Dr. Tam's. During his sojourn here, Steve had learned that Tam's house was an absolute stronghold into which neither friend nor foe could find a way without Tam's due permission.

Yet, The Shadow had come and gone invisibly within the last five minutes!

The proof lay in Steve's hand, a brief note written on a small slip of torn paper that somehow fluttered to the table beside his tobacco pouch. It was addressed to Steve, and it stated:

Our mission is immediate. My car is waiting near Gotham Court. Take it and deliver the jet dragon. Let no one know.

The Shadow.

Grimly, Steve wadded the paper, its tiny writing on the inside. Thrusting the wad in his pocket, he felt the carved dragon that he still carried. A death token to which he was immune, being under the protection of The Shadow. That, Steve knew, was the reason why The Shadow wanted him to carry it.

A challenge to the Black Dragon, and now to carry it further, The Shadow wanted Steve to deliver the token somewhere. To whom and why, Steve neither knew nor cared. It was The Shadow's order; that was enough. It could only be The Shadow's order; otherwise it could not have arrived here. That was where The Shadow held the advantage over the Black Dragon. The Shadow knew where Steve was; the Black Dragon didn't. So this was The Shadow's order and Steve would follow it.

Picking up his tobacco pouch, Steve found he'd already filled it. The empty can was lying on the table, fragments of its paper lining beside it, where Steve had crumpled them. Funny. Steve didn't remember filling his pouch, though he must have, because he'd been smoking his pipe steadily.

Maybe The Shadow had thrown some hypnotism Steve's way in order to pay the unseen visit. That was it, for Steve was sensing The Shadow's presence as he had that night in the opium den. He was moving steadily, almost rapidly, out through the door and toward a stairway. Below, Tam's men would be on guard, but they were watching for intruders and therefore not concerned with Steve.

Free run of the place—that was what Tam had given Steve in return for a promise not to leave. So there would be no questions from Tam's men and no regrets on Steve's part. He wasn't breaking his word to Tam while following orders from The Shadow!

The night air ended Steve's exit. He was outside, somewhere in Chinatown, though how he'd managed it so swiftly he couldn't understand. Right now Steve's worry was his legs: they were getting draggy. Seeing a cab, Steve stumbled into it. The driver's face showed through a cloud like something from a nightmare. Its features, though, were plain. This wasn't Shrevvy, so naturally this wasn't The Shadow's cab. Steve laughed.

How could it be?

The Shadow's cab was waiting outside Gotham Court, which meant that The Shadow was probably checking on Carlton Sauber. That suited Steve perfectly, so he muttered:

"Gotham Court."

The cab began to revolve. Next it started forward, so its locomotion took a corkscrew effect that made Steve very dizzy. At last the spiral ended and the cab became an arrow that shot right to its mark, stopping like something hitting smack against a target.

Steve handed the driver something that looked like an eleven-dollar bill, judging from the two ones that he saw side by side. No good, eleven-dollar bills, but they couldn't be counterfeit because there weren't any genuines to begin with. Maybe the one and one made two, but that didn't matter, either. Two-dollar bills were bad luck. The cab driver could have it.

The tail-lights chuckled and the cab was gone. It could go; Steve didn't want it. He wanted The Shadow's cab and here it was, flapping its door and saying: "Get in!" The Shadow's cab, all rigged up nice and new. They'd put a leaf in it, making it longer, like a dining room table, and painted it so it would look like Commissioner Weston's official car.

Smart fellow, The Shadow, fixing the cab like this for Steve. No cops would think of bothering the commissioner's car. More power to The Shadow.

STEVE'S wish was The Shadow's own. At that moment, The Shadow was wishing for more power as he stood with Dr. Tam, viewing Steve's empty room. Ming Dwan, peering over their shoulders, arched her eyebrows as she sniffed the atmosphere. The opium scent was heavier here than at Li Huang's.

"My men did not know," apologized Tam. "They thought that Trask was looking somewhere for me. He seemed in no hurry, yet suddenly, he was gone!"

The Shadow did something very suddenly. Striding to Tam's office, he skimmed his hat across the desk, let his cloak drop from his shoulders. About to play the part of Cranston, he wanted to look like Cranston, even though he was only making a telephone call. After all, he would have an audience: Dr. Tam and Ming Dwan. He could judge from their reactions whether or not his act was convincing.

It was convincing. Tam and the girl stared open-eyed as they viewed Cranston in a state of fervor, something that he so rarely displayed. His call had gone through to police headquarters, and he was talking directly to Inspector Joe Cardona.

"Yes, this is Cranston..." The Shadow was putting strain into his tone. "The commissioner just left the Cobalt Club. That's why I'm calling you, Inspector... A message from the commissioner? No! One from the Black Dragon!

"Yes, the Black Dragon called me... His voice? I couldn't describe it! But what he said was even worse. He intends to murder the commissioner... Absolutely! He says that Commissioner Weston will never leave his car alive, not even if the whole force tries to save him!

"Excellent, Inspector! The shortwave will help... They may have taken over the commissioner's car, as you say... Yes, in that case, it will try to get away... But wherever it is, it will be reported. Good!"

Real sweat was streaking Cranston's forehead as he finished his intensive hoax. Mopping it with a black handkerchief that he took from his cloak, this man who was The Shadow leaned back and smiled at Dr. Tam and Ming Dwan.

"If Steve is where I think he is," declared Cranston, "the police will find him for us."

"Unless they find the commissioner's car first," observed Tam with a worried expression. "In that case, the search will be ended."

Cranston picked up the slouch hat and turned toward the door.

"They won't find the commissioner's car first," he assured quite calmly. "In fact, they won't find it at all."

Tam stared, puzzled, as did Ming Dwan. They saw Cranston raise his cloak collar and place the slouch hat on its head, its brim still upward, so that they could see his face. Sensing an immediate departure, Tam queried:

"Why not?"

"Because Commissioner Weston is at the Cobalt Club," declared Cranston. "His official car is parked right out front, the one place in all New York where the police will never look for it."

Cranston pulled down the hatbrim. As darkness obscured his features, his hidden lips delivered the famed laugh of The Shadow. With it, he was gone.

CHAPTER XII
THE MAN WHO MOCKED DEATH

POLICE sirens were on the shriek when Steve Trask alighted from the car that he had met at Gotham Court. By this time, Steve had straightened a few facts to his own satisfaction. For one thing, he'd decided that this wasn't The Shadow's cab converted into something else.

It probably was the commissioner's own car, though Steve wasn't sure about the chauffeur. However, everything fitted plausibly. Probably Cranston had managed to borrow the car for the evening. Being Tam's friend, Cranston might know The Shadow, too. It all fitted.

As for the sirens, they didn't matter. Nobody would bother the commissioner's car. Steve watched it pull away, then turned to look at the place where the car had dropped him. As he did, a sense of unreality seized him.

The place looked like an oversized mausoleum, a granite structure two stories high that didn't belong in New York at all. It occupied the corner of a short, dead end street where Steve saw a blocking wall of stone that ran across to an old brick building that looked deserted.

For that matter, the gray pile looked empty, too, and when Steve looked at the inscription carved above its door he could almost read the word "Mausoleum," which was already in his mind. Then, while his bewilderment was actually increasing, his eyes made out the inscription more plainly.

Steve's imagination had added a few letters that weren't there. Instead of "Mausoleum," the inscription said: "Museum."

There was another word above, a name which Steve finally identified as "Norland." He had never heard of the Norland Museum.

Seeing a big bell beside the barred front door, Steve rang it. The door opened promptly, and Steve was ushered into a foyer from which he could see the interior of an exhibit room, which was lined with stuffed heads of queer animals, along with elephant tusks, turtle shells, snake skins and other sizable knickknacks.

Footsteps sounded from a corridor. Steve turned and saw another attendant joining the one who had admitted him. Odd characters, these, men who were furtive, yet ugly. Maybe it was the poor light that gave their faces a clay color above the frayed collars of their drab uniforms.

Home to Steve came the sudden, startling thought that these attendants were too like some of the Oriental dregs who served the Black Dragon. Polynesians of a mixed caste was the best way to define them—or the worst. Yet the men were polite as they bowed Steve into the large trophy room, which seemed the principal portion of the Norland Museum.

As Steve's footsteps echoed hollow on the tiled floor, he heard others coming toward him. Stopping abruptly, Steve faced a man who stepped from a doorway at the rear. The man was an American whose face was long and oval in shape. Steve was taking in details of thin eyebrows, thin hair above an elongated forehead, when the man's eyes fixed upon him.

Droopy eyes, with lids like shields, above straight nose and lips. With the merest flicker, the man raised his eyelids just far enough to survey Steve thoroughly. Then the man spoke in a drawly tone.

"I am Craig Norland. I suppose you came to look at the collection of weapons? Most people do."

Norland gestured Steve into the rear room, which was smaller but well-stocked. It contained many odd weapons, but Steve was unable to identify any except boomerangs and blowguns, so Norland politely classified others for him. The droopy man pointed out a weapon which was hanging on a small door at the rear of the room. Norland stated:

"A Filipino barong."

The barong was a two-foot sword that widened between hilt and point, but the really curious feature was its scabbard. The blade was sheathed between two fitted slabs of wood, held crudely together by thongs. Through the primitive lacings, Steve could see a very sharp edge. So tight were the thongs that Steve began to wonder how anyone could unsheathe a barong, if in a hurry.

"My grandfather went in for big game," remarked Norland. "So I made weapons my hobby. I thought the combination would be appropriate, particularly as we both traveled extensively in the Orient."

Steve was about to ask what part of the Orient interested Norland most, when he stopped himself. Glancing warily back across his shoulder, Steve heard Norland chuckle. A moment later, the back door of the museum was opening outward and Norland's hand was clamped firmly on Steve's shoulder, guiding the visitor through.

They were stepping into a high-walled garden in back of the museum, but for the moment Steve wasn't interested in such nearby surroundings. He was looking off above the wall toward the top of a great, sweeping superstructure that curved from one huge pillar off to another that seemed distant in the night.

The structure was one of the great suspension bridges that crossed the East River. This garden in back of the Norland Museum was located on the river bank itself. Oddly, the wall seemed specially designed to prevent anyone from looking into the garden.

For example, Steve could see the superstructure of the bridge, but not the roadway. Beyond the rear wall, he spied the passing smokestack of a steamer, but couldn't quite see the topmost deck.

The museum itself cut off any view from the Manhattan side, and putting those facts together, Steve lowered his gaze to the garden to learn why it was too unique to be submitted to public gaze. In one glance, Steve understood.

This was a Japanese garden!

LITERALLY, this product of Nippon might have been uprooted from the yard of Hirohito's own palace and transplanted to New York. It was a chunk of Japan in miniature, with an undersized pagoda no higher than the wall, a squatty Shinto shrine, humped bridges crossing a canal that ran between two pools that teemed with golden carp.

There were beds of exotic flowers, a crude waterwheel that turned under the constant pressure of a small, flowing stream. As Norland gestured Steve around the premises, more features came into view; one, for instance, being a pool so thick with lily pads and flowers that it looked like a solid, earthen bed.

They reached the squatty Shinto structure which stood shoulder-high. Norland opened its door and disclosed a peculiar curved sword in a scabbard of the same shape.

"A Japanese samurai sword," explained Norland. "It must never be drawn from its scabbard except for shedding blood. I am a stickler for such traditions, Trask."

Steve stared. He couldn't understand how Norland had guessed his name. Whereat Norland laughed quite heartily.

"I have no love for the Japanese," sneered

Norland. "None except so far as their arts and crafts are concerned. I shipped these mementos back here, piece by piece. Why should I sacrifice them because Japan has become unpopular?"

With a smile at his own mild way of putting it, Norland gestured toward the wall around the garden.

"Instead, I have seen that these souvenirs should remain hidden," resumed Norland. "I consider myself a man without a country, hence free to collect the trophies of every land. You have an oddity which I should like to add to those I already own."

REMOVING his strong hand from Steve's shoulder, Norland extended his palm upward and ordered:

"Give me the jet dragon." Mechanically, Steve placed the death token in Norland's palm, where it looked quite puny. Norland grated a laugh.

"I suppose the Black Dragon thought he could scare me by having a notorious murderer bring this token. Is that it, Trask?"

Things flashed home to Steve. Norland was using guesswork. First, he'd guessed who Steve was; that part was correct. But now he was guessing wide, in classing Steve as a server of the Black Dragon.

"You have it wrong, Norland," argued Steve. "That little knickknack is one the Black Dragon handed me through a Jap stooge named Sujan. The curse was supposed to get me, but it didn't."

"Crawling out of it!" scoffed Norland. "Well, I should have expected it. The Black Dragon knows enough about me."

WITH a swoop, Norland produced a sizeable tin box from a shelf above the samurai sword.

"Here's what the Black Dragon wants!" he stormed. "The money I brought back from Shanghai. His crowd tried to get it from me there, and there were two less when I finished. You think you're a killer, Trask." Norland's sneer was back. "The Black Dragon must think it, too, or wouldn't have sent you. He knows I'm a killer, because I've never tried to hide the history of my souvenirs. I've used every weapon to dispose of a victim, and in most cases it was outright murder!"

Norland gestured toward the open door of the museum where the barong was hanging in sight, as a sample of other deadly weapons. Replacing the tin box on its shelf, Norland folded his rangy arms, as though inviting Steve to attempt the first thrust. The long, strained silence was broken by the howl of police sirens, wailing weirdly through the neighborhood.

"Killer meets killer," snorted Norland. "The difference between us is only this, Trask. I do my murders outside the realm of jurisprudence. You can't call it crime, where there isn't any law. That's how I acquired the wealth that the Black Dragon wants."

Norland's tone rang too true to be doubted. He was a man who mocked death, particularly that of his own making, a calloused murderer, self-admitted, contemptuous of those belonging to his ilk, in which he included Steve.

"I could kill you with pleasure, Trask," continued Norland in a grating tone. "I have a weapon that is itching for someone's blood!"

Thinking of the barong, Steve swung hastily about. Across one of the humped bridges he saw the open door, with its hanging, slab-sheathed sword. Steve was nearer to that vantage point than Norland, but it didn't help.

In the doorway stood the two clay-faced attendants, both with drawn revolvers; behind them, another pair, evidently here at Norland's order!

"There is no escape," sneered Norland, his voice coming from Steve's shoulder. "You were recognized the moment you arrived. One of my men phoned the police commissioner at his club to tell him that you were here, bringing a death token."

Steve could still hear sirens wailing outside the garden walls. He wondered how the police had arrived so soon. But the sooner they appeared, the sooner Steve's death would be. For it was quite obvious that Norland intended to kill Steve. He was a man with blood-lust, Norland, and he would receive no penalty for disposing of a victim already wanted for murder!

Wondering why the servants didn't shoot, Steve turned suddenly and saw Norland. Gunfire wasn't necessary in Steve's case. From the Shinto shrine, Norland was taking the samurai sword, which once drawn from its scabbard, would have to be dyed with blood!

In order to use both hands, Norland was pocketing the tiny jet dragon. As he did, Norland announced:

"There is only one reason why the Black Dragon sent you here, Trask. He knew that when you delivered this, I would dispose of you for him. The messenger who brings such a token is never the killer. Murder is always left to others."

Murder left to others!

Even as Norland was drawing the samurai sword, a wave of hope swept Steve. Eager to take Steve's life, Norland had forgotten that he, himself, was marked for death by the fact that he had received a jet dragon!

Springing suddenly away from Norland's blade, Steve sped a glance to the museum door and saw that the guns of the foremost attendants had not budged. They weren't trained on Steve, those weapons; they were pointed straight at Norland!

The attendants were traitors bought out by the Black Dragon!

They were giving Norland his chance to kill Steve. After that, they would blast Norland by order of the Black Dragon. As Steve dashed for a humped bridge, with Norland close behind him, the two servants charged from their doorway.

SOMETHING whirred the air behind Steve's neck. It was the samurai sword, missing by a mere three inches. Steve tried to take a shortcut across a flower bed.

By mistake, Steve picked one of the shallow lily ponds. Tripping knee-deep among the pads, he was hardly out the other side before Norland was full upon him, poising the samurai blade for a terrific, murderous downswing.

From another angle, the two attendants were arriving with their guns, to cut Steve off from the museum. Under the shelter of the eight-foot pagoda, Steve was trapped in the most distant corner of the garden. His lurch ending in a sprawl against the stone wall itself, he could no more than turn and fling his arms upward in an effort too futile to ward off the coming swing of Norland's sword.

At that moment, when the death stroke seemed as good as home, Steve heard the only token that could bring a respite.

The laugh of The Shadow!

CHAPTER XIII
TRIUMPH'S FAILURE

THE SHADOW'S laugh ended in a shivering crash. Not the sort of crash that its echoes would normally produce, but a splintering sound that came with an increasing smash. Looking up, Steve saw blackness enveloping everything, blotting out Norland and his waving sword, eradicating the two gunners who were also lunging into the scene.

A block of blackness, much larger than The Shadow—such was the thing that ripped a path among the murderers. The squatty pagoda, pride of Norland's Japanese garden, was hurling downward like a mammoth bludgeon upon the inhuman killers just beneath it!

From the low roof of the toppled tower, Steve saw a cloaked figure spring to the ground beyond. Landing on his feet, The Shadow was full about with a drawn automatic, ready to add new feats of rescue.

Only The Shadow could have staged this sudden surprise. With all the police in town hot on the trail of the commissioner's car, it hadn't taken them long to spot the vehicle that passed for it. They'd reported the chase by shortwave, from the very start, and The Shadow, listening in, had promptly headed for the neighborhood where it began.

The most conspicuous building thereabouts was the Norland Museum. Knowing something of its history. The Shadow had picked it as the place where Steve must have gone. Rather than batter at the huge front portals, he'd tried the wall along the waterfront.

He was just in time, The Shadow, to see the chase reach the pagoda corner. He'd needed more than gunfire to take out three fighters at a clip, particularly when they were coming below his angle of range. Full force, he'd hurled himself upon the flimsy, ornamental pagoda and thrown it from its moorings and in among his foemen!

As yet, The Shadow hadn't learned that the attendants were traitors to their employer, Norland. What The Shadow had glimpsed looked like a mass attack, directed at Steve. Though jarred by the cracking pagoda, Norland and the other two weren't out of battle permanently. Moreover, The Shadow could see another pair of armed men coming from the rear door of the museum.

Hauling Steve to his feet, The Shadow started him on a quick circuit of the garden toward the museum door.

Half obscured by The Shadow's cloaked figure, Steve wasn't seen as he stumbled along. The Shadow didn't use the bridges, the way the second pair of attendants did. He cut through the flower beds, without picking lily ponds by mistake, made a detour past the waterwheel, and finally gave Steve a quick shunt in through the open doorway.

By that time, snarls could be heard from the far corner of the garden, where the second pair of attendants were helping the others from the debris of the pagoda. Steve was hoping that they would find Norland in the wreckage and treat him as the Black Dragon had ordered.

That thought made Steve turn to tell The Shadow what it was all about. A bad mistake on Steve's part. He was forgetting that those traitors intended to let Norland kill him first!

Dumbly blocking The Shadow off from the doorway, Steve didn't have time to explain things. Already The Shadow had drawn a second gun, planning to stave off any attack. Half turned, he shouldered into Steve and lost his stride toward the doorway. Then, before Steve could gulp a single word, Norland was upon them!

THE man who reveled in murder had evidently dodged the pagoda's crash sufficiently to be at large again, with comparatively short delay. He'd made a shortcut across the garden while The Shadow was taking the longer way about.

Still anxious to murder Steve, Norland was intent upon chopping through any obstacles. Among such, he included The Shadow, at present the only thing that blocked his path. Again the curved samurai blade was sweeping under the impulse of a murderer's hand, this time for The Shadow's head!

What The Shadow did was most amazing.

Coming up and around in cross-armed style, he threw a hand straight for the whipping sword. In that hand, The Shadow gripped a heavy gun that caught the stroke in midair. But the force of the terrific blow drove the .45 from The Shadow's fist, hooking it through the doorway that Steve had unwisely abandoned.

Moreover, The Shadow was carried with the swing, landing against the open door itself. He hadn't time to get his other automatic into play; in fact, he needed a free hand to stop his fall. Again, The Shadow performed in uncanny style, letting the second gun go riding over his shoulder, straight to a man who could use it without delay: Steve Trask!

A perfect toss, The Shadow's. Victory would be in the bag the moment Steve caught the lobbed automatic. Instead, Steve muffed it!

Bounding from Steve's frozen fingers, the gun landed in a flower bed. Madly Steve dived after it, to the tune of a whiplash from the samurai sword, another stroke meant for The Shadow. Norland's slash sliced half a sleeve from The Shadow's cloak, but missed the target underneath, for The Shadow was adding a roll to his fall. Then Steve, groping for a gun he couldn't find, looked up to see murder in its final process.

Coming up beside the door, The Shadow was grabbing the only weapon he could find, a Filipino barong. But the short sword was still in its thong-bound wooden scabbard as The Shadow tugged it from the door, whereas Norland's samurai blade was bare.

Down came the curved sword with a fury that could not be warded. Only the bite of a rival sword edge could divert such a slash. Blade for blade, The Shadow would have had a chance, but his weapon was still encased in its primitive scabbard.

Norland's face, alight with the joy of murder, seemed to outvie The Shadow's defiant laugh. Steel against wood, with Norland the man who held the metal! Steve thought it was all over with The Shadow as the two strokes passed.

FIRST to land was The Shadow's barong, and with the stroke its scabbard flew apart. What met Norland's shoulder was not a mere sheath composed of two wooden slabs, but a biting blade that hewed its course through the leather thongs, cutting them apart in the process!

Norland reeled, his own stroke going wide. The Shadow couldn't have deflected the samurai sword, so he diverted Norland's arm instead. In its blow, the unleashed barong cleaved half through Norland's shoulder, literally unhinging the arm below it. And Steve, a witness to that short-lived fray, was realizing that the correct way to unsheathe a barong was to use it!

Unique among weapons, a barong did not have to be drawn from its scabbard, as The Shadow had demonstrated!

Rolling after his own wide stroke, Norland sprawled. Blood was pouring from his shoulder down to the samurai sword, staining the long, curved weapon. Norland, at least, was maintaining the tradition; the Japanese weapon was tasting blood—Norland's own!

It didn't satisfy Norland. Savagely, he tried to come to his feet, swinging the curved sword with his other hand. Instead of fending with the barong, The Shadow made a long dive through the doorway, a thing which made Steve wonder until he heard the blast of guns.

The men in the far corner of the garden were opening fire. They were aiming at The Shadow, until he made his quick feint away from their first shots. Then, seeing Norland reeling to his feet, the charging crew of half-breed Japs gave him a point-blank volley.

As Norland sprawled, Steve found the missing gun. He aimed for a skulker in a flower bed, only to hear another shot from atop a bridge. Steve pulled the trigger and a roar deafened him. It wasn't the blast from the gun he had regained, but from another, fired out through the doorway.

The Shadow, too, had reclaimed an automatic, the one that Norland had slashed through the doorway. He was taking over in his usual style, his first shot being a crippling delivery that toppled the gunner who had aimed straight at Steve. There was a howl, followed by a splash, as the foiled marksman went over the rail of the bridge and landed in the canal.

Plucking the second gun from Steve's hand, The Shadow sent the rescued man off through a flower bed. Again guns barked, and when Steve reached the corner wall, he turned to witness the results. The Shadow was contending with three marksmen in a bizarre setting where they were quite at home.

Shots seemed to come from everywhere—stabs of flame from beneath the bridges, out of the lily pads, through the revolving spokes of the ancient waterwheel. Like Norland, these killers were trying to get rid of The Shadow in order to have a chance at Steve.

But from his safe corner, Steve could hear The Shadow's laugh, accompanying the return shots. In attempting to outshoot The Shadow, those assassins were committing another form of hara-kiri. The Shadow's laugh was everywhere, his gun stabs anywhere—except those places where the skulkers aimed.

STEVE saw a patch of blackness flit across the lighted block that represented the museum doorway, but none of the snipers noticed it, for they were on the other side. A gun stabbed suddenly from beside the waterwheel, to test The Shadow's response.

It came promptly, that response, straight through the spokes of the wheel. An assassin sprawled, and another fired, too late. The Shadow had already spotted him and was one snipe ahead. As a figure rolled into a lily pond, Steve heard a gurgly cry:

"*Hayai! Hashi!*"

Steve was to learn later that those words meant: "Quick—the bridge:" Apparently one of the sagging Japs was telling the last of the tribe where to find The Shadow. Up sprang a crouched killer, his gun chattering a stream of bullets into the hump of the nearest bridge as he charged for the span itself.

Tuned to a weird laugh, came a single shot from near the Shinto structure in the garden's center. The Shadow's final jab sent the last Jap spinning from the bridge. Only then did Steve realize that The Shadow, himself, had gargled those words in Japanese.

While the last assassin was taking his sprawl across the bridge rail, shots came from within the museum. Flashlights were glaring from the doorway, directed by men in blue uniforms. Attracted by the gunfire, the police had crashed their way through the front door of the old museum!

While the amazed cops were staring at the scene before them, a hand gripped Steve and started him upward to the wide base of the overturned pagoda. Another boost from The Shadow, and Steve was going over the wall itself. Police saw him and shouted, but by then he was across, with blackness following after him.

At least they'd recognized Steve, for guns were barking, but the bullets were merely bashing the wall or whizzing above. Not only was Steve in the clear, but The Shadow was with him, thrusting him into a small rowboat that was moored beside the wall.

Using an oar as a paddle, The Shadow was propelling the boat silently beneath the great bridge. Past the bridge, they came ashore beside a dead-end street just as a police boat came scooting down the river, to play its part in the coming manhunt.

Moe's cab was waiting on the dead-end street. Soon it was snaking a course past converging police cars that were all bound toward the East River, while The Shadow and Steve were riding westward. From the darkness beside him, Steve heard a whispered laugh.

It was The Shadow's token of triumph, another victory over insidious crime, amplified by the details which Steve related concerning Craig Norland, the murderer who had defied the Black Dragon.

In that tone, Steve detected a prophetic note, as though The Shadow had already begun some new mission. For The Shadow had a way of packing one triumph upon another in rapid succession.

This time the rule was working in reverse. From triumph, The Shadow was traveling to failure!

CHAPTER XIV
THE UNSEEN HAND

THE cab came to an abrupt stop. It was somewhere in Greenwich Village, a district well distant from the Norland Museum. Steve noticed a slight stir beside him; the swish of a cloak as the cab door opened. Then The Shadow's whispered tone:

"You will wait here. Certain of my agents will soon join you and introduce themselves. Should they be needed, they will be summoned, you among them."

With that, The Shadow was gone. Gripped with the urge for action, Steve would have followed, but for the fact that Moe shoved his hand through from the front seat and prevented Steve from opening the door that The Shadow had just closed.

"He'll be back," assured Moe. "He's just gone up to make sure that everything is all right with Myra."

"Who is Myra?" inquired Steve.

"Ming Dwan," explained Moe. "Her real name is Myra Reldon. She should have stayed at Doc Tam's. Instead, she went home."

"To Li Huang's?"

"No. To her own apartment."

Steve could now understand how the girl had flashed warnings that night at Li Huang's. It hadn't been East meeting West. Myra had simply dropped her Chinese pose for Steve's benefit.

Steve's thoughts jumped from the past to the present. The Shadow had told him of events at Li Huang's tonight. In disposing of Li Huang, the Black Dragon had nearly taken Myra's life as well. Spies of the Dragon Clan might have been watching for the pretended Ming Dwan after she left Tam's. In that case, her present peril could be greater than before!

Such was the reason why The Shadow was entering the apartment house where Myra Reldon lived as her real self!

Already a swirl of blackness was filtering through the dim entry of the apartment building. Reaching the automatic elevator, The Shadow entered it imperceptibly. The car started upward when he pressed the button, and immediately afterward the cloaked fighter drew a brace of guns. Should foemen be listening for the elevator's buzz, he would be ready to meet them the moment the car stopped at Myra's floor.

The Shadow was ready for all eventualities, except the thing that happened!

As it stopped, the elevator gave a sudden jar. A cable gave a clack above the car. Then the car simply lost all holds and dropped!

Down plummeted the elevator with The Shadow boxed inside it. The twang of a broken cable sounded like a giant's harp string, tuned to a note of death!

There was a crash as the car hit the bottom of the shaft. New sounds clanged up from the basement level, where the car had struck. Clashing discords, like a hideous chorus of brazen-throated ghouls!

Then silence from the shaft. Low, babbling voices took up the tale from lurking spots within the apartment house. Creatures who served the Black Dragon were posted here, awaiting the crash that would mark The Shadow's doom. As if in vengeance for the members of their clan who had died at the Norland Museum, these lurkers had heard the clatter that turned The Shadow's triumph into failure!

QUITE oblivious to her present menace, Myra Reldon was emerging from a bathtub where she had soaked for nearly half an hour to dispose of the special dye that formed her Ming Dwan complexion. Myra was smiling as she slid her arms into a dressing gown and stepped into a pair of slippers. A weight in the pocket of her gown caused her smile to fade.

The weight was a gun. It reminded her that she might still be hearing from the Black Dragon, whose efforts to gain a hold in Chinatown had been thwarted largely through Myra's own endeavors. Myra tried to shrug away the illusion of danger as she stepped into the living room and turned toward the bedroom door.

A hiss jogged Myra's memory anew. Coming about, she saw a man she recognized. He was one of Li Huang's former servants, a traitor who had worked for a traitor!

The man with the Mongolian look was toying with a knife. He watched for Myra's reaction to see if she would betray herself as Ming Dwan. But the resemblance between Myra and her Chinese counterpart was nil. In American style, Myra displayed her bewilderment, whereupon the man with the knife hesitated.

There was another hiss. Myra turned to see the second of Li Huang's former servitors. This fellow was angry at the other's hesitation. Still, Myra continued to bluff, hoping that these invaders wouldn't find her Ming Dwan costume which she had stowed deep in the bedroom closet.

For Myra was confident that The Shadow would soon rescue her from this predicament. Her cloaked friend was one who never failed. Hopefully, Myra looked toward the door from the outside hall, expecting The Shadow to materialize.

Instead, a snaky figure crept forward. It was the third of Li Huang's servants, the most insidious of the trio. Reaching Myra, the creeper whipped a hand into sight and extended it palm upward. In the bowl of his hand rested a jet dragon with eyes of jade!

The death token!

This was the real test. If Myra quailed, she would admit herself to be Ming Dwan. The recollection of a jet dragon that had become a living lizard charged with deadly venom was something that could not be quickly eradicated.

Despite herself, Myra recoiled with a shriek.

The scream gave her away. The knife men lunged with their deadly blades. Still staggering backward, Myra gave a frenzied glance toward the door.

No sign of The Shadow; no sound of his laugh. Too late for the mighty rescuer to deliver the aid that Myra needed. Tripping, Myra sprawled. As she toppled, she saw the glitter of the knife blades flashing toward her.

Then blackness obliterated all.

With the toss of those knives, every light in the apartment house was extinguished. Flat on the floor, Myra heard the passing whispers of the knives above her. Darkness had arrived just in time to spoil the aim of the assassins. Only The Shadow could have supplied so sudden an interruption. He had not failed!

COMING to her feet, Myra encountered a foot stool, the thing that had so luckily tripped her. But she still wasn't safe. The killers whose knives had missed were lunging toward her in the dark! The lights came on again, and Myra kicked the footstool at the nearest assassin, sending a slipper with it. The lights went off.

On and off—on and off—

Such was the behavior of the lights as Myra dashed about the living room, flinging everything she could find: chairs, tables, even books. The whole thing was a mad dream in this kaleidoscopic setting where blinking lights produced a deceptive blur.

Better than darkness, those blinks. Knowing the apartment, Myra, could gain her bearing, whereas her pursuers couldn't. All the while, the lights kept up their eccentric behavior, sometimes short, then long in their flashes.

The man with the Mongolian look was toying with a knife!

They were spelling a word in Morse code: "*Come*!"

Help was on its way. The Shadow was bringing it, even though his own plight might be serious! As a blink showed the bedroom door, Myra dodged through, escaping the grasp of grabbing hands that managed only to catch the corner of her gown. Wrenching from that lone hold, Myra slammed the door home and turned the key. Amid the blinking light, she reached an open window which had a ledge leading to an adjoining roof.

Blinks ended and the lights stayed off. Men were pounding up the stairs in order to reach Myra's apartment. Assassins quit hammering at the inner door and dashed out to the corridor where they were met by guns and flashlights brandished by The Shadow's agents.

Steve was a witness to what followed. Before Li Huang's former servants could use their regained knives, gunfire stopped them. One assassin was clipped at the stair top; he plunged across the rail and went down the narrow well to the ground floor, his howl trailing behind him.

The second flung himself through a window at the end of the hall and grabbed for something outside. A gun stab jounced him and he sprawled in space. Another screech drifted back from the depths.

The third, caught between a pair of guns, forgot about the elevator's fate. Yanking the door open, he dived for the car as though he expected to find it. His wail was hollow, like the crash that followed it.

There were four in the rescue party, not counting Steve. One, Clyde Burke, dashed into the apartment to call for Myra. The others threw flashlight beams into the elevator shaft. Seeing the broken cable, they started down the stairs. Steve followed them.

Spotting fresh members of the Dragon Clan, The Shadow's men began to use their guns along the ground floor. There was a scurry that reminded Steve of rats in flight, then the harried Dragon men reached a door to the basement, unbolted it and fled below.

Beyond the open door of an elevator that was bent but not broken, stood The Shadow. He was holding himself against the wall, clinging weakly to the master switch that controlled the lights in the apartment house. As enemies reached him, The Shadow tried weakly to draw a gun. The Dragon crew seized him. Hoisted on their shoulders, The Shadow disappeared around a corner of the cellar.

Unable to fire, The Shadow's agents followed, only to be blocked by a door that was slammed in their faces. By the time they pulled the door open and reached the rear street, the agents were nonplussed. Police were arriving, some on foot, others in patrol cars. Even an ambulance was scouting about to pick up the victims of a fray that had roused the entire neighborhood.

The Shadow was gone and his captors with him, as though some power of the Black Dragon had spirited them all into thin air!

CHAPTER XV
THE DRAGON'S DECREE

THE sound clashed through The Shadow's groping thoughts. *Clang!*

It didn't belong with the falling elevator or the light switch in the cellar. Not even with the shouts that The Shadow had heard his agents give!

Clang!

The sound meant motion, for it went with the vehicle in which The Shadow rode. He heard voices babbling beside him, but when he tried to rise, he couldn't. His hands and feet were tightly bound.

Clang!

This time the signal meant "Stop." The Shadow was lifted on a stretcher and carried out through a door that opened in the middle. In the light of a dim street, he looked back and saw the vehicle which had brought him: an ambulance!

The Dragon Clan had managed the impossible. They had captured The Shadow. They'd needed the ambulance for a getaway only, a purpose which it filled to perfection. Neither the police nor The Shadow's own agents had thought of trailing an ambulance, working on an errand of mercy.

Small mercy for The Shadow!

In the solid-walled room where his captors flung him, The Shadow looked up into the glaring light to see the Black Dragon attired in his writhing costume.

The forced voice hissed:

"This is your finish, Shadow! You have found me, and the deed itself means death! You are helpless, so helpless that you cannot even preserve the secret of your identity!"

With that, the Black Dragon whipped away the slouch hat and looked at the face of Cranston in the light. There was just a trace of surprise in the sharp hiss that the Dragon gave. Then, planting the hat at an angle on The Shadow's head, the hooded man sneered:

"Perhaps I should also unmask. It would give you satisfaction to know who I am. That happens to be the reason why I shall not disclose my identity."

Wearily, The Shadow laughed. His tone carried a trace of Cranston's bored style.

"Quite unnecessary," he said. "You have made the whole thing very obvious. I know who you are."

The Dragon snarled in sudden derision. Turning about, he ordered his followers to shift the light. When they did, The Shadow saw a square-walled room with a door at the other side. At the Dragon's gesture, a pair of pock-faced men lifted The Shadow and carried him to the door. The Dragon opened it, kicked a doorstop and let The Shadow watch the closet floor slide open.

Below was a pit, approximately twelve feet wide. From each of its four walls projected knifelike spikes, a few inches in length. The Dragon reached for a wire that ended in a switch. Pressing the switch, he produced an electric buzz; with it, the spikes issued slowly from the walls. When they had emerged a few inches, the Dragon turned off the current.

"A comfortable nest," sneered the Dragon. "In it, a person could survive about five minutes. By then the spikes will be fully extended, intermingling to cover the entire pit. It will not be a pleasant death. Or should I say—it would not?"

The Shadow studied the pit. Its interior measurements were about six feet by six. The Dragon's five-minute estimate was approximately correct.

With a sweeping motion, The Dragon ordered his men to cut The Shadow's bonds. They did so; then the Dragon personally supplied the quick shove that sent the cloaked prisoner down into the pit. Grazing the spikes in one wall that he passed, The Shadow knew that they were sharp.

"Five minutes," the Dragon repeated. "During that time, anything you care to say will be heard through a loudspeaker in this room above. Simply call me by name—my real name—and I shall stop the spikes. But remember"—the tone came harsh—"no guesses are allowed. One false statement ends my offer!"

Unlimbering, The Shadow stood upright in the pit, his head six feet below the edge. He touched the spikes with his fingertips and gave an indifferent shrug. Reaching for his guns, The Shadow found that he no longer had them. The gesture pleased the Dragon. He beckoned to a man beside him and received one of The Shadow's automatics.

"I appreciate the suggestion," scoffed the Dragon. "After all, Shadow, if your guess fails, you will have to accept the spikes. I shall then have no way of knowing how far you quailed at death. So I shall be generous, and give you this gun! Should I hear it fire, I shall know that your bravery is a myth."

The Black Dragon kicked the doorstop in order to bring the floor shut. As the space narrowed, he dropped the gun. Before The Shadow could catch the weapon, the floor was shut. There was a sharp clicking as hidden catches took hold within the wooden floor.

Swinging the closet door shut, The Black Dragon

turned on the current that started the interlocking spikes. The first sound that came over the loud-speaker was the defiant laugh of The Shadow. Arms folded, the Dragon waited, his breath coming with a hiss.

THERE were less minutes than the five that he had promised. That period marked the time when the spikes would be fully home. The Shadow would have to speak before then or take the punishment of the stabbing points. So the Black Dragon waited only briefly, before he snarled through a microphone:

"All right, Shadow. Who am I?"

A laugh sounded in amplified tone. Then came The Shadow's reply:

"Commissioner Weston!"

With a fling, the Black Dragon threw aside the switch that alone could stop the spikes. Turning on his heel, he paused by the microphone for a final statement.

"A fatal jest, Shadow," he said. "Not knowing who I really am, you thought that you could taunt me or arouse my sense of humor. Your life will be very short from now on. You know it better than I, for you can see the closing spikes. Of course, you still have the gun I gave you!"

Striding across the room, the Black Dragon paused by the door and waited. His head had a tilt that added greater realism to the open-mouthed hood. He was a dragon indeed, this creature, as he listened for the token that would brand The Shadow as a coward. So well timed was the estimate that the Dragon was uncoiling himself toward the door, his hands dropping like flapping scales, when the sound came.

A gun blast from the spiked pit!

One of the Dragon's followers moved toward the cord that terminated in the switch. With a snarl, the Dragon ordered the fellow back. That switch wasn't to be touched until the spikes were home. Beckoning for other men to follow, the Black Dragon strode out through the door.

There was a clang from the ambulance as it took the Black Dragon to his next destination. More clangs, that faded in the distance. The last was echoing back when the buzzing ceased, telling that The Shadow, dead or living, was impaled upon four bristling batches of spikes. If The Shadow still lived, he wouldn't survive that hideous ordeal long.

Convinced of that, the Black Dragon had been free to leave. His departure, however, was spurred by a more positive belief. The Black Dragon was sure that he had heard The Shadow deliver a suicide blast, a thing which pleased the Dragon more. In any event, the decree of the Dragon was fulfilled.

Death to The Shadow!

CHAPTER XVI
TWO KEYS TO CRIME

EXCITEMENT still reigned outside the Greenwich Village apartment house. Indoors, heavy footsteps were pounding up the stairs, denoting police who were coming to search the premises. Steve Trask was only half a floor ahead when he reached the door of Myra Reldon's apartment.

Outside the door stood Clyde Burke. Head tilted, the reporter was listening to the sounds from below. When Steve arrived, Clyde reached out a hand, took the breathless man's arm and steered him right into the apartment.

A moment later, Clyde was inside, too, closing the door behind him. The reporter said, "Sit down. The police won't bother us. That broken elevator cable will worry them for a while."

Steve couldn't have accepted Clyde's invitation unless he'd chosen a seat on the floor. Every chair in the room was overturned; some of them were broken. The room looked like a hurricane exhibit.

Anxiety swept Steve's face.

"What about Myra Reldon?" he panted. "Did... did they—"

"They didn't," interposed Clyde.

He picked up a chair and planted it for Steve. "Myra dodged them while the lights were blinking. She got into the other room and bolted the door just before we arrived to break up the party. Myra will be out in a few minutes."

Clyde picked up two knives that were lying in a corner of the room, where they'd rebounded when they struck the fireproof wall. He handed Steve the souvenirs, then strolled to the window. Clyde beckoned and Steve came over.

Looking across rooftops and down between, Steve saw the cab that Clyde indicated. It was nosing from an alley a few blocks distant, timing its departure between the passing of patrol cars. It was The Shadow's cab, leaving with the other agents.

Stout fellows, those. One, Harry Vincent, had impressed Steve by his clean-cut style, which seemed an equal measure of his fighting ability. Another, Cliff Marsland, was more rugged in appearance, and as hard-fisted as he looked. But the third, a diminutive man with wizened face, who answered to the name of Hawkeye, was by no means a supernumerary. To say that Hawkeye was a pint of human dynamite wouldn't be doing him justice. He packed a wallop more like TNT.

Each of the trio had accounted for one of the Dragon's followers, and now the three were departing while the police were gathering the remains. The police would certainly be stymied for a while when they found the assassin who had dived down the elevator shaft. They'd wonder why he wasn't inside the wrecked car, instead of lying on top of it!

"They're off to hunt for the chief," observed Clyde grimly. "There's no better hackie in town than Moe Shrevnitz. If there's a trail within a mile, he'll smell it. But the way The Shadow vanished taking that whole crowd with him—well, I just don't get it."

The bedroom door opened and Myra Reldon stepped into the living room. Her dark-blue dress was smartly fashioned, American style, well-suited to a striking brunette like Myra. It did justice to her trim build, quite as well as the Chinese costume which she had worn as Ming Dwan. The girl's real change was in her face.

FOR the moment, Steve was startled. He thought that Myra was deathly pale, on the point of wilting from her recent experience. Then Steve realized that the effect was his own imagination. Remembering Myra as Ming Dwan, he'd classed her complexion as that of yellow-ivory. The illusion of pallor faded from Steve's mind when he studied Myra's face in terms of normal white.

Methodically, Myra began to straighten the room. Steve and Clyde helped. She smiled when she set the footstool where it belonged, but her lips went a trifle grim when she saw the knives that Steve had laid aside.

Then, picking up a dressing gown from the floor, Myra rolled the knives inside it with a pair of slippers and took the whole bundle into the bedroom, where she stowed it deep on a closet shelf with the Ming Dwan costume. Returning, Myra looked from Steve to Clyde, her eyes asking an anxious question.

"No word yet," said Clyde a bit solemnly. "Moe just took the boys to the hunt. We'll hear from Burbank if they find the chief."

Who Burbank was, Steve didn't inquire. Glancing from the window, Steve saw a big official car nose into the front street, pause as though poking into matters, and then continue on its way.

"Look, Burke!"

"No soap, Trask," said Clyde, when he saw the car that Steve pointed out. "That's the commish in person. The phony job is out of circulation. Half the force grabbed it."

"They questioned the driver?"

"Yes. I was covering the story when you and the chief went by in Shrevvy's cab. The chauffeur was an A-1 dope who thought he was really working for Weston. He'd stopped at Gotham Court to pick up a passenger for Norland's. He was going back to some old garage when the law clamped down on him."

Steve felt an inward groan. There wasn't any way to beat the Black Dragon's game, the way all the trails evaporated the further they were followed. Nobody had even begun to beat it, except The Shadow, but his technique lay in putting things in reverse. For instance, tonight, The Shadow had let the police swarm after the fake, official car, just so he could locate where it had come from—namely, Norland's house.

A thought hit Steve like a sunburst. He wanted a key to crime and he had one. Why not carry The Shadow's system further, by tracing back to an earlier starting point? The fake, official car had been at Gotham Court before it went to Norland's. There was the place to use crime's key!

Steve didn't express the thought to the others. Myra was becoming really worried, so Clyde was using the phone to call Burbank just in case there was some word of The Shadow. A glance from the window showed that the street was deserted, so Steve strolled from the apartment unobserved and quickened his pace as he started down the stairs.

THERE wasn't any copyright on the idea of checking backward trails. Clyde, Myra, the rest of The Shadow's agents all had the thing in mind. They'd rejected it because the trail they wanted led ahead to some hidden location where The Shadow had been carried as a prisoner.

So far, the agents hadn't an inkling as to where that place might be. Even if they'd found it, the atmosphere would have harrowed them. For the pall of doom was heavy in the square-walled room where the Black Dragon had decreed death to The Shadow.

Death delivered!

Two of the Dragon's followers were still present in that room, toying with revolvers they wouldn't have to use. Their ugly faces were exchanging evil leers. They had been ordered to wait, this pair, before withdrawing the spikes that impaled The Shadow's body. Now the time was up. One watcher gripped the door handle; the other turned to kick the stop that controlled the sliding floor. The door stuck as the first man tugged it. He yanked harder.

Flying wide, the door brought a mass of living blackness that reeled half across the room, came about with a sideward stagger, and disgorged a hand that swung a heavy gun. Blackness materialized into a cloaked figure, whose hidden lips trailed a strangely echoed laugh.

The Shadow, free from the spiked pit of death!

Frozen were the men who viewed this fabulous return. To the eyes that bulged from mud-hued faces, this was not The Shadow in bodily form. The babbled words they uttered were synonyms for the one term: "Ghost!"

The sweep of The Shadow's cloak displayed the proof. The garment was marred with rips from the spikes that must have pierced the human form within. In any language, The Shadow was a ghost, for only such a creature could have emerged as he had.

Reeling toward the man who had yanked the door, The Shadow was an open target for the watcher's gun. Too open, for The Shadow's own drive wavered. He couldn't seem to bring his automatic to aim. A few shots, point-blank, would have drilled The Shadow, but the man with the revolver didn't fire.

Of what use were bullets against a ghost?

Missing in aim, The Shadow swung his gun. His foeman went prostrate ahead of the weapon's sweep. Stopped when his stroke thwacked the door, The Shadow stumbled half across the figure that was bowing, pleading at his feet. He turned, steadying himself against the door, to aim at the other man.

NO aim was needed. That watcher was prostrate, too, hoping that he'd share The Shadow's grace. Both babbling men were tossing their guns along the floor, to prove that they wouldn't think of using such weapons, even in a case where bullets couldn't count.

Again The Shadow uttered his chilling mirth.

His tone, like his actions, proved that he hadn't fully recuperated from the plunge in the elevator, but his laugh was all the more ghostly. It was preferable to keep it so, to preserve the illusions held by these Dragon men.

Superstitious creatures, these, who had often witnessed the Black Dragon's vanish from his gilded throne and believed it to be real sorcery. They were of the right breed to accept The Shadow's reappearance as superior wizardry. Even their brief sight of The Shadow's face had not shattered their ghost theory. Lacking his slouch hat, The Shadow was displaying the features of Lamont Cranston. That detail was easily rectified.

The Shadow stepped to the closet. Its sliding floor was already open; the shot which the Black Dragon had mistaken for The Shadow's suicide had served another purpose. With it, the cloaked prisoner had blasted the woodwork above the pit, releasing the simple catch that held the sliding floor.

And now The Shadow demonstrated how he had escaped the sharp-pronged spikes.

He pressed the switch that controlled them. As the spikes receded, The Shadow waited until sufficient space showed in their boxed center. Down into that spiked vortex he descended, using the slowly moving spikes as the rungs of an improvised ladder!

At the bottom, The Shadow paused until the spikes had withdrawn a few more inches; stopping, he reclaimed his slouch hat. Deliberately, he duplicated his original escape, deftly climbing the pointed rods, shifting conveniently from one wall to another, but always avoiding the sharpened spike-tips.

In the first climb, the final spikes had caught his trailing cloak while he was gaining a grip inside the closet door. In wrenching the black garment free, The Shadow had caused those rips that had so impressed the guarding dragon men.

The cowed guards were still prostrate, their noses flat to the floor. The Shadow spoke in a commanding tone. Shaky, but willing, they arose and lunged toward the outer door.

Out into the waiting night, The Shadow marched the cowering pair, confident they would direct him to their former master, the Black Dragon!

CHAPTER XVII
PATHS TO THE DRAGON

DR. TAM looked up from his desk and studied the two nondescript Orientals who faced him. Though they were of mixed lineage, Tam could see that they were of Japanese strain, this pair that had been captured by The Shadow.

Being familiar with the Japanese language, Tam put questions in that tongue. They replied volubly under the nudge of guns that bulged from blackness behind them. The fact that The Shadow was still present caused them to magnify his prowess.

In the opinion of the prisoners, The Shadow was a *Kitsumi-tsuki*, a being who controlled the foxes and made them do his bidding. So powerful was The Shadow that he might even be *Inari*, the fox god, in person.

When that outburst ended, Tam pretended to class the prisoners as Li Huang's former servants. Sternly he asked if they had delivered the kogo to Li Huang. Since *kogo* was the Japanese term for a small box with a lid, Tam's question was an implication that these men had personally seen to Li Huang's death by giving him the jewel case that contained the poison lizard.

When both protested innocence, Tam said he would believe them if they told him where to find the Black Dragon's *kura*, or hidden treasure room. They said they couldn't, but they did know where the Dragon Clan would meet—later tonight.

When the pair had given the necessary details, Tam summoned his own men and had them remove the prisoners. Whereupon, blackness laughed, and materialized itself into the form of The Shadow. Bowing to his cloaked friend, Tam declared that he would send men to raid the meeting place, but The Shadow had a better plan.

"I shall go alone," he declared. "The whole spirit of the clan hinges upon the Black Dragon.

Once his boasts are nullified, his followers will desert him. I proved that with the pair I captured."

Tam frowned. In whispered tone, The Shadow assured him that this plan would work. Though he nodded, Tam retained his frown because of something else.

"You were missing for quite a while, Ying Ko," reminded Tam. "During that time, Steve Trask disappeared. Your contact man, Burbank, phoned me and said your agents were unable to find him."

"Tell Burbank to send them to Sauber's," ordered The Shadow. "That is where Trask would go to look for trouble. They should be able to keep him from finding it."

The Shadow's own destination was the meeting place that the prisoners had named and described to Dr. Tam. If ever there had seemed a false trail, this was it, for it seemed the last place in New York where the Dragon Clan would dare to assemble. That fact, in itself, convinced The Shadow that the trail was real.

THE spot in question was the old building directly across the dead-end street from the Norland Museum, a structure almost under the shelter of the great bridge that spanned the East River!

It happened that The Shadow could understand the Black Dragon's purpose in choosing such a rendezvous. Had things gone as the Dragon planned, this place would have been perfect. The police would have found Norland dead, presumably murdered by Steve, who in turn was to have died at the hands of the museum attendants. The Dragon had counted on the police releasing those killers on the ground of justified action.

Instead, the treacherous attendants had met their own doom from The Shadow. That fact, however, had closed the case more definitely. With Steve alive and at large, the police were spreading their search, which meant that the Dragon Clan could still meet at its chosen place.

Nearing the building in question, The Shadow approached it from the bridge side. Noting activity along the waterfront, he saw that the police were still trying to trace Steve's course. They had found the rowboat and were making inquiries from persons in the neighborhood.

Soon, the police would be gone, but The Shadow's plans called for immediate investigation of the premises where the meeting was to be held. Having brought along a black bag filled with varied equipment, The Shadow adopted a unique method of entering the three-story building.

Instead of approaching by the street, he took an obscure route leading up to the bridge itself. Gliding along a deserted footwalk by the rail, The Shadow reached a spot directly above the building that squatted below.

From his bag, The Shadow produced a cylindrical object like a huge measuring tape, a dozen inches across. He hooked the device to the outside rail of the bridge. Gripping a small stirrup that projected from the cylinder, The Shadow swung himself across the rail and dropped into space.

There was a weird whine as a thin but powerful wire uncoiled from the cylinder. Like a living spider, The Shadow dropped in dangling fashion to the rooftop more than fifty feet below. The process was very simple, except for the outward swing that was needed to clear the space between the bridge and building, which were not quite on a vertical line.

Nevertheless, The Shadow made it with a comfortable margin. Nor was his drop too rapid, for the coil was braked by a mechanism in the cylinder. Indeed, The Shadow spent less than half of the wire's length in reaching his destination. Settled on the roof, he released the stirrup and the wire drew it upward with a powerful spring action. The cylinder itself could be retrieved later, after this adventure was completed.

From the bag, The Shadow took a portable jimmy that fitted on the end of an automatic. He pried open a trapdoor and descended into the forgotten structure that had once been an office building. When he reached the second floor, he found that the prisoners hadn't lied to Dr. Tam.

The stage was set for the meeting. There was an outer office, square and of sizeable proportions, with ornamental screens along its walls. Since there were several of these, the screen behind the Dragon's throne did not look suspicious.

Knowing the throne's trick, The Shadow sat down and pressed the arms. As he tilted back, the deceptive glass slid down to produce its mirror effect. The back of the throne revolved with the central panel of the screen, and The Shadow arrived in an inner office which was quite dark.

Through the rear window The Shadow saw a fire escape, the convenient route which the Black Dragon would use. So The Shadow descended silently and reached the window of another empty suite directly below the meeting place.

A whispered laugh was absorbed by darkness as The Shadow entered the lower window, carrying his bag. This first-floor office would serve as his own headquarters until the Dragon Clan arrived. There were certain preparations to be made, after which The Shadow could move about the neighborhood as he chose, since the police were giving up their hunt along the waterfront.

A final duel was impending between The Shadow and the Black Dragon—a duel wherein skill in mysterious ways would constitute the weapons!

MEANWHILE, Steve Trask was exactly where The Shadow expected him to be, outside Sauber's house in Gotham Court. Steve was just about to try the front door when a big car pulled up outside the archway. Steve dropped quickly from sight below the steps, because he recognized the car as Weston's.

At least it couldn't be the spurious vehicle belonging to the Black Dragon! That false car had been taken into custody, so it constituted a menace no longer.

With Commissioner Weston was Miles Fenmore. The pair were admitted to Sauber's house by Pelly, the secretary. As soon as the door closed, Steve ascended the steps and tried the doorknob. It proved unlatched, so Steve entered.

The ground floor was dimly lighted, and there wasn't a servant in sight. Steve moved stealthily toward a stairway, then rapidly sought the darkness behind it as he heard footsteps coming from the second floor. Looking up through the banister rails, Steve saw Weston and Fenmore coming down, with Sauber right behind them.

In his usual style, Sauber was protesting ignorance of anything and everything that concerned the Black Dragon. He even doubted that the fray in Greenwich Village could have anything to do with the Dragon problem. His argument on that score was still the same: the whole business of the Black Dragon was a myth.

Neither Weston nor Fenmore offered comment, but their faces showed annoyance. At the front door, they met Cardona coming up the steps, and the inspector went along with them. Steve heard Weston telling Fenmore that he'd drop him off at his house; then the three were on their way to the commissioner's car, without even saying good night to Sauber.

The curt departure didn't hurt Sauber's feelings. If anything, it pleased him. Bolting the door, the tawny-faced man turned toward the stairs, and Steve, well-huddled from sight, saw a gleam from narrowed eyes that suited the sly smile of Sauber's almost lipless mouth.

When Sauber started up the stairs, Steve followed. What worried him was the absence of Pelly. But when Sauber entered an office on the second floor, Steve saw that the secretary was awaiting him. Deep in the office was another door with a large, upright cabinet shoved halfway through it. Steve decided that he could spy best by sneaking around to that adjacent room.

Steve reached his goal easily enough, but found the room stacked with trunks and crates, like other rooms that he passed on the way. Evidently the containers held the excess imports that Sauber had ordered on a lavish, wholesale scale when he foresaw that sources would be cut off.

Working in among the crates, Steve saw some with Japanese letters and the word "Silk." Others were labeled "Tea" and "Quinine." Most curious of all was a huge box marked "Tapioca," which Steve decided to climb upon so he could look across the cabinet that blocked the connecting door to the office.

To Steve, this emphasis on imports could be the cover-up for Sauber's real game—the Black Dragon racket. Certainly Sauber must know much about the credits—and cash—of businessmen returned from the Far East. Knowing who had money and who hadn't, the Black Dragon could stretch his insidious claws into the affairs of anyone he chose.

Such were Steve's thoughts as he peered across the blocking cabinet in order to spy on Sauber and his secretary, Pelly. Like The Shadow, Steve Trask was seeking the Black Dragon. But through Steve's brain was surging the idea that he had already found the monster in question—in the person of Carlton Sauber!

CHAPTER XVIII
HIGH-LEVEL BATTLE

THOSE shrewd eyes of Sauber's still had their sly look as his gaze ran through some papers that Pelly handed him. Finished with the sheets, Sauber crumpled them, touched them with a match and threw the burning wad into a metal wastebasket.

"Good work, Pelly," complimented Sauber. "These reports tally. Therefore, we can assume that the men who supplied them are properly informed, since you say that they do not know one another."

What the reports were, Sauber did not specify. While they burned, he opened the drawer of an ornamental desk and brought out a bundle of letters.

"Take these to Fenmore," ordered Sauber. "Tell him I found them after he left. They prove that he is right and I am wrong—that there is a Black Dragon. It is just as well that I should find it out. A man's status is always improved when he admits that he can be wrong."

Pelly left with the letters, and Sauber, softly drumming the desk, listened until he heard the front door close. Giving a sly glance at the ashes of the burned report sheets, Sauber brought a Japanese puzzle box from the desk drawer. Finding the secret spring, Sauber pressed it. The box popped open, and into Sauber's hand dropped a jet dragon with tiny, bead-green eyes!

Pocketing the death token, Sauber arose and approached the cabinet in the doorway. Steve slid out of sight to the tapioca crate and listened to a sharp click, so close to his ear that it could only mean that Sauber was opening a secret compartment, deep in the cabinet.

When Steve raised his head for another look, he saw the thing he expected. Carlton Sauber was putting on a costume that he had taken from the hiding place—a costume that seemed alive because of the writhes it gave. A robe of silver and gold, literally enfolded in the coils of an embroidered dragon absolutely black in hue!

The costume was a perfect disguise when Sauber finished by drawing the hood over his head and face. To Steve's amazed gaze, the hood became a dragon's mouth, yawning wide, with an eye-slit between its fangs. More monster than man, Sauber writhed out of the room and down the stairs to the front door!

As fast as he could, Steve followed. From the front door, he saw the dragon shape snaking out through one of the archways. At the other, a cab was pulling to a stop, and Steve decided there was no time to lose. Full speed he dashed for the cab, to be met by persons coming from it.

They were friends: The Shadow's agents!

Myra was with them, and when they motioned Steve inside the cab, he found himself beside the girl. Harry was on the other side, while Cliff and Hawkeye perched in the folding seats. The cab, of course, was Moe's, and the speedy driver was off like a whippet the moment Steve told what he'd learned about Sauber.

Around the corner, Moe spotted a car ahead. It could only be Sauber's, so Moe took up the trail. But they hadn't gone many blocks before Hawkeye, peering back in his sharp-eyed style, spotted a pair of cars behind them.

The situation was self-evident. Those cars were on hand to eliminate any trailing vehicle such as Moe's cab!

THE triple chase kept on, threatening to break into something more serious. When the chase was swinging into an area which Steve identified with the old Norland Museum, things began to happen fast.

Sauber's car took a turn leading toward a dead-end street. As Moe's cab darted in pursuit, the trailers roared into the attack. They wanted to overtake the cab before its riders saw where Sauber went, and they would have—if sudden intervention had not come.

From beside a ramp that led up at a right angle to the great bridge across the river, came the sudden jab of guns. Behind those weapons was a black-clad marksman whose presence here was proving of the timeliest sort.

It was The Shadow literally knocking the triple chase apart!

Sauber's car took a quick dart through an alley. That detour took the dragon-garbed man from the fray, but it was to cost him considerable time in reaching the meeting place, because the alley was a long one, with its outlet well above the bridge.

Recognizing The Shadow as the marksman, Moe performed accordingly. The skillful cabby took the shortest way out, to give The Shadow a chance at the pursuing cars which obviously contained members of the Dragon Clan. Moe's choice was the ramp leading up to the high-level bridge.

The pursuing cars were almost side by side. One took The Shadow's first shots and did a roundabout skid, that swung it across the other's path. To avoid a crash, the driver of the second car veered away and through sheer luck found the ramp. To add to such undeserved fortune, the veering car was shielded by the crippled vehicle and thus escaped The Shadow's gunfire!

Foreseeing what could happen next, The Shadow did not remain upon the scene. He disappeared like a puff of smoke, off between two buildings to the stairs that he had used before, those long steps leading up to the footwalk of the great bridge.

The Shadow's route was far the shorter. But when he reached the top, Moe's cab was already past, with the pursuing car close behind it. Guns were blazing back and forth as The Shadow's agents opened fire to stave off these members of the Dragon Clan. Far ahead, The Shadow saw a car swerve as it came from the other end of the bridge.

With Dragon servers coming from many places to attend their meeting, luck had again turned their way. The car from the other end was blocking off Moe's cab to put The Shadow's agents between two fires!

THE SHADOW had stopped beside the cylinder that contained the coiled wire. One gun drawn, his other fist was clutching the hand stirrup. Seeing that the cab was being trapped near the center of the bridge, The Shadow dashed along the footwalk. As he reached the end of the cable length, he hooked the stirrup over a huge bolt-head projecting from the bridge rail.

Then, with both guns drawn, The Shadow opened a rapid fire at the place where two cars had stopped with a cab at an angle in between them. Timely, indeed, was that gunnery. It halted men of the Dragon Clan in their tracks just as they were leaping from their cars to riddle the occupants of the beleaguered cab!

The Dragon fighters scattered, giving The Shadow's agents a chance for a counterattack. Leaping from the cab, the agents showed their stuff in no uncertain fashion. They were taking over the scene and capturing the two cars in the bargain, but a new brunt was being thrown on The Shadow.

Anxious to reach their meeting place, the foiled

Dragon men scurried for the footwalk. There, for the first time, they located The Shadow's gunfire. They ripped shots in response, an enfilading fire along the footwalk itself!

The Shadow had no chance to dart between big girders. Shots were coming from too many guns, and such a course would have boxed him in. Besides, The Shadow had no desire to prevent the meeting of the Dragon Clan. Having carried this fray away from the meeting place, he was anxious to get back there.

Hence, The Shadow sped ahead of the gunfire. Wild shots ricocheted from the steel posts all about him. Shooting foemen saw him only as a vague shape. The Shadow suddenly swerved beside the bridge rail and threw himself across and over it.

As he went, The Shadow seized the stirrup from its bolt. The wire twanged as it swept downward into the darkness.

Stretched to its full length, the wire was like a mammoth pendulum with The Shadow as its base. Seemingly, The Shadow was bound for a plunge into the river, but the steel wire stood the test. It was tugging, gathering into its cylinder, as The Shadow swooped toward water level.

Then, with the bridge high above him, The Shadow reached the limit of his dip. He was coming up again, shoreward, with the squatty building waiting to receive him, but he was too low to reach its roof!

This time, The Shadow hadn't made an outward leap. He profited by the fact, for as the wall came looming at him, he twisted just enough to miss its corner and take to space between. His swing was losing its momentum as he passed the far corner of the building. There, The Shadow made a grab.

Then he was literally crawling along the wall, supported by the cable that couldn't get away until he chose to release it! Reaching the fire escape, The Shadow grabbed hold and let the stirrup go. It thwacked the wall, flapped past the corner, and sailed up to the high bridge.

The Shadow had reached the meeting place ahead of Sauber, whose detour had delayed him. He was ahead of the Dragon men who were hurrying this way along the bridge. As for The Shadow's own agents, they were wondering where their chief had gone.

It would take the agents and Steve some time to find the meeting place. Which suited The Shadow's plans to perfection, since he would still have time to confront the Dragon Clan alone, as he originally intended.

Low, sibilant was The Shadow's whispered laugh as the darkness of a waiting window swallowed him—a prelude to his final duel with the Black Dragon!

CHAPTER XIX
THE VANISHED MASTER

CREAKS were sounding in the darkened hall outside the old office that formed the new meeting room of the Dragon Clan. Whispers passed among lurkers who were stationed there. Those lurkers belonged to the Dragon Clan, and their whispers proved that no genuine Chinese were mixed in this ugly business. Chinese couldn't whisper; their language depended on inflections, which made it impossible.

Obviously, the Dragon men were expecting someone. It was quite in keeping with the methods of their chief, the Black Dragon, to turn his meeting room into a trap. Hence, the hallway was dark, to encourage the intruder who was moving toward quick doom.

The creaks kept on. They reached the door of the meeting room and continued through. A surprising thing, considering that the door was closed. Whispers ended instantly. Only The Shadow could have opened and closed a door so silently. The thing was uncanny; nevertheless, the lurkers took it as a matter of course. Shiftily, they moved to new positions, producing other floor creaks.

It was like a calm before a storm, this coming of the meeting hour for the Dragon Clan. A storm which The Shadow had boldly determined to invoke. But there were outside elements concerned in it; how soon they would be due was a question.

For one thing, Carlton Sauber couldn't yet have reached this meeting place in the reptilian guise that branded him as the Black Dragon. As for The Shadow's agents, they would be at least ten minutes behind the double-dealer whose departure Steve had witnessed.

Meanwhile, the drama was centered in the meeting room, and it was drama indeed. First, the creaks. They weren't the sound of footfalls; rather they were only the groaning of loose floorboards, purposely arranged so that even the tread of The Shadow would disturb them. Reaching the center of the room, the creaks stopped amid the absolute darkness.

A long time seemed to pass, but only because moments lingered in this place that was like a tomb, a purpose for which it happened to be intended. The proof that an insidious climax was at hand came when lights appeared, creeping from mere flecks of redness into a gradually increasing glow that soon revealed the room and the stranger it contained.

Standing in the center of the room was The Shadow. As the lights disclosed him, the cloaked figure hunched lower and began to turn about. His posture showed that he was ready to whip guns from beneath his cloak, should enemies invade this room. But so far The Shadow was alone. At moments he gazed toward the gilded throne, but observing it to be empty, he continued to look elsewhere.

The Shadow's back was almost turned when a puff came from the throne. There, as if conjured from thin air, sat the Black Dragon. As if startled by the puff of smoke, The Shadow wheeled about, too late. One of the Dragon's hands had already flipped a signal that went with the sharp hiss from his fang-embroidered mouth.

The walls of this room had more than ears. They held fighters. With a rip, panels crashed from the ornamental screens. Guns stabbed the openings that ripped further to disgorge a dozen members of the Dragon Clan, all aiming for their cloaked enemy—The Shadow!

Knives, too, were flaying through the air, to find their mark in that hated figure of justice. In one instantaneous swoop, the murderous horde had overwhelmed The Shadow before he could fire a single shot in return!

Halted, the assassinating band expected to see the bullet-riddled victim collapse. Instead, The Shadow laughed!

SNARLS came from killers as they shrank back toward the broken panels. Those snarls were drowned by the sharper, louder hiss of the Black Dragon as he arose from his throne. He would end this illusion, nullify this strange chance whereby The Shadow, through some sheer trick, was standing dead on his feet, his lips forcing a laugh that they had begun before the hail of knives and bullets reached him.

Advancing with a drawn knife of his own, the Black Dragon stopped just short of The Shadow, intending to slash the blade into his rival's heart. The Dragon paused, his hiss triumphant. The figure of The Shadow was swaying; its collapse had begun.

Such was the introduction to another marvel.

The Shadow did not fall. His sway became a shrink. He was dwindling, before eyes that now included the Dragon's in their astonished circle, to something that was formless! A thing that couldn't be The Shadow, yet was, for from the shape that folded into itself came the same challenge that amazed men had heard before:

The laugh of The Shadow!

Down to the floor where it spread like an enormous ink blot that crept, with its hemmed cloak transformed into tentacles, toward the murderers who couldn't kill! Such was the action of this thing that had once been The Shadow, and still was!

From the blot, itself, issued The Shadow's laugh, louder, more strident than before!

To dispel the illusion that so outmatched his own arts, the Black Dragon stooped forward to clutch at the spread cloak and the slouch hat that tilted from the top of the cloth blot. Then, his hiss changed to an angry snarl, the Dragon waved his hand instead, as though such menial work belonged to others. None of the Dragon Clan sensed their master's fear. One was bold enough to obey the Black Dragon's order.

Springing forward, a rangy killer grabbed the hat and flung it, at the same time scooping up the cloak. Timed to the action came a louder mockery, with it a gun spurt from the midst of the blackened folds. The Dragon man who had dared defy The Shadow, paid his penalty before the cloak could leave his hand.

Face forward, the killer sprawled, gave a kick that turned him over and lay face upward, his eyes staring into the ruddy glow. There was horror in those dead eyes, as though they had seen the invisible hand that could deliver vengeance from nowhere!

The Shadow's laugh ended at the same instant. Madly, the Black Dragon seized the hat and cloak himself and shook them in order to learn their secret. They were empty, those garments, due proof that The Shadow was indeed a ghost. But this ghost had proven that it could deliver vengeance to any—or all—of the Dragon Clan!

INSTANTLY, the power of the Black Dragon was gone. The Shadow ruled triumphant in the minds of the superstitious clan. Anxious to appease The Shadow, they saw the Black Dragon as their real foe. He was the one who had defied The Shadow's challenge and pronounced the doom of the pit upon a fighter who could return from the world beyond!

"Death to the Black Dragon!"

With that shout, the assorted killers hurled themselves upon their former chief. With a frenzied writhe, the Black Dragon reached the throne, striking his hands against the arms and rolling around, to land deep in the seat. He didn't wait to throw a puff ball that would dramatize his disappearance. He used the mechanism as fast as it could send him, which was just ahead of the bullets that shattered the dropped glass, ending its utility as a mirror.

Bullets fired from the doorway, by an arrival whose hand was quicker than those of the Dragon's followers! The motley clan still didn't guess the trick, for by then the throne was empty. Nor did they stand gaping at the broken glass, for their attention was diverted the other way. The thing that brought them full about was more than mere gunfire.

It was the laugh of The Shadow!

Fierce, vengeful mirth that seemed to hold this tribe responsible for the escape of the Black Dragon. There in the doorway stood The Shadow, fully cloaked, smoke trailing from his drawn guns. The Shadow, no longer a ghost, but a superhuman fighter who had switched from the invisible to the indestructible!

Like the pair who had seen The Shadow return from the spiked pit, the whole brutal throng flattened on their faces and pleaded with The Shadow to spare their worthless lives. Leaving them thus, The Shadow turned and started for the stairs.

His laugh, trailing back, was like an omen, telling the cowed killers that their case would pend while The Shadow was settling scores with their banished leader, the Black Dragon.

CHAPTER XX
THE DRAGON'S RUSE

OUTSIDE, a cab was stopped beside the curb a short distance from the meeting building. On its steps stood a figure robed in gold and silver, adorned with a writhing dragon that ended in a hood.

Gun in hand, this monster who represented murder was about to point the weapon at a doubtful cab driver and order him to start away, when The Shadow wheeled from the doorway of the building and delivered a weird laugh.

Instantly, the creature in the dragon's costume changed his tactics. Instead of firing at The Shadow, he sprang away from the cab and rushed for shelter across the street. The lights of another cab disclosed him and he tried to dart from the glare. Out of the cab sprang other fighters, The Shadow's agents.

Between The Shadow and his agents, the fugitive hadn't a chance. Lowering his gun, The Shadow watched the roundup. It looked as if four men were trying to capture a slippery snake, so wildly did this Dragon writhe. He was coming across the street again, forgetful that The Shadow awaited him, when another car bore down on him.

Only by a mad scramble did the Dragon reach the sidewalk. Even then, he tripped across the curb. But his pursuers were blocked off by the stopping car and, for the moment, the Dragon was in the clear. Then, a new champion was leaping from the limousine, in the person of Miles Fenmore.

In his hand, Fenmore had a revolver, which he tried to center on the Dragon. It was the writhing effect of the costume that fooled him and gave the other man time to come about. By then, there was no question as to the Dragon's identity. The man in the costume was Carlton Sauber; he had thrown back the dragon's hood, because the eye slits were out of their proper place.

Seeing Fenmore aim, Sauber returned the favor. The gesture was almost useless, considering the advantage that Fenmore held. But to Steve Trask, springing around the front of Fenmore's limousine, the situation looked serious. With more fervor than wisdom, Steve hurled himself toward Sauber, shoving a gun toward the man who wore the regalia of the Dragon.

Only the speed of The Shadow could outmatch Fenmore's steady aim, Sauber's hasty return, and Steve's frenzied interference. Like a whirl of smoke, The Shadow went across the path of aim, but he met Steve with the solid effect of a stone wall. Flinging one hand upward, The Shadow struck Steve's revolver with the hard clash of an automatic and knocked the gun away.

Out of the same whirl, The Shadow aimed his other gun in backward style and fired. The illusion of the dragon costume seemed to baffle him, for he missed Sauber by scant inches. The shot, continuing onward, reached Fenmore's shoulder. Jolted at the moment when he pulled the trigger, Fenmore shoved his gun high. His shot carried over Sauber's head.

Before The Shadow could change that situation, Sauber's gun was full in line. It spoke, like an echo of the others, and drove its leaden message straight to Fenmore's heart. With a long, slow pitch, Fenmore flattened to the sidewalk into the posture of the Dragon Clan that The Shadow had so recently left.

There was no longer any writhe to Sauber's costume. The man was standing like a thing of stone. The Shadow's agents reached him and he made no effort to flee. The Shadow gestured toward Steve, and they pushed Sauber in that direction. Steve plucked the gun from Sauber's hand and gave it to The Shadow. All the while, Sauber kept staring at Fenmore's body.

MINUTES must have passed while Steve stood frozen, watching Sauber, who was equally rigid. Not a word from Sauber; the mere sight of his handiwork, in the form of Fenmore's body, held him speechless. A big car pulled into the street and from it stepped Commissioner Weston, with Inspector Cardona right behind him.

Weston took charge of Sauber, while Cardona was bringing out a fresh pair of handcuffs for Steve. Hoping that The Shadow would at last explain things, Steve looked for his cloaked friend and saw, quite to his dismay, that The Shadow had gone. Nevertheless, the process of the law was rudely interrupted.

Out from the entrance of an office building came a curious parade. It began with a dozen men, hands all lifted, who by their ugly looks and indiscriminate attire belonged to the Dragon Clan. Behind them, stimulating the forced march, were The Shadow's agents. They turned their prisoners over to arriving police.

Puzzlement was showing on Cardona's swarthy face. He weighed the handcuffs, but didn't slap them on Steve. Joe Cardona was beginning to get one of his very famous hunches, but he didn't express it aloud. Commissioner Weston didn't like Joe's hunches.

"Well, Inspector!" Weston was gesturing toward Sauber. "Here is our Black Dragon. Poor Fenmore was right. The fellow was a killer. Too bad we didn't bear down on Sauber this evening!"

Steve watched Cardona. An odd thought struck him. Inspector Cardona was as badly muddled as Steve. He was hoping, too, that The Shadow would reappear. But there wasn't any sign of The Shadow; not even a trailing laugh.

Lamont Cranston stepped up from somewhere. He arrived in his usual leisurely style, probably from a limousine parked around the corner. Despite himself, Commissioner Weston smiled. His friend Cranston was always arriving late.

"If you'd been at the club," snapped Weston, "you could have come with us, Cranston. Fenmore called and told us where we could find the Black Dragon."

Cranston looked from Fenmore's body to Sauber's equally rigid, though upright form. From the appearance of things, he might have suggested that the Black Dragon had found Fenmore. But Cranston didn't comment on Sauber's costume. Instead, he questioned casually:

"Who told Fenmore about the Black Dragon?"

"That fellow Pelly," began Weston. "You know—Sauber's secretary. He came to Fenmore's this evening and said he'd learned that Sauber was the Black Dragon. You see, Pelly found a note that came to Sauber's—"

"What is it, Commissioner? I would like to hear the rest."

"I'm wondering where Pelly *is*!" said Weston, somewhat puzzled. "He was coming here with Fenmore."

Cranston finished lighting a cigarette, turned about and blew the smoke toward a limousine, where a silent chauffeur was seated.

"There's Fenmore's car," observed Cranston. "Why not have a look inside, Commissioner?"

WESTON stepped over to the car. When he opened the door, a thing like a wildcat flew out. It was coming, with a gun, but it stopped with a whimper and dropped the weapon. The human wildcat was Pelly, and the thing that stopped him was another gun, gripped by the complacent Mr. Cranston, who had shoved the stubby revolver right into Pelly's ribs.

"Good work, Cranston," complimented Weston. "I'm glad I gave you that gun permit you wanted. It came in very handy."

"This isn't my gun." With a smile, Cranston handed the revolver to Weston. "It's yours, Commissioner. It was falling from your pocket, so I caught it."

Before Weston could think that one over, Cranston reached into Fenmore's limousine and dug deep beside the seat. He came out with a thing that looked like a deflated sea serpent. Spreading the object out, Cranston looked surprised to find that it was another dragon costume. He gave a glance toward Sauber's dejected figure.

"Offhand, Commissioner"—Cranston took another look at the outfit he was holding—"I would say that this was the original." He took a look toward Pelly, who was receiving the handcuffs originally meant for Steve. "Is it yours, Pelly?"

"It's Fenmore's!" blurted Pelly. "Or it was! He was the Black Dragon. But I had to work for him, or he'd have sent me a dragon token, like he did with Sauber!"

With a nod, Sauber dug deep beneath his costume and brought out the little jet dragon.

"I received this long ago," he said. "It had me scared. That's why I hid it. I couldn't understand why the Black Dragon let me live until I realized that I was being framed. So I tried to get back at the Black Dragon. I knew what his costume was supposed to be, and I rigged this duplicate. I wanted to get to a Dragon meeting and bluff that crowd of his.

"They were laying for me at Li Huang's, the first place I tried. They tried to get me the night you brought Trask to my house. I had Pelly make inquiries among people who might know something about the Black Dragon. Pelly found out more than I had hoped, because he was actually working for the Black Dragon, though I didn't know it.

"The moment I saw Fenmore, I knew the truth. He couldn't have come here, unless Pelly had told him, and Pelly wasn't supposed to tell. Fenmore wanted to kill me so I'd be marked as the Black Dragon. But The Shadow must have gotten here first, to break things up."

Cardona was quizzing Pelly, who admitted that he'd been waiting behind the building in Fenmore's car. There, Fenmore had joined him and discarded the original dragon costume. Tonight's trap had been planned for Sauber, who was to be found dead in the meeting room in the dragon costume. It was to look as though Sauber had run into some trouble with his own followers.

"Fenmore was finished with the racket," declared Pelly. "He was running out of victims. He didn't have to do any checking on them here; all the data he needed was sent him from Japan. The vault in his house is the kura that contains his wealth. He threatened many persons like Miljohn and Pendleton. Most of them paid."

LIKE the situation, the scene cleared. Cardona

was gone, along with Pelly and the other prisoners. Sauber had left with Commissioner Weston to probe matters up at Fenmore's. Cranston was supposed to come there in his own car, bringing Steve, whose case was completely understood. But Cranston wasn't in a hurry to start.

Looking about, Cranston appeared surprised by the fact that all The Shadow's agents had strolled from the picture after delivering the Dragon Clan. One stepped into sight: Myra Reldon. She gestured toward the building where the Dragon Clan had met.

"Dr. Tam received word from The Shadow," said Myra. "He wants us to bring along a few things that he left."

Cranston nodded and they went inside.

In an office on the ground floor, they found a long rod, formed in telescopic fashion. Cranston whipped the thing full-length and found it rigid. Seeing the outline of a stairway in a corner of the office, he began poking the rod up beneath. There were creaks from the stair boards that had continued as Cranston poked the rod along the line of the upstairs hall, then in the direction of the meeting room.

"A clever chap, The Shadow," observed Cranston. "He must have used this rod to make the Dragon Clan think he was sneaking into the meeting room. I suppose, at first, they thought it was Sauber."

Myra was pointing to a tiny hole in the ceiling. Cranston couldn't seem to understand its purpose. Finally, he pushed the rod up through and told Myra to hold it that way. Taking Steve upstairs, The Shadow found a hat and cloak lying on the meeting room floor. It was Steve who pointed to the rod that projected through the floor and exclaimed:

"Try them on that!"

Cranston tried them and found that the end of the rod opened umbrella fashion. Adorned with hat and cloak, the skeleton contrivance made a perfect replica of The Shadow that became wonderfully lifelike when Cranston called down to Myra to revolve the rod. Then, for a finish, Cranston added:

"Draw it right down through."

Myra did. The cloak and hat collapsed and fell away to a formless blot. When Cranston lifted them, the rod was gone.

Myra had drawn it through, the sprouting ends closing right through the hole. Further amazed by the ingenuity of The Shadow, Cranston picked up the hat and cloak and carried them on his arm, to return to the friend of his friend, Dr. Tam.

THEY rode to Fenmore's, to find that Weston and Sauber had uncovered the Black Dragon's stolen hoard, thanks to Fenmore's servants, honest men, who didn't know they'd been the front for their master's double life. By the time they left Fenmore's, Steve was all straight on the Sauber question.

Twice, he'd mistaken Sauber's gestures as a summons to men of crime; whereas Sauber, like Steve, had simply been trying to get away from murderers!

Cranston summed up other details as they left Fenmore's house. He was dropping off at the club and sending Steve and Myra home in his limousine.

"Fenmore put you in a jam the first night you saw him," Cranston told Steve. "That should have aroused your suspicion. Then there was the time that I was there, when Pelly muffed around with Sauber's papers just for an excuse to stay at Fenmore's. That was when Fenmore gave Pelly the real death token that eventually reached Li Huang."

Cranston paused, as though he felt that he'd really missed the facts on that occasion.

"What really tipped off The Shadow," declared Cranston impersonally, "was that message you received at Dr. Tam's. The one which bore The Shadow's name, but came from The Black Dragon."

Immediately agog, Steve asked if Tam had learned the secret of that odd riddle. Whereupon, Cranston nodded.

"The Shadow solved it," said Cranston. "The note was written on the paper in your tobacco tin. You tore it loose while you were filling your pouch. Later, you mistook it for a note."

"That's right!" exclaimed Steve. "I left my tobacco tin on Fenmore's desk! That's when he fixed it. But why was I such a dope to mistake that piece of paper for a real note?"

"You were really a dope," put in Myra laughingly. "Fenmore just didn't fix the wrapping. He planted a nice dose of opium in the tobacco, too. A few pipe loads and you were in a mood to mistake almost anything."

There was one thing on which Steve wasn't mistaken: The Shadow. All through the weave of fact and fancy, he could see the hand of the master genius who had ended the Black Dragon's reign of crime. But the identity of The Shadow was still a puzzle that remained unsolved.

So strange a puzzle to Steve Trask that when he and Myra Reldon were riding from the Cobalt Club, Steve actually thought that he heard a distant laugh, trailing like an echo from the past. Mirth that was more than memory, for it symbolized The Shadow's conquest over crime.

As those echoes faded, Steve Trask looked back. He saw only Lamont Cranston waving a good night from the doorway of the Cobalt Club.

THE END

It was one of the most famous faces in American literature. It stared out from the covers of literally hundreds of pulp magazines, was caricatured on comic book covers and floated in the imaginations of millions as they listened to the radio every Sunday night.

Even shaded by the brim of the familiar slouch hat, the lower part of his face hidden behind the high scarlet collar of an all-concealing black cloak, it was an unforgettable profile—strong, intensely masculine, forbidding, and unforgettable. It was too dynamic to be just a face. It was a countenance, a mien: It was the distinctive visage of The Shadow!

The Shadow was known by many names: Lamont Cranston, Henry Arnaud, and his true identity, Kent Allard. Many people played the role over the years: Orson Welles, William Johnstone, and Bret Morrison on radio; Rod LaRocque, Victor Jory and Alec Baldwin on the silver screen. Some people like to think of Walter B. Gibson, who developed the character and wrote most of the 325 novels published in *The Shadow Magazine* bylined "Maxwell Grant," as The Shadow. But only one man wore The Shadow's classic profile.

His name is William J. Magner. He was a silent film era feature player who turned professional artist's model in 1920. It was in this capacity he first went to work for George Rozen, who became cover artist for Street & Smith's phenomenally successful *Shadow Magazine* in 1931 when his twin brother, Jerome, relinquished the assignment soon after it was promoted to monthly publication.

At that time, Walter Gibson and Street & Smith were still developing the character and searching for a recognizable Shadow "look." It was eventually decided the Dark Avenger should have an instantly recognizable profile, something like Sherlock Holmes'. Gibson dubbed it "hawklike," and legend has it that it was inspired by the rather pronounced aquiline nose of S&S art director Bill Lawler. Lawler, they say, sometimes posed for Rozen right there in the S&S offices, using a floppy hat and cape kept handy for deadline emergencies. But pulp cover artists did most of their work at their studios, not in art directors' offices.

Still, Lawler seems to have been used as Rozen's model in those very early days, if we can believe a postcard sent out to Shadow contest winners in 1931. An early *Shadow* cover, dated January 1932, showed a *hooded* Shadow inspired by publicity stills from The Shadow's radio program, may be a portrait of Lawler, as were some other early depictions. As late as 1937, Lawler's photograph appeared on a cover intended to tie in with the Rod LaRocque-starring feature, *The Shadow Strikes*. To this day, most people still believe it's LaRocque on that cover, but it's actually Bill Lawler.

But somewhere along the line—probably by 1933 at the latest—George Rozen hired a model of his own. Enter William Magner, by then a very busy artist's model whose face was nearly perfect for the The Shadow. He had an intense face, frightening, almost evil. Piercing blue eyes peered out from under bushy black brows. True, he was balding, but The Shadow never appeared on the cover of his own magazine without benefit of headgear, so that minor imperfection was immaterial.

Best of all, from an artist's standpoint anyway, Magner possessed wonderfully articulated fingers. Any painter will tell you that hands are exceedingly difficult to capture on canvas. Whether because it had been a cover motif before Magner came along, or was directly inspired by those impressive digits, Rozen painted painted many, many *Shadow* covers in which The Shadow's hands, set off by a mystic fire-opal ring, dominated the scene. His face wasn't even shown. Those hands were enough.

The one big drawback was Magner's nose. It was large, pronounced, with appropriately flaring nostrils, but it lacked the famous hawklike hook. So Rozen simply exaggerated it to get the desired effect. Sometimes, he exaggerated *too* much, and The Shadow's profile became a parody of itself. With two issues of *The Shadow* coming out each month, no one was likely to notice the variation much. They were too busy reading.

Rozen scoured second–hand shops for an appropriate slouch hat. The famous cloak was a dress cape belonging to Rozen's wife, Ellen, who often appeared on *Shadow* covers herself. The slouch hat is now the proud possession of Sanctum Books publisher, Anthony Tollin, a gift from the late Jerome Rozen. George died in 1973.

Without doubt, William Magner modeled for the overwhelming majority of *Shadow* covers during the classic period of the magazine, which is to say, the Great Depression. A rough estimate would indicate that Magner's face, profile, or hands were depicted on about 150 separate covers. When Rozen lost the Shadow contract in 1939, Magner was probably just as happy to hang up the black cloak and felt hat for good.

That was not to be. As it happened, that same year, artist Rafael de Soto replaced John Newton Howitt on the covers of *The Shadow*'s chief rival and imitator, *The Spider.* Most of the New York pulp illustrators knew each other, and frequently posed for one another. They also shared models. De Soto, suddenly tasked with the lucrative job of painting the Spider every month, hired Magner for the job.

The Spider dressed very much like The Shadow—black suit, cloak and slouch hat. In the novels, these were augmented by a fright wig and vampire fangs designed to transform millionaire Richard Wentworth into a truly terrifying figure. But Popular Publications deemed this Halloween visage too extreme for the covers, so the artists were instructed to simply suggest the longish hair, coarsen the features, and add a black domino mask for a mysterious effect.

De Soto did just that, although there was a very brief period in 1940 when he experimented and portrayed the *real* Spider on the covers. That lasted all of seven issues. But for the most part, de Soto painted Magner in strokes so bold that even in a slouch hat and cloak, no reader ever suspected that the face of the Spider was also the face of The Shadow. One reason was that de Soto painted Magner's nose as it truly was. For another, The Shadow's mouth was always hidden; The Spider's was invariably set in a tight grimace, if not a snarl.

There was more variety working for de Soto, Magner found. Because he wasn't tied down to a fixed twice-a-month magazine contract, de Soto put Magner's already-overexposed countenance on an incredible variety of pulp covers. In pith helmet and jodhpurs, he looked manly on the covers of *Adventure.* With his bald pate showing, he would be a murderer or a murder victim on *Dime Detective.* He graced many a *Black Mask* cover during the 40s, too. In a long, stringy wig, syringe in hand, he became a *Terror Tales* mad scientist.

William Magner stayed with de Soto even after *The Spider* was canceled in 1943, and beyond the pulp magazine era. When de Soto made a very successful switch to painting paperback covers, Magner appeared on those, too. Some of the accompanying photographs of Magner were taken during the '40s by de Soto, who used them as painting guides. They show Magner as he looked just a few years after he was principal model for The Shadow, and in his mid-40s.

"I think I was the original Shadow," he once said of those days. "I started working in silent pictures, and I went into posing because it was more steady. I worked in the first picture that Warner Bros. made, *The Fighting Roosevelts*. I played Archibald, one of the sons. I think that was in 1918 or '19."

Magner was also featured in Lewis J. Selznick's first film, *The Woman God Sent*, starring Zena Keefe. Among his friends from his three-year acting career were Adolph Menjou and future *Batman* TV Commissioner Gordon, Neil Hamilton. "I danced with Billie Burke in a picture once," he recalled fondly of the woman who played the Good Witch in *The Wizard of Oz*. All of these films were shot at the Fort Lee studios in New Jersey.

When the New York studios migrated to

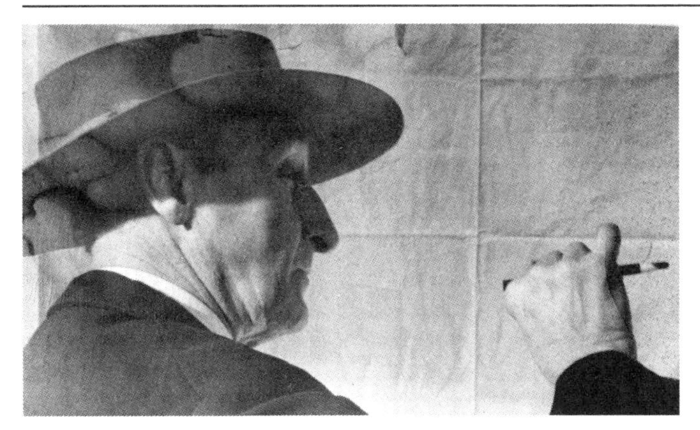

Hollywood around 1920, Magner chose not to follow. He was hired to pose by artist Clarence Underwood, then painting covers for *Cosmopolitan*. Over the years, he modeled for an incredible variety of artists from Charles Dana Gibson to Edward Dalton, who as "Dalton Stevens" did most of the covers for *Master Detective* and *True Detective*. Magner appeared on almost every cover for several years.

One of his fellow models was aspiring actor Fredric March, later to star in *Dr. Jekyll and Mr. Hyde*. Another was woman named Mildred Gillars. They were working in the same artist's studio when she received an offer to work in Germany. After World War II, when the notorious "Axis Sally" was arrested and tried for treason, Magner recognized the face in the newspapers as that of Mildred Gillars.

Once, Magner posed for the Ellery Queen story, "Death Counts Five," which was inspired by the notorious "Three-X" killer of Queens, New York, and was shocked years later when another artist copied his face in Hearst's *Sunday Journal,* claiming it was his "conception" of "Three X's" face. Magner contemplated suing Hearst because, he said, "I live in Queens," but he decided against it.

Why was he chosen by George Rozen for The Shadow? "I suppose it was because I have a sort of long, drawn face," Magner recalled. "Back in those days there weren't too many models around—maybe half a dozen. Modeling was hard work because you had to pose direct. They didn't take photographs until later. And I had a reputation because I had worked for so many men. I had a good face to draw from. It wasn't that I was handsome or anything. It was just the idea that I was very drawable." He was paid a flat dollar an hour and worked with so many artists at the same time, he was constantly traveling between studios.

Once, while working for watercolorist Walter Baumgartner, he travelled West and visited an Indian reservation, where they were initiated into the Blackfoot tribe. Baumgartner was renamed Walter Bull. Magner earned the Blackfoot name of Bill Eagle—ironic given that The Shadow had been nicknamed the Dark Eagle.

Magner didn't recall very much his Shadow posing days. In fact, he never kept any copies of the magazine. *"The Shadow Magazine* with a 10-cent article and the others like *Cosmopolitan, Woman's Home Companion, Master Detective* and *True Detective* were a quarter, and those were the ones I saved because they looked like me, you see, and Dalton Stevens spend so much time doing them. He didn't just knock them out."

In spite of his long association with The Shadow, no one ever came up to him on the street and asked if he was Lamont Cranston. Once, however, a woman on the subway mistook him for Basil Rathbone. It's not surprising, then, to learn

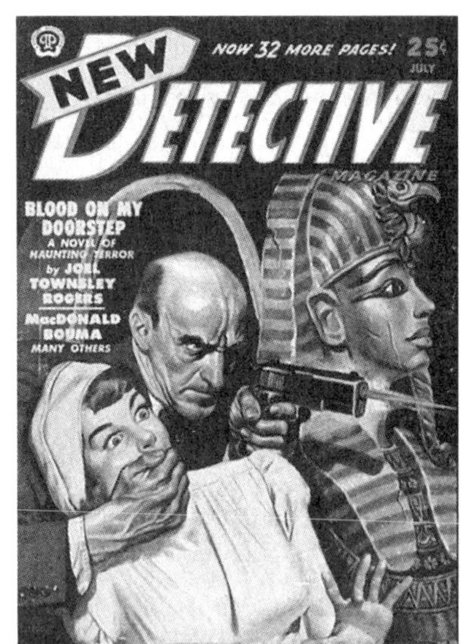

that he posed for a series of Sherlock Holmes paperback covers by Jack Faragasso. Despite his imposing appearance, Magner characterized himself as a very shy person.

In later years, Magner still sat for the occasional portrait, but not for commercial artists. "I can't take action poses at my age," he admitted. When John F. Kennedy was president, noted artist William F. Draper was asked to paint his portrait. Kennedy posed for the face, but William Magner sat in for the body and hands, wearing a suit on loan from J.F.K. He also performed the same service when Draper painted Joseph P. Kennedy. "I've had an interesting life up to this point," Magner explained.

Born in January 1897, William Magner died in Queens, New York on June 15, 1986, at the age of 89. Ironically, he was living near *Shadow* editor John. Nanovic. Another coincidence: Magner's mother's maiden name was Savage!

It should be mentioned that others took up The Shadow's guise after 1939. George Rozen was immediately succeeded as *Shadow* cover artist by Graves Gladney, whose rather pronounced features enabled him to dispense with the modeling fee. Gladney used his own face. At that time, Edd Cartier and later his roommate Earl Mayan produced the black-and-white interiors. Mayan inherited Bill Lawler's cloak and slouch hat, donning them for photographs, from which he drew. His stark illustrations are so intense they often resemble high-contrast photos.

William Magner posed for the hands and body on William Draper's portrait of President Kennedy.

In 1941, George Rozen was welcomed back into the Street & Smith corporate bosom and resumed painting *Shadow* covers. Because William Magner was too busy looking fierce on the covers of *The Spider*, Rozen was forced to hire a new model. He was an Englishman named Al Drake, an ex-ironworker and bartender turned artist. (He is not to be confused with Stanley Albert Drake, who did pulp covers for Popular Publications, and went on to fame as comic strip artist.) Al Drake often modeled. Magner knew him well, but other than the fact that they both had brown hair and blue eyes, he noted, "Al looked entirely different from me." Drake didn't have a hawklike nose, either. But by this time pulp cover styles had changed enough that it didn't matter. Most of the time, Rozen painted a full-figure Shadow in an action pose, so the famous profile was underplayed.

George Rozen again departed Street & Smith in 1942, not to return until 1948, when he painted the final quartet of *Shadow* covers. His model at that time is unknown. Perhaps, after nearly 200 Shadow portraits, he didn't need one, the fearsome visage leaping from his brush spontaneously. If he did paint those final covers from memory, there is no doubt whose face inspired him. It had to be the countenance of William Magner—the true face of The Shadow. •